ONE HUNDRED YEARS IN CEYLON

or the centenary volume of the church missionary society in ceylon 1818–1918

Rev. J.W. Balding, C.M.S.

MAVEN BOOKS

Chennai   New Delhi   Tirunelveli

Honour Copyright
&
Exclude Piracy

This book is protected by copyright. Reproduction of any part in any form including photocopying shall not be done except with authorization from the publisher.

MAVEN BOOKS

An Imprint of **MJP Publishers**

ISBN 978-93-87826-40-3   **Maven Books**

All rights reserved   No. 44, Nallathambi Street,
Printed and bound in India   Triplicane, Chennai 600 005

MJP 442   © Publishers, 2018

Publisher: **C. Janarthanan**

PUBLISHER'S NOTE

The legacy of a country is in its varied cultural heritage, historical literature, developments in the field of economy and science. The top nations in the world are competing in the field of science, economy and literature. This vast legacy has to be conserved and documented so that it can be bestowed to the future generation. The knowledge of this legacy is slowly getting perished in the present generation due to lack of documentation.

Keeping this in mind, the concern with retrospective acquiring of rare books has been accented recently by the burgeoning reprint industry. Maven books is gratified to retrieve the rare collections with a view to bring back those books that were landmarks in their time.

In this effort, a series of rare books would be republished under the banner, "Maven Books". The books in the reprint series have been carefully selected for their contemporary usefulness as well as their historical importance within the intellectual. We reconstruct the book with slight enhancements made for better presentation, without affecting the contents of the original edition.

Most of the works selected for republishing covers a huge range of subjects, from history to anthropology. We believe this reprint edition will be a service to the numerous researchers and practitioners active in this fascinating field. We allow readers to experience the wonder of peering into a scholarly work of the highest order and seminal significance.

Maven Books

PREFACE.

IN consequence of my having had the honour of compiling the general History of the Church Missionary Society, I am now asked by the Ceylon Committee that has arranged for the celebration of the Centenary of the Ceylon Mission, to introduce this present work, which tells the story of the Hundred Years of that Mission, and this I do with pleasure and thankfulness. The author, the Rev. J. W. Balding, is now the senior C.M.S. missionary in Ceylon, so far as length of service in the Island is concerned, having joined in 1881, and having therefore thirty-seven years' experience. That honoured veteran, the Rev. W. E. Rowlands, indeed, went out fifty-seven years ago (1861), but he retired in 1884 and rejoined in 1907, so that his actual service in the field is less than Mr. Balding's. The book, therefore, is authoritative in an unusual degree.

In 1868 a small Jubilee volume was prepared by the Ceylon missionaries. It was not an encouraging recital of the fifty years.

Few Missions have had, in so long a period, more apparently scanty results to report. In my History, published thirty years later, I noticed this, and explained the causes (Vol. ii, p. 288), and I added that if a record of those thirty additional years were written, the tone would be very different (Vol. iii, p. 547). In the supplementary fourth volume, published in 1916, I was thankfully able to present a much more hopeful account. Although I had even then to acknowledge that progress had been, as compared with that of several other Missions, exceptionally slow, yet on the other hand, the Mission had been exceptionally interesting in respect of the individual cases of conversions reported (Vol. iv, p. 257). This general impression will be confirmed by the present work, and the careful reader will find much to strengthen his faith in the Gospel and his thankfulness to God.

Colombo, with Galle Face Church, the Ladies' College, etc.; Cotta and Baddegama, as centres of village work; Kandy, with Trinity College; the Itinerancies; the Tamil Coolie Mission; Jaffna, and its isolated but important influence;—all these present features of real interest, though they may have little of the romance of Uganda, or the Punjab, or parts of China, or the Arctic Circle.

In one respect Ceylon is unique. The Anglican Church there furnishes the spectacle of a self-governing body comprising white and coloured races working together in harmony and fellowship, with the native Christians in a decided majority, while the foreign Christians are no negligible minority, differing therefore from Colonial Churches like those of Canada or New Zealand on one side, and from Churches almost purely native as in China and Japan on the other.

The Church in Ceylon has its own constitution and its own Synodical administration, although

PREFACE

ecclesiastically a single diocese in the Province of India and Ceylon. It presents, on a small scale, a picture of what we hope in time to see on the larger field of India itself.

I heartily commend this book to readers both at home and in the mission field, and to the Divine blessing.

EUGENE STOCK.

January, 1918.

CONTENTS

		PAGE
PREFACE	...	iii
INTRODUCTION	...	1

CHAPTER

I.	CEYLON	5
II.	THE SINHALESE	11
III.	BUDDHISM	16
IV.	THE TAMILS	24
V.	HINDUISM	28
VI.	CHRISTIANITY IN CEYLON	32
VII.	EDUCATION	48
VIII.	C.M.S. IN CEYLON	53
IX.	KANDY	68
X.	JAFFNA	88
XI.	BADDEGAMA	108
XII.	COTTA	128
XIII.	THE KANDYAN ITINERANCIES	143
XIV.	COLOMBO	155
XV.	THE TAMIL COOLY MISSION	173
XVI.	C.E.Z.M.S. IN CEYLON	188
XVII.	THE GREAT WAR AND RECENT PROGRESS.	196
XVIII.	RECENT EDUCATIONAL DEVELOPMENTS	201
	CONCLUSION	205
	A HYMN FOR CEYLON	206

CONTENTS

	PAGE
APPENDIX A—	
Ceylon C.M.S. Missionaries (Men)	207
Sinhalese Clergy	225
Tamil Clergy	228
Women C.M.S. Missionaries	231
APPENDIX B—	
New Constitution for the Ceylon Missionary Conference	236

INTRODUCTION.

DR. EUGENE STOCK, in the 'History of the Church Missionary Society' published in 1899, in connection with the Centenary of the Parent Society, refers to the 'Jubilee Sketches,' or an 'Outline of the work of the C.M.S. in Ceylon during fifty years, 1818–1868' written by the late Rev. J. Ireland Jones, and published in Colombo, in the following terms :—' In 1868, the Ceylon Mission celebrated its Jubilee. The missionaries then brought out a small volume of " Jubilee Sketches," giving the history of each station during the fifty years. This little book is singularly modest in its estimate of the work done and the results achieved. If the interesting little book were now to have a new edition, the whole tone would be different. Few missions had been, at the end of fifty years, more scanty in results. Few missions have presented in subsequent years more manifest signs of the working of the grace of God.'

Early in 1915, in view of the near approach of the centenary of the C.M.S. in Ceylon, the Standing Committee of the Conference suggested the formation of a Centenary Central Committee, so that the Centenary in 1918 might be widely and properly commemorated.

A representative committee was accordingly formed, with the Secretary of the Mission (the Rev. A. E. Dibben) as chairman. Two secretaries, one clerical

INTRODUCTION

(Rev. A. M. Walmsley) and one lay (Mr. W. Wadsworth) and a treasurer (Rev. J. W. Ferrier) were also appointed.

In addition, members of committee were nominated by the District Church Councils.

It was proposed that the Centenary should be made the occasion of the raising of a sum of at least Rs. 50,000, as a thank offering, and that this should have four objectives :—

(1) a Capital Fund for advance Missionary Movements, (2) a Pension Fund for Catechists, Biblewomen and School Teachers, (3) a Capital Fund to meet opposition in Educational Work, and (4) to provide funds for Itinerating Bands.

Several 'Centenary Pamphlets' have been published, and the writer of No. 3 says, ' We do not want to make this centenary effort merely a matter of raising funds. To do so, would be to fall very short of our real needs. What are they? First of all, this must be a time of increased prayer and re-consecration. If we are all in the line of God's will, praying earnestly for the extension of His kingdom, the effort and the means will be forthcoming, but money, without His Spirit to direct and control and bless it, can never fulfil its purpose. Let the Centenary be borne to us on a great wave of prayer, and we shall find it stored with a rich cargo of blessings. Let us remember three watchwords :—(1) Thanksgiving, for the past, with all its mercies and blessings. (2) Humiliation, as we think of the present, with its many unanswered calls, unused opportunities, and unentered doors. (3) Advance, in the future, as we remember that

INTRODUCTION

in the future lies the coming of the Lord, so closely connected with the evangelization of the world.'

Further, it was agreed that a history of the work of the C.M.S. in Ceylon should be written, which it was hoped ' would find its way into many homes, and thus sustain and deepen interest in our work, and prove a source of information and renewed effort.'

This I was asked to undertake, and the following pages are the result, which I trust will draw forth praise and thankfulness for God's goodness and help in the past, and call forth more prayer and work in His cause in the future.

I have chosen as the title for the book, ' One hundred years in Ceylon, or the Story of the C.M.S. there from 1818 to 1918.' It is the natural title to take for a centenary volume, and other writers on Ceylon seem to have been impelled to describe their books in terms of years, for instance,

' Two Happy Years in Ceylon,' by Miss Gordon-Cumming.
' Seven Years in Ceylon,' by Miss M. Leitch.
' Eight Years in Ceylon,' by Sir Samuel Baker.
' Eleven Years in Ceylon,' by Major Forbes.
' Fifty Years in Ceylon,' by Major Skinner.
' A Century in Ceylon,' by Miss Helen Root.

Although I have been a missionary in Ceylon for more than a third part of the one hundred years, I cannot lay claim to much that is original in the pages of this history, as I have drawn and compiled, largely and liberally, from the ' Jubilee Sketches ' published in 1868; the small pamphlet, the ' Ceylon Mission ' published by the C.M.S. in 1900; the 'History of the C.M.S.' published in 1899; the 'Historical Sketch of Ceylon' published by the S.P.G.; 'Ceylon at the Census of 1911,' by Mr. E. B. Denham; the 'Book of Ceylon' and 'Golden Tips,' by Mr. H. W. Cave; 'Ceylon,' by Dr. J. C. Willis; 'History of Ceylon,' by Mr. Donald Obeyesekere; the 'Ceylon Handbooks' published by the Messrs. Ferguson; the local 'Reports of the C.M.S. Ceylon Mission;' and many other writers. To each and all of these I am much indebted and tender grateful thanks, as well as to the many friends who have given valuable advice and assistance, and last but not least to the kind writer of the preface.

J. W. BALDING.

CHAPTER I.

CEYLON.

No country in the world, except possibly Egypt, has such a long continuous history and civilization, with tradition, fable and legend encircling it from the remotest times. The Mohammedans assert that Ceylon was given to our first parents, Adam and Eve, as a new Elysium to console them for the loss of Paradise. According to the Indian poem, the Ramayana, (500 B.C.) a prince named Rama is said to have come with a great army from India to Ceylon about three thousand years ago and conquered and killed the king.

It is also supposed to have been part of the region of Ophir and Tarshish, from which the ships of King Solomon obtained ' gold and silver, ivory, apes and peacocks.' The ancient Greeks and Romans knew the island as ' Taprobane,' and the poet Milton has preserved the name in his great poem,

> Embassies from regions far remote,
> From India and the golden Chersonese,
> And from utmost Indian isle, Taprobane.

To the people of India it has been known for centuries as ' Lanka the Resplendent,' and the ' pearl-drop on the brow of Ind,' whilst the Siamese called it ' the divine Lanka.' To the Chinese it was ' the island of jewels,' to the Persians ' the land of the hyacinth and ruby,' to the Arabs it was ' Serendib ', to the ancient Sinhalese ' the island of the lion race,' and to travelled Europeans ' the Eden of the Eastern wave.'

It has been immortalized by Bishop Heber, in the well-known missionary hymn,

>> What though the spicy breezes
> Blow soft o'er Ceylon's isle
>> Though every prospect pleases. . . . .

By another poet it is

>> Confessed to be the brightest gem
> In Britain's orient diadem

Ceylon lies to the south-east of the continent of India, and is about the size of Ireland. Its length from north to south is 271 miles, and its greatest width 137 miles. Its area is about 25,000 square miles. The south of the island lies within six degrees of the equator, and the average temperature near the coast is between eighty and ninety degrees in the shade, a climate always humid and enervating. In the hills however a temperature as low as twenty-six degrees is sometimes experienced. The annual rainfall varies from thirty-six inches in the driest parts of the island to two hundred inches in the wettest whereas the rainfall of Great Britain ranges from a minimum of twenty-two inches to a maximum of seventy inches. Time is five hours and twenty minutes ahead of Greenwich, so it is about noon in Colombo when England is only half awake.

Ceylon has a population of over four millions of people, and among these, eighty races are represented. The Sinhalese number 2,714,880, the Tamils 1,060,432, the Moors 266,876, the Burghers 26,857, the Malays 13,092, the Europeans 8,555 and the Veddahs 5,342.

The Veddahs are supposed to be the descendants of the aborigines—the yakkos or devils, as they are called in native legend. These were conquered by an invading race who in 543 B.C., swept down from the valley of the Ganges, commanded by Wijayo, the son of a king of Bengal. He founded the royal dynasty which held sway for about 2,300 years. The Sinhalese (from Sinha, a lion) are the descendants of these conquerors. They speak an Aryan language of the Sanskrit type, and are divided into two great sections, Kandyan and Low-Country Sinhalese. Both are descended from the same stock and are only distinguished outwardly by difference of dress. The Tamils are of Dravidian origin, and are the descendants of mercenaries and invaders from Southern India who settled in the Island ages ago. Others are recent immigrants who come over in large numbers from India to work on the tea and rubber plantations. The Moors, who are energetic and enterprising traders, are probably descendants of Arabs, who conquered some coast towns in the eleventh century, and intermarried with the women of the land. They are Mohammedans, as are also the Malays, who were brought to Ceylon by the Dutch.

The Burghers are the descendants of the Portuguese and Dutch settlers, and form an influential part of the community. The Dutch Burghers are largely employed in Government offices, law and medicine.

The Europeans consist chiefly of Government officials, the military, merchants, planters, and missionaries.

The principal seat of Government is at Colombo, which under the name of Kalambu, was described by the Moors in 1340, as 'the finest city in 'Serendib.' It has one of the finest harbours in the world, and all steamers going to or from the East make it a port of call.

Kandy, the capital of the interior, is situated in an amphitheatre surrounded by wooded hills and forest-clad mountains, seventy-two miles from Colombo, nearly two thousand feet above the sea, whilst in Nuwara Eliya, six thousand feet above sea level, 'Europe amid Asia smiles.'

Ceylon is an island of indescribable beauty. Nature has showered her charms with lavish hand, and has welded together giant peaks, rippling streams, dense jungles and pleasant plains into one sweet fairyland. There is beauty everywhere, in the wealth of vegetation and foliage, the rich colourings of birds and insects, and a thousand other objects. A belt of rich alluvial soil round the coast waves with dense groves of coconut, palmyra, sago, areca, and other palms. There is an abundance of fruit, such as mango, rose-apple, guava, durian, prickly-pear, sour-sop, lovi-lovi, custard-apple, cashew nut, pomelo, tamarind, pomegranate, pineapple, mangosteen, orange and lime.

Melons and cucumbers, papaws and bananas, breadfruit and jak, cinnamon, cacao, cardamoms, pepper, nutmegs, cinchona, tobacco, cotton, sugarcane, lemon and citronella grass all have their place.

There are about three thousand species of native plants, two hundred and thirty different kinds of ferns, and over one hundred and sixty-eight species of orchids growing wild. Paddy or rice cultivation has been the chief agricultural pursuit of the people from time immemorial, and although sixty varieties of rice are grown, the quantity raised is not sufficient for the wants of the people. For many years coffee cultivation was the staple industry of the European planters, but a fungoid pest, *Hemeleia vastatrix*, practically destroyed this shrub, and tea took its place. In 1873 only 23 lbs. of tea were exported, but now nearly 200,000,000 lbs. are exported annually.

The fauna of the island includes a number of species which are not found in any other country. There are superb butterflies, black and grey monkeys, lemurs, civet-cats, cheetahs and bears, wild elephants (protected by Government), wild buffaloes (also protected), crocodiles, porcupine, pangolin, sambur, wild pig, jackals and twenty-two species of bats. Amongst the owls there is one called 'the devil bird' uttering most fearful cries, which have been compared with those of a woman being murdered, or a child tortured. Forty-three of the one hundred and thirty-three species of reptiles, have not been found elsewhere. Of the snakes, eight species are poisonous, the most dangerous being the cobra and tic polonga. One thousand five hundred species of beetles are found in the country, and mosquitoes, ticks, sand flies, leeches and other creatures make their presence felt and known.

The seas abound in fish, trout have been introduced into upcountry streams, singing fish live in the hot water wells on the east coast, another fish only thrives when half buried, in mud, and a kind of perch can make its way across dry land unaided by legs.

The island is also renowned for its precious stones, the chief of these being the ruby and sapphire, to which may be added the catseye, the star ruby, star sapphire, amethyst, alexandrite, moonstone, garnet, chrysolite, chrysoberyl and tourmaline.

Iron is also found, and plumbago, otherwise known as graphite or blacklead, and pearls are fished up from the oyster banks on the north-west coast.

Mr. H. W. Cave in his 'Book of Ceylon' writes: 'To those who have the most extensive experience of East and West, the claim of Ceylon to be regarded as the very gem of the earth will not seem extravagant. The economic results due to its situation in the eastern seas, a spot on which converge the steamships of all nations for coal, and the exchange of freight and passengers, its wealth and diversity of agricultural and mineral products, the industry of the inhabitants both colonists and natives—these, together with its scenery and the glamour of its unrivalled remains of antiquity, entitle Ceylon to a place of high distinction among the dependencies of the empire.'

Sir Emerson Tennent, who resided in the island for some years as Lieutenant-Governor and Colonial Secretary, in his interesting and valuable work on the colony, writes :—

'There is no island in the world, Great Britain itself not excepted, that has attracted the attention of authors in so many distant ages and so many different countries as Ceylon, there is no nation in ancient or modern times possessed of a language or literature, the writers of which have not at some time made it their theme. Its aspect, its religion, its antiquities and productions, have been described as well by classic Greeks as by those of the lower empire, by the Romans, by the writers of China, Burmah, India and Cashmere, by the geographers of Arabia and Persia, by the mediæval voyagers of Portugal and France, by the annalists of Portugal and Spain, by the merchants and adventurers of Holland and by the travellers and topographers of Great Britain. . . . Ceylon, from whatever direction it is approached, unfolds a scene of loveliness and grandeur unsurpassed, if it be rivalled, by any land in the universe. The traveller from Bengal, leaving behind the melancholy delta of the Ganges and the torrid coast of Coromandel, or the adventurer from Europe recently inured to the sands of Egypt, and the scorched headlands of Arabia, alike are entranced by the vision of beauty which expands before him as the island rises from the sea, its lofty mountains covered by luxuriant forests, and its shores, till they meet the ripple of the waves, bright with the foliage of perpetual spring.'

CHAPTER II.

THE SINHALESE.

THE origin of the Sinhalese has given rise to much speculation. The Mahawansa[1] (chapter VI) states that the grandmother of Wijaya was Suppadevio, a princess of Bengal, who secretly fled with a caravan chief bound for the Maghadha country. In the jungle in the land of Lala, she was carried off by a lion, by whom she had a son called Sinhabahu, who slew his lion father and became king of Lala, and founded a city called Sinhapura. Wijaya was his son, who with his followers arrived in the island about 543 B.C.

By whatever means the monarch Sinhabahu slew the Sinha (lion) his sons and descendants are called Sinhala (the lion slayers). Lanka having been conquered by a Sinhala, it obtained the name of 'Sinhala' or 'Sihala.' It is probable that the 'lion' was a bold and daring bandit, known by the name of 'Sinha,' the lion.

The most generally accepted theory however is, that the progenitors of the Sinhalese were Aryan settlers from the north of India. This is borne out by language, customs, and subsequent history. The ancient poem Ramayana (500 B.C.) and the inscriptions of Asoka (250 B.C.) prove early intercourse between India and Ceylon. The Sinhalese language is one of the group of Indo-Aryan languages of which Sanskrit is the literary type. It is unknown in India, and its preservation in Ceylon is valuable evidence of the distinct development of the Sinhalese race. It has borrowed largely from Sanskrit, Pali

[1] An ancient History of Ceylon.

and Tamil, and many Portuguese, Dutch, Malay and English words have become naturalized in it.

The Sinhalese literature consists of works written in pure Sinhalese, now called Elu, free from Sanskrit foreign words. The Buddhist scriptures, or the sayings of the founder of Buddhism, were first reduced to writing in Ceylon, in 85 B.C. The language of most of the sacred books is Pali, which is not understood by the common people, and many of the Sinhalese commentaries are written in an antiquated style.

The 'Mahawansa' is a dynastic history of the island written by Buddhist monks, to cover twenty-three centuries from 543 B.C. to A.D. 1758.

Before the dawn of civilization in England, the Sinhalese were a nation possessing beautiful cities and wonderful temples, and maintaining a high type of civilization. Being keen agriculturists they brought the whole country into a high state of productiveness by means of irrigation. The inhabitants of the Sinhalese highlands, of which Kandy is the capital, are called Kandyans or Upcountry Sinhalese. They are of a stronger and more independent character than the people of the plains, or low-country, and preserved their freedom intact throughout the Portuguese and Dutch periods. A Sinhalese writer says ' The Kandyan and Low-country Sinhalese are as distinct from each other in their dress, manners and customs and in their very ideas and manner of thinking as if they formed two different races, rather than two sections of one nation.'

The distinction is every year lessened, by increasing intermarriage, opening up of the country by improved means of communication, the creation of new standards of comfort, and the spread of education and Christianity.

Marriages take place at an early age, though not so early as in India, the daughters as a rule marrying before the sons.

Superstition abounds and lucky days are sought, for beginning any important work, for marriages, and even for sending children to school. Astrologers are consulted on every event of life. Devil ceremonies for the sick are of nightly occurrence, and planet-worship is practised. Charms are worn by the mass of the villagers, and pots spotted with lime are hung up in the vegetable gardens to avert the evil eye. Fishers on the sea and reapers in the harvest field use a language they suppose the evil spirits will not understand. Caste, in the matter of marriages is extremely rigid, and sometimes strong in social intercourse, but as affecting trade it is almost dead.

The Sinhalese are a graceful race, with delicate features. The men wear a jacket, and a cloth round the waist reaching to the ankles. They usually wear their hair long, drawn back from the face and tied in a knot at the back. A semicircular tortoise-shell comb on the top of the head is frequently used by the men of the low-country. Many are now adopting short hair and English dress as well as language.

Intellectually they are capable of anything, but as a race they are perhaps lacking in energy. Educated Sinhalese now take high and honourable positions in the various professions, and in Government service up to the Legislative Council and the Supreme Court bench. Agriculture is the chief employment of the people and there are good artisans who excel in wood-carving, carpentry and brass work. It is not easy to win the confidence of the people at first, as they are of a very independent and somewhat suspicious turn of mind, but are responsive to kindness and confidence. European habits and customs have a great attraction for them, and the more progressive have a great desire for English education.

The following is the judgment of Sir William Gregory, a former governor, written after he retired from the island:—

' The people are pleasant to govern, they are quick-witted and intellectual, and the higher classes singularly well-bred and taking in their deportment. I think too, there are indications of the quality of gratitude, in the existence of which in the East I had long disbelieved. I am sure much may be done with them by kindness, courtesy, and respectful treatment. I have known some whom I would trust as implicitly as I would Englishmen, and I am as confident as one can ever be of human conduct, that if future rulers of Ceylon will endeavour to induce the natives to trust them and rely on them, much more of the administration of the country may be vested in them. Weakness and moral and physical timidity are their main faults, and as you well know, cowardice is a difficult defect to cure. The way to deal with such a race is to give them confidence and encouragement, to reward even ostentatiously good conduct, fidelity and strength, but to be down on offenders with relentless severity. I have pursued this course, and without egotism I can say that I believe no Governor ever before succeeded in inspiring such a universal trust in his motives.'

A rebellion of the Kandyan Sinhalese occurred in 1817-19. The first outbreak was in Uva, and the Government Agent of Badulla was killed by the rebels. The people were not altogether pleased to be governed by foreigners, and the chiefs were discontented when they found they were less respected, and the greater part of their power taken away. Some of the rebels were beheaded, and others banished to the Mauritius. A change was also made in the relations between the British Government and Buddhism. When the British took Kandy in 1815, a treaty was made in which Buddhism was declared 'inviolable,' and its rites and temples were promised protection and maintenance. It was found that the Buddhist priests were the chief promoters of the rebellion, so in the new treaty it was stated that 'the priests as well as the ceremonies of Buddhism shall receive the respect which in former times was shown to them.'

There were two small risings of the Sinhalese in 1820 and 1823, but in 1848 a small rebellion broke out in Matale and Kurunegala. There had been unrest for some time and resentment towards the new taxes on dogs, guns and boats, the stamp-tax, and especially the road-tax. Riotous meetings were held protesting against the taxes, and a rebellion broke out, but it was at an end in less than three months. Some of the ringleaders were banished to Malacca. In 1866 there were serious food riots in Colombo, Kandy and Galle, owing to the high price of rice.

For the next fifty years everything was peaceful, till in May 1915 serious riots occurred in many places, which led to considerable loss of life, the proclamation of martial law, and the imprisonment of some 6,000 men, under sentences varying from a few weeks' detention to death. Religious and economic considerations led the Sinhalese mob to attack the Mohammedans or Moors. The Mohammedans had protested against a Buddhist religious procession passing their mosque at Gampola, and their protest had been upheld in the law-courts. They also boasted that they would interfere with the great Kandy *perahera* in August—the most important procession in Ceylon—and tried, though in vain, to prevent the erection of a *dansala*, or booth, in Kandy for the free distribution of food on Buddha's birthday. These steps aroused religious animosity, which was intensified by the economic hatred of the Moors, caused chiefly by jealousy on account of their superior success as traders. The riots broke out on the morning of the 29th of May, when a mosque which had been specially aggressive in its objections to dansalas and processions, was wrecked by the Sinhalese, and in the evening of that day bloodshed began. The riots were quelled after a few weeks, the ringleaders punished, and heavy fines imposed upon the inhabitants to repair the damage done to property.

CHAPTER III.

BUDDHISM.

THE population of Ceylon in 1911 was 4,110,367 ; of these 2,714,880 were Sinhalese. In the Census returns for that year 2,474,170, entered themselves as Buddhists.

Gautama Buddha, the founder of Buddhism, lived and died in Northern India in the sixth century B.C. At the age of twenty-nine years he undertook what is called the 'Great Renunciation' by forsaking his family and departing into the jungle, to discover by his own unaided efforts how deliverance from the ills and changes, to which mankind was subject, could be realized. At the end of six years of meditation he achieved his aim and while sitting near a Bo Tree (*ficus religiosa*) became Buddha, i. e. the enlightened one. He declared he was free from all desire and was capable of comprehending all things—past, present and future. With regard to the beginning of matter and life, he asserted that it was unknowable. In one of his first sermons he took as his text the words, 'Everything burns,' and said that nothing is permanent, and that the comprehension of this fact was essential to the attainment of the *summum bonum* of his religion—nirvana. Buddha commenced to preach at the age of thirty-five and died at the age of eighty.

In the seventeenth year of the reign of Asoka, king of Maghada, in India, in the third century after Buddha's death, a convocation of Buddhists was held and it was decided to send missionaries to Ceylon. Prince Mahindo, the son of the king, was sent about the year 307 B.C. and succeeded in converting Tissa, the king of Ceylon and many of his subjects. Tissa sent to Asoka for the right collar bone of Buddha, and over this was erected the Thuparama dagoba, in Anuradhapura. Shortly after this Sanghamitta, the younger sister of Mahindo, came to Ceylon bringing with her a branch of the sacred Bo Tree. Buddha is said to have visited the island on three occasions, knowing that 'Ceylon would be the place where his religion would be most glorified,' and on the last occasion is said to have left the impression of his foot on Adam's Peak. In 85 B.C. five hundred priests met in a rock-temple at Aluwihare, near Matale, and there the 'Tripitaka' or 'Threefold Collection' of Buddha's sayings, with notes, were written down. Previously the doctrines were committed to memory and handed down orally.

In A.D. 313, the relic, Buddha's tooth, was brought to Ceylon by a Brahman princess, hidden in the folds of her hair, to prevent its falling into the hands of enemies.

In A.D. 1305 King Bahu IV built many temples, and during his reign the 'Jatakas' or five hundred 'birth stories' of Buddha were translated from Pali into Sinhalese.

The canonical scriptures of Buddhism contain more than two million lines, about two feet each in length of manuscript, and treat of the most abstruse and metaphysical subjects, as well as of moral duties. The *raison d'être* of Buddhism must be looked for in the pantheism and sacerdotalism which prevailed in Buddha's time and country. The Brahmans taught that every particle of matter was a visible portion of the unseen God and that worship addressed to it was the same as worship addressed to Him. They also had become unpopular on account of their extreme pretensions to superiority with regard to caste. The Ceylon priests in a petition to the late King Edward regarding their temple-lands, said that Buddha did not inculcate the worship of any God, and that the temples were not built for, nor dedicated to, the worship of any supernatural being. 'Answer 122' in the Buddhist Catechism, published by the late Colonel Olcott says, 'The Buddhist priests do not acknowledge or expect anything from a divine power. A personal God is only a shadow thrown upon the void of space by the imagination of ignorant men.'

Buddha repeatedly told his followers to look to themselves alone for salvation, so prayer to a superhuman being is unknown and unpractised. Professor Monier Williams says, 'It is a strange irony of fate that Buddha himself should have been not only deified and worshipped, but also represented by more images than any other being ever idolized in any part of the world.'

The obliteration of the doctrines relating to the Supreme Being of the Universe and the soul of man has made Buddhism generally inoperative in the lives of its adherents.

Buddhism teaches that a man's present existence was preceded by unnumbered lives in past ages, and will be succeeded by countless others, unless, like Buddha, we snap the chain of desire which links us to life. The arbiter of any particular state of being is 'karma'—action. This is taught in the oft-quoted saying of the Buddhists, who, when wishing to show what is the doctrine of rewards and punishments, say, ' Kala, kala dē, phala, phala dē,' the equivalent of ' As a man sows, so shall he reap.'

Dr. R. S. Copleston, in his valuable work ' Buddhism, past and present,' says : ' Buddhism does not hold that there is any such thing as a permanent independent soul, existing in or with the body and migrating from one body to another. The self or personality has no permanent reality ; it is the result of certain elements coming together, a combination of faculties and characters. No one of these elements is a person, or soul, or self, but to their combination the term self is popularly given. The death of a man is the breaking up of this ombination, not the separation of soul from body, but the dissolution both of body and of the aggregate of faculties and characters on which life depended.'

On the death of any living being whose Karma is not yet exhausted, another being comes into existence, to whom the residue of the karma is transferred. This second being is the same as the first and yet not the same.

Buddhism lays stress upon four fundamental truths called the ' Four noble Truths,' viz:—

(1) All existence is suffering, (2) The origin of suffering is desire, (3) The cessation of suffering is brought about by the removal of desire, (4) The way to the attainment of cessation of suffering is by carrying out the precepts, until Nirvana is reached.

The course of conduct which, if adopted, will lead to the removal of desire is called the ' Noble Eight-fold Path,' viz :—

(1) Right opinion, (2) Right resolve, (3) Right speech, (4) Right employment, (5) Right conduct, (6) Right effort, (7) Right thought, (8) Right self-concentration.

Every priest is bound to abstain from the following ten things, (*dahasil*):—1. Killing, 2. Theft, 3. Unchastity, 4. Falsehood, 5. Alcoholic drink, 6. Solid food after midday, 7. Dancing, 8. Perfumes and ornaments, 9. High or broad beds, 10. Receiving of gold or silver. The lay adherent is only bound to abstain from the first five of these *(pansil)*.

Buddha himself issued no regulations about religious ritual or worship, because it was opposed to that state of self-reliance which he insisted on. All that we find now relating to temples, images and offerings was instituted later. He established an order of celibates, who were to devote the whole of their lives to the subjugation of their passions, and to exhort others to join their order. Buddhism has adopted many ceremonies of the Hindus in order to obtain popular sympathy and processions with dancing, jugglers, music, clowns and elephants are frequently held to attract the public. The people give alms to the priests, feed beggars, make pilgrimages, prostrate themselves before images, relics, trees, dagobas and footprints, visit temples at the changes of the moon, and recite their creed, ' Buddham saranam gachchami, Dhammam saranam gachchami, Sangham saranam gachchami '—I take refuge in Buddha, in the doctrine, in the priesthood.

For some years past there has come into prominence the belief in the coming of another Buddha, the Maitri or Metteyya, the loving one. Buddha made the following prophecy : ' Man's average age will dwindle through sin to ten years, and will then rise again to eighty thousand years ; there will then arise a Buddha named Metteyya, endowed with all wisdom.'

Many of the Buddhists now centre all their hopes of Nirwana in the coming of this Maitri Buddha, who is to be righteousness, knowledge and love, believing that the love he will inspire by his personality and preaching will do what they cannot now do. Animism or demon worship which existed before the introduction of Buddhism, still holds its own, and the devil priests are important functionaries in the village communities, having less philosophy but more power than the Buddhist priests. Bishop R. S. Copleston says, ' It is the devil priest and not the Bhikku who is the real pastor of the people.'

According to the Census of 1911, there were in Ceylon, 7,774 Buddhist priests, 3,019 ebittayas, or attendants on the priests, 948 persons engaged in temple service, 1,305 devil dancers and 468 astrologers. Buddhism has wealthy endowments, and four hundred thousand acres of land belong to the temples.

About thirty years ago a ' Buddhist Temporalities Ordinance ' was passed by the Government, and a few years later a Mr. Bowles Daly, LL.D. of Dublin University, and once a clergyman of the Church of England, was appointed

'Commissioner' to enquire into the working of the Act. For some years he had made Ceylon his head-quarters, identifying himself with the Buddhists, and endeavouring to excite among them a revival of religious zeal. He visited 1,300 of the *Pansalas* or monasteries, and, in his report to Government, is scathing in denunciation of the general character of the priests.

For the last thirty years the Buddhists have been very active and aggressive, through what is called the 'Buddhist revival' which was commenced by American and English Theosophists. A catechism was published, with the approval of the high priest, and in the preface it states 'The signs abound that of all the world's great creeds, that one is destined to be the much talked of religion of the future which shall be found in least antagonism with nature and with law. Who dares predict that Buddhism will not be the one chosen?' It further says, 'Various agencies, among them, conspicuously, the wide circulation of Sir Edwin Arnold's beautiful poem " The Light of Asia ", have created a sentiment in favour of Buddhistic philosophy, which constantly gains strength. It seems to commend itself to Freethinkers of every shade of opinion. The whole school of French Positivists are practically Buddhists.' This Catechism further states 'The word " religion " is most inappropriate to apply to Buddhism, which is not a religion but a moral philosophy.'

In addition, vernacular schools as well as English and Boarding schools have multiplied rapidly, some of them taught by European teachers, and itinerant preachers penetrate to remote villages copying Christian phraseology and Christian missionary methods. Sunday schools, Young Men's Buddhist Associations, tract distribution, carol singers during the Sinhalese New Year, parodies of Christian hymns, Buddhist cards for Buddha's birthday, newspapers, a Buddhist 'Daily Light,' an 'Imitation of Buddha,' a

'Funeral Discourse,' pictures of events in the life of Buddha, a Buddhist flag, have all been brought into being.

We agree with the words of the Rev. J. A. Ewing in the 'Resplendent Isle,' viz. 'We rejoice in all this opposition, for it rouses the people from apathy and indifference. It has led also to the spread of primary school teaching among the children—the duty utterly neglected by the Buddhist monks in respect of the boys, and, of course, nearly always of the girls. Christianity has everything to gain ultimately by the change. It is in the days of strenuous struggle that the Gospel wins its greatest triumphs, not in the days of ease and compromise.'

Mr. K. J. Saunders, late of Trinity College, Kandy, on the last page of his 'Modern Buddhism in Ceylon,' writes, 'Already we have to thank God for signs that Buddhists are awakening from the long sleep of centuries, a new enthusiasm for national life, and a revival of the old yearning for the coming one, both due, we believe, to the quickening touch of Christianity. The problem before the Church of Ceylon would seem to be so to preach Christ that He should be accepted as the realization of their ideal of a loving one, who has superseded Law by Love, and counteracted karma by His redemptive power, and that His kingdom shall stand for the Fulfilment of all those dim yearnings after national greatness which are struggling to find expression.'

Mr. Harold Begbie, in his introduction to 'In the Hand of the Potter,' writes truly 'Christianity is *janua vitae*, Buddhism, *janua mortis*. Christianity is an ardent enthusiasm for existence, Buddhism is a painful yearning for annihilation, Christianity is a hunger and thirst after joy, Buddhism a chloral quest for insensibility. The Christian is bidden to turn away from sin that he may inherit the everlasting joy of eternity, the Buddhist is told to eradicate all desire of any kind whatsoever lest he be born again.

Buddha sought to discover an escape from existence, Christ opened the door of life. Buddha forbade desire, Christ intensified aspiration. Buddha promised anaesthesia, Christ promised everlasting felicity.'

CHAPTER IV.

THE TAMILS.

AT the last Census (1911) there were 528,024 Ceylon Tamils and 530,983 Indian Tamils, making a total of 1,059,007, in the Island, or slightly more than a quarter of the whole population.

The first invasion by the Tamils from South India occurred in 205 B.C. when an army led by Elara, a prince of the kingdom of Chola, now called Tanjore, landed in Ceylon, and marched victoriously to Anuradhapura, where he defeated and slew Asela, the king of the Sinhalese.

The Ceylon Tamils or 'Jaffna Tamils' as they are more popularly called, are the descendants of the old conquerors, who mostly came from the far north of Southern India. The Indian Tamils are chiefly the estate coolies, who are temporary migrants from the extreme south of India. The name 'cooly' is derived from the word 'kuli' which means 'daily hire or wages,' therefore a cooly means a day labourer.

Jaffna is the stronghold, or Mecca, of the Ceylon Tamils, whilst the Indian Tamils look upon 'the coast' as their home. Jaffna has always been supplied with educational advantages, and this has encouraged emigration. Many of the Jaffnese find work in the Madras presidency, and others find employment in Colombo, and the far East, as accountants, clerks, overseers and conductors on estates. There were seven thousand Jaffnese in the Federated Malay States and

Straits Settlements at the last Census. Owing to the emigration of so many men, Jaffna is the only district in Ceylon, with the exception of Galle, where there is a preponderance of females. The Tamils have of course their failings like other mortals, but it is always more gracious and pleasant to look at the bright side of things than at the dark. No one who knows anything of Tamils will deny the fact that as a race they are industrious, enterprising and clever. The energetic and industrious coolies are the backbone of all island labour. It has often been said that Tamil cooly labour is the 'best labour in the world,' and certainly it is surprising how much work a Tamil labourer will get through in a day on a minimum of food.

In days of old these immigrants invaded Ceylon as ruthless conquerors, now they come as valuable helpers in every enterprise, and are invaluable on the tea and rubber estates.

They are also an enterprising people, for they are to be found in many parts of the world, as far away as Capetown, the Mauritius and Jamaica, where they make money by their industry and thrift. This readiness to emigrate in search of work is a singular characteristic in an Eastern people.

That they are clever is clear from the many wise sayings which are found in their classical works, and from the fact that many of them take high honors at our universities. It is a fact, of which the Tamils may be justly proud, that the first Indian to be raised to the Episcopate, the Right Rev. V. S. Azariah, D.D., of Dornakal, is one of their race. Another point of interest is their literature. The great epic poem, the Ramayana, was rendered into Tamil some centuries ago and is most popular to-day. Among the most interesting of their classical works is the Cural, which is considered one of the finest poems in the Tamil language. Here are a few examples of its ethical teaching culled from E. J. Robinson's book on ' Tales and Poems of South India.'

Woman.	What is there not, when she excels ?
	Where she is useless nothing dwells.
Children.	The rice is all ambrosial made,
	In which their tiny hands have played.
Love.	The soul of love must live within,
	Or bodies are but bone and skin.
Slander.	Who loves to backbite makes it clear
	His praise of virtue's insincere.

A question which naturally arises is, Have the Tamils made their mark upon Christian literature in any degree ? The answer is in the affirmative. One of the greatest Christian poets that has arisen among the Tamils is Vethanayagam Sasthriar of Tanjore. Perhaps the most popular of his hymns is one that is connected with Ceylon. The story of how it came to be written has its humorous side, and by some may not be considered very complimentary to the fair island. The story is that on one occasion the poet and his choir of singers visited Jaffna, and their robes being somewhat soiled, it was thought expedient to send them to the 'wash.' But, alas, they never returned, the washerman having set envious eyes on them. The poet and his choir had, therefore, to appear in their ordinary clothes. To comfort his own mind the poet wrote a hymn which is often sung by the Tamils in time of sorrow. Of course, there is no mention made of the dhoby and his thievish tricks. The following is a translation of the hymn, which may be entitled ' Trusting at all times.'

> Though sinners hate thee sore
> And would entrap thy way,
> Though trials and distress
> Befal thee day by day,—

Though all should persecute,
  And grievous cares arise,
Though devils should appear
  Before thy trembling eyes,—

Though all men should forsake
  And battles rage around,
Though pain and suffering come
  And poverty abound,—

Though men despise and scorn
  And ill for good requite,
Though evil hosts combine
  To rob thee of thy right,—

My soul, be not distressed,
  Remember Zion's Lord,
By anxious thoughts oppressed,
  Faint not, but trust His word.

CHAPTER V.

HINDUISM.

THE Ceylon Hindus may be described as pure Animists, Animists and Sivites, and orthodox Sivites. The Animists are principally composed of all castes from the barber caste downwards, who are not allowed to enter a consecrated Hindu temple, and who are not ministered to by Brahmans. The orthodox Sivite worships certain gods, of whom Siva, Parvati his wife, Ganesha their son, Skanda and Virabhadra are the principal; but these gods merely represent ideals for meditation. The worship of Skanda is considered the most important, and Kataragama is the chief shrine in Ceylon. The circle of gods is considerably enlarged by the admission of various other gods of local, caste, or traditional significance. Each caste has its own protecting deity. Hinduism was originally nature worship, but has become polytheism of a gross kind. In the Hindu mythology there is a triad of principal gods,—Brahma, Vishnu and Siva, the first of whom is not now worshipped. The legends of Vishnu represent him, in his various incarnations, as guilty of all sorts of immoralities. Siva represents the reproductive force of nature, and in his temples an upright black stone, called a lingam, is worshipped. Saivas or Sivites, the followers of Siva, are distinguished by the three stripes of white cow dung ash, smeared on their foreheads, and often on their arms and breasts. Many also have a round white mark on the centre of their foreheads to represent the third eye of Siva. In Ceylon, the most familiar names of deities, or

HINDUISM

perhaps as they should rather be called, demons, are Mari-amma (mother of death), Suppramaniam, Muniyandi, Katharesan, and Narayanan. Mari-amma is the small-pox goddess or demon. Muniyandi is the demon most commonly worshipped by the coolies, and has many little temples on the tea estates. Muniyandi was once a cooly himself, in the early coffee days. He was of the lowest caste (shoemaker). One day he went to cut some branches from a tree for his goats, when a branch fell on him and killed him. That very day a terrible storm broke over Hunasgiriya estate, near Kandy, where Muniyandi worked. Two men chanced to take shelter in a cow-shed and one of them was struck by lightning. Next day, his companion consulted a fortune teller, as to the cause of the misfortune. He was told that it was the spirit of Muniyandi that had taken revenge on his companion, and he was urged to worship Muniyandi with proper rites. Muniyandi has ever since been regarded as a worker of mischief on the estates. The following is the mode of worship of the coolies. The worshipper, accompanied by a few companions, takes some incense in a pot, a banana leaf, some bananas and betel nuts, some ashes and camphor, a coconut, a bottle of arrack and a live cock. Arriving at the spot sacred to Muniyandi, he burns the incense, arranges the bananas with the betel nuts on the banana leaf, covers the ashes with camphor, sets fire to it and cuts the coconut shell in halves, care being taken to cut the shell with one cut. He then places the bottle of arrack beside the banana leaf and kills the cock, pouring its blood over the rude stone that serves as an idol, as well as over the banana leaf and its contents. He then pulls the feathers off the bird, and, having cut it down the breast, holds it over the camphor fire for a few minutes. This done, he either prostrates himself before the idol or stands with his hands clasped over his head, and prays to Muniyandi to prosper him and forgive anything amiss in his worship. He then takes the ashes, now sacred, and having put some in his mouth and smeared some on his forehead, he distributes some among his companions, and reserves the remainder for his family. He then takes up the cock and the arrack, and after pouring a little of the latter before the idol, he cuts the kernel of the coconut into pieces and pours some arrack into the coconut shell. He then cuts the fowl into pieces and distributes it with the coconut and arrack among himself and his companions. Once more, with due reverence, he places a piece of coconut and betel before the idol and returns home.

There are three chief religious festivals in Ceylon. (1) The Thai Pongal, which takes place early in the year, is a relic of an aboriginal nature worship of the sun. (2) The Tee-Vali in October commemorates the defeat of a tyrannical giant who had mightily oppressed both gods and men. It is also called the feast of lamps. (3) The Vale is connected with the worship of Suppramaniam, a son of Siva. In Colombo this festival is the occasion of a curious procession between two temples at opposite extremities of the town; and of celebrations lasting many days.

The religion of the higher classes is a religion of fear, for Hinduism presents God in a terrible aspect. No one can visit the temples in India and Ceylon without being struck with the representation of God. As in all false systems of religion, purity is unknown in Hinduism. This is clear from the fact that 'dancing girls' are attached to nearly every temple. These unhappy girls are called 'the slaves of God,' while in reality they are the miserable slaves of men's worst passions. Every candid Hindu will admit that the presence of these women at their festivals is a blot on the escutcheon of their religion. And yet there is a certain amount of light in Hinduism, for the doctrines of expiation, sacrifice, the

HINDUISM

incarnation and the unity of the Godhead are all found in it. Bullocks, sheep and fowls are commonly offered as expiatory sacrifices. Hinduism teaches moreover, that the God Vishnu has become incarnate, under different forms, nine times, and a tenth incarnation is eagerly looked for by every devout Hindu.

Again, the Trinity in Unity, is not a strange doctrine to the Hindu, for he believes that Brahma is God, Vishnu is God, and Siva is God, and yet they have a saying, 'Let earth be put into the mouth of any one who denies that Vishnu and Siva are one.'

It has been well said that 'a man's religion consists of what he is, what he does, and what he hopes for.' What then is the hope of the Hindu? His highest ambition is to lose his own personality and be absorbed in the deity. To attain this he must perform many acts of self-mortification, or of charity, which bring with them the reward of merit, but before this highest stage can be reached, he must pass through many transmigrations. Hinduism presents but little hope to women. Here is a story the truth of which can be vouched for. A Hindu woman was seen in devout and earnest prayer. When she had concluded her devotions, a Zenana missionary asked her, 'For what have you been praying?' and the woman replied, 'I have been praying that when I die, my soul may enter into a cow.' It is often said, 'Why trouble to preach the Gospel to the Hindus?' Surely, the Hindus, men, women and children need the Gospel, the Gospel of love and purity. While the Hindus are expecting another incarnation of their God Vishnu, it is the duty and privilege of the Christian Church to proclaim far and wide the one true incarnation which, when compared with the false incarnation of Vishnu, is as light compared with darkness.

CHAPTER VI.

CHRISTIANITY IN CEYLON.

THERE is a tradition of the existence of Nestorian Christianity in Ceylon, in the time of the Emperor Justinian. Cosmas, a Nestorian Christian, writing about A.D. 550 says, on the authority of one Sopater, a Greek merchant, that in Taprobane (which was the ancient Greek name for Ceylon) there existed a community of Persian Christians, tended by bishops, priests and deacons, and having a regular liturgy.

St. Thomas, St. Bartholomew, and the eunuch of Candace, whose conversion by St. Philip is recorded in the Acts of the Apostles, are all alleged to have preached Christianity in the island.

The historical evidence of the planting of Christianity is the arrival of the Portuguese in 1505, who brought with them Franciscan Fathers and who did their utmost to press Roman Catholicism upon the people. The most famous of their workers was St. Francis Xavier, the 'Apostle of the Indies' who came over from India in 1544 on a mission to the Tamils in the North. He, being unable to accept the invitation of the people of Manaar to 'come and teach them also' sent one of his clergy, through whom about seven hundred persons received baptism, a baptism which was straightway crowned by martyrdom, as these early converts were forthwith put to death by the Rajah of Jaffna, who was a worshipper of Siva. In 1650 the Dutch arrived, forcing the people by every means in their power to embrace the doctrines of the Reformed Church of Holland. Baptism had come to be regarded as a Government regulation, and was known as 'Christiyani karnawa,' or making Christian.

In 1795 the low country, and in 1815 the upcountry, came under the rule of the British, who proclaimed religious liberty. Emerson Tennent says, 'It had been declared honourable by the Portuguese to undergo such a ceremony, " making Christian," it had been rendered profitable by the Dutch, and after three hundred years' familiarity with the process the natives were unable to divest themselves of the belief that submission to the ceremony was enjoined by orders from the civil government.' When the pressure of compulsion was removed by the advent of the British power, thousands openly returned to their former superstitions, while the great majority of those who kept up their connection with Christianity had been so educated and trained in hypocrisy and false profession, that while outwardly, as a body, conforming to Christian worship, and anxious, as a matter of respectability, to obtain Christian rites, they held as their religious belief the doctrines of Buddhism, and practised in secret all its ceremonies and rites. In the first ten years of the British rule, the number of Buddhist temples in the Sinhalese districts had increased from between two and three hundred to twelve hundred.

In 1801, out of an estimated population of about one and a half million, the number of those who professed the Protestant form of the Christian faith was estimated to exceed 342,000, while the Roman Catholics were considered to be still more numerous. In 1804, the Protestant Christians were estimated at 240,000, in 1810 they had dropped to 150,000, in 1814 to 130,000 and fifty years after in 1864, there were said to be 40,000 Protestants and 100,000 Romanists.

The writer of the 'Jubilee Sketches' of the C.M.S. in Ceylon says, 'About the time that the first C.M.S.

Missionaries came to the island, the people were becoming aware of the fact that the outward profession of Christianity was no longer necessary to secure their civil rights, and were going back in large numbers to the open practice of Buddhism which, all along, they had secretly believed. The gradual cessation of efforts to instruct the people, which preceded and followed the advent of the British rule, left the mass of nominal adherents, who still retained their outward profession of Christianity, in utter ignorance of its real nature, and thus confirmed in them the idea that connection with it, although no longer compulsory, still placed them in a more advantageous position and that the reception of its rites, (Baptism and Marriage) still secured to them the countenance of the ruling powers, and gave them a respectable standing, which, for their worldly advancement and profit, it was necessary to retain.'

At the commencement of the Dutch rule, and for a long period of its continuance, earnest and systematic efforts seem to have been made by that Government to bring the people of the island to a knowledge and profession of Christianity. Had those efforts been continued in full vigour, both by the Dutch Government and our own, Buddhism would doubtless have been uprooted from the land, and a nominal profession of Christianity established in its place. Whether or not that would have been more favourable to the real progress of the Gospel than the present state of things, is a question which it is difficult to decide, and concerning which diverse opinions will always be held. For a long period of their rule, the Dutch made vigorous efforts, and liberally expended funds, it endeavours to convert the inhabitants to the Christian faith. Not only did they establish schools, but they also built churches and employed ministers in direct missionary work among the adults. Yet these efforts seem to have been marred by their mistaken policy, in making the reception of

CHRISTIANITY IN CEYLON

baptism and the outward profession of Christianity necessary in order to secure to the people their civil rights and privileges, and as a passport to Government employment. The result of this false policy was to make the outward profession of Christianity almost universal, but, at the same time, it so opened the floodgates of hypocrisy, that the tide of false and insincere professors completely overwhelmed the real converts, and overspread the land with a spurious Christianity which although imposing in extent, was utterly false and unsound. In the ' Historical Sketch of Ceylon ' by Dr. R. S. Copleston, published by the S.P.G., the writer says, ' When the English took possession in 1798, more than 300,000 natives are said to have been registered as members of the Dutch Church. Of these a few were genuine Protestants, a large number were really Romanists, but the majority were merely nominally Christians, and actually Buddhists or Hindus. Still, it was a grand opportunity which was thus set before our own nation and our own Church. For, although much of the Christianity we found in Ceylon was unsound, still the heathenism was feeble, ignorant, and discredited (to a depth far below what is now the case), and Christian education had done much to bring the children at least within our reach. But unhappily the England of that time was little alive to such a responsibility, the opportunity was lost, almost all that was done was to remove the pressure which had kept so many people nominally Christian. With the gradual withdrawal of that pressure (which was not completely done till 1860, when marriage, other than Christian, obtained equal registration), the great majority of the nominal Protestant Christians resumed the open profession of their real religion. In many cases this was Roman Catholicism, in more it was heathenism. Thus during nearly the whole century, at the beginning of which more than 300,000 persons outwardly professed the Church of England as representing the Government religion, the number of adherents of the Church has steadily decreased.'

For some time after the British annexation, Dutch Presbyterianism was recognized as the established Church of the Colony, and Mr. North afterwards Lord Guilford, the first British Governor, not only took active measures for restoring one hundred and seventy of the Dutch village schools, but also offered Government assistance to the clergy if they would itinerate through the rural districts, and so keep alive some knowledge of the Christian faith.

The first Protestant missionaries to visit Ceylon from England were four agents of the London Missionary Society in 1805, but for some reason, they all soon left for India, except the Rev. J. D. Palm who settled down as the Pastor of the Dutch Church at Wolfendahl in Colombo. The pioneer of modern missions in Ceylon was the Rev. James Chater who landed in Colombo on April 16, 1812. He was sent out by the Baptist Missionary Society in 1806 to join the Serampore Mission in North India, but his landing was opposed by the Indian Government, so he went on to Burmah and commenced work there. Civil war in the Burmese dominions and the ill-health of his wife forced him to relinquish work there and try Ceylon. The Governor-General Sir Robert Brownrigg, and Lady Brownrigg, were in full sympathy with missionary effort and gave him a hearty welcome. The beginning of all the principal missions in Ceylon took place during this Governor's regime.

The centenary of the Baptist Mission was celebrated in 1912, and a most interesting story of the hundred years was written by the Rev. J. A. Ewing, under the title, 'The Resplendent Isle—a hundred years witness in Ceylon.' In it, the writer says, 'The Baptist cause in Ceylon has never been strong numerically. There have been years of abundant harvest, as well as periods of barrenness and drought,

CHRISTIANITY IN CEYLON 37

but every effort is made to receive only sincere adherents, believing that only thus will the Church ultimately become strong and self-supporting.' The principal stations are at Colombo, Kandy, Matale and Ratnapura. There are twenty stations and out-stations, four men missionaries, nine women missionaries, thirty-nine native evangelists, thirty-one independent churches, 954 native members, 106 school teachers, forty-six schools with 3,831 scholars, and 2,787 children in the Sunday schools.

The Ceylon Auxiliary (originally called the Colombo Auxiliary) of the British and Foreign Bible Society was established at Queen's House, Colombo, on August 1, 1812, mainly by the zealous efforts of Sir Alexander Johnston, Chief Justice of Ceylon, with the Governor, Sir Robert Brownrigg as President, and the Rev. J. Bisset, Assistant Colonial Chaplain, the Honorary Secretary. From the day of its birth the Society has pursued an unwavering course and stands at the centre of all organized efforts for the evangelization of the island. The position which it holds in respect to all Protestant missions is unique, for it is the partner, helper and friend of all.

The auxiliary celebrated its centenary in 1912, and in the Annual Report for that year, a summary of the year's work is given as follows: 'The Scriptures circulated totalled 84,326 volumes, in twenty-five languages, against 72,783 for the previous year, an increase of 11,543 copies. The average number of Colporteurs employed was twenty and of Biblewomen sixty-four. The receipts from sales reached no less a sum than Rs. 7,622 : 27 and the subscriptions and collections contributed locally came to Rs. 8,424 : 92.'

The Wesleyan Methodist Mission commenced its work in Ceylon in 1814, being the first oriental station of this denomination. The first party of six missionaries, two of whom were married, with Dr. Coke as their leader, sailed from

England on December 30, 1813, and arrived at Point de Galle on June 29, 1814. Dr. Coke and Mrs. Ault, wife of one of the missionaries, died on the voyage.

Evangelistic, educational and industrial work have been prosecuted vigorously in many parts of the island. The principal educational institutions are Wesley College in Colombo opened in 1874, Richmond College, Galle, 1876, Kingswood College, Kandy, 1891 and the Wellawatte, Industrial Home, 1890. In Wellawatte, the mission owns a valuable printing establishment, and in Colpetty a high school for girls. It has also established a mission to seamen and a 'city mission' in Colombo. Other important stations have been established in the Jaffna peninsula and on the East coast. In 1916 there were twenty-seven European men missionaries, twenty-eight women missionaries not including wives, sixty catechists, 343 elementary schools with 927 teachers and 27,500 scholars, eleven boys' high schools with eighty-six teachers and 1,572 scholars, four colleges with eighty-two teachers and 1,583 students, 6,545 church members and 10,438 on probation.

The American Board of Foreign Missions (Congregationalist) commenced work in Jaffna in 1816, and have ever since confined themselves to that part of the island. The first missionaries had been designated for Madras, but on their way their vessel was wrecked off the north-west coast. This they accepted as an indication of the Divine will that they were to go no further. The medical work of the mission has been a great feature, and has been attended with much success. In 1824 the Uduvil Girls' Boarding School was commenced, probably the earliest effort of the sort in a heathen land. One of the missionaries, Miss Eliza Agnew had charge of this school for forty-three years. Upwards of a thousand girls studied under her care, and of these more than six hundred left the school as really earnest

Christians. Although the Mission has concentrated its effort on a comparatively small field, it has twenty-one outstations, twenty-one churches, 2,252 members, five men missionaries, nine women missionaries, eleven pastors, 375 teachers and 126 schools with 11,548 scholars. The mission celebrated its centenary in 1916, when a history was compiled by Miss Helen Root entitled 'A Century in Ceylon.'

The Friends' Foreign Mission Association commenced work in Matale in 1896 and in Mirigama in 1903. In 1915 there were six missionaries, sixty-three native workers, 313 adherents, twenty-three schools, 1,373 scholars and three dispensaries at which 4,800 patients were treated that year.

The Salvation Army commenced work in Ceylon in 1883, the Heneratgoda Faith Mission in 1891, and there are a few private or 'free lance' missions at work.

The Ceylon branch of the Christian Literature Society for India, formerly called the Vernacular Education Society, was founded in 1858 as a memorial of the Mutiny by a union of all the chief missionary societies to do a work which (in their own words) 'could not be done by them separately except by the wasteful expenditure of much money.' It is accordingly controlled by committees composed mainly of their missionaries. The Central Depot and Head Office of the Ceylon Branch is situated in Dam Street, Colombo. During the year 1915, there were sold 16,237 copies of General Literature, 2,015 Bibles and 11,278 Testaments and portions, whilst there were distributed free 240,000 four-page tracts and 120,000 twelve-page booklets. During the same year 123,500 copies of school books, 44,000 copies of general literature, 140,300 copies of periodicals and 240,000 copies of tracts, having a total of 11,233,500 pages, were printed. Six colporteurs were employed whose sales produced nearly Rs. 1,500. The object of the Society is to disseminate among the masses pure, healthy literature of a

Christian spirit and tone, chiefly in the vernacular. The Edinburgh Conference of 1910 reported that 'Christianity has been most intelligent, influential and progressive when mental activity has been most carefully nourished and stimulated by Christian literature,' and an Indian missionary says, 'After an experience of fifty years among the millions of these vast regions, I have no hesitation in saying that I regard this agency as second only to preaching and teaching among all the forms of labour employed in the missionary world.'

The Society for the Propagation of the Gospel began work in Ceylon in 1840, and in November of that year the Rev. C. Mooyart became its first missionary, being stationed in Colombo. In 1842 the Rev. H. Von Dadelszen was appointed to Nuwara Eliya and the Rev. S. D. J. Ondaatjie to Kalutara. In the following year a District Committee was formed at Colombo. 'The S.P.G. began by aiding existing churches, not by going into entirely new fields. In some cases, a Sinhalese or a Tamil clergyman, who was already employed as a chaplain under Government to minister to Christians of his own race, would be assisted by a grant from the S.P.G. and placed upon its lists of missionaries, that he might in this capacity be encouraged and enabled to extend his work to the heathen, and such missionary chaplains employed catechists, and opened schools. In other instances, where Government could be persuaded to make an allowance for a Catechist, the S.P.G. grant, in addition to the Government salary, made it possible to maintain a priest.'

'The S.P.G. has been a promoter and helper of missionary work rather than a proprietor of distinct missions. In one or two districts it has independent and valuable work, but more often the S.P.G. has worked in close conjunction with Government chaplains or diocesan clergy, rather than by a staff and missions of its own.' In 1851 with the assistance of the S.P.G., St. Thomas' College was opened and has received continuous aid. The Society has been gradually reducing its grant to Ceylon which now only amounts to £500. It was through the help of the Society that the Bishopric Endowment Fund was originated and completed in 1898.

The statistics for the year ended June 1916 were Christians 2,906, commmunicants 816, catechumens 44, baptized during the year 94, schools 28, teachers 148, pupils 2,792.

The preponderance of Roman Catholicism in the island is very marked. In seven out of the nine provinces more than seventy per cent of the Christians are Roman Catholics. There has been great activity not only in multiplying dignitaries, but in promoting higher education. There are three principal Roman Catholic Missions, the Oblates of Mary Immaculate, the Oblates of St. Benedict and the Society of Jesus. The Archbishopric is of Colombo, with Bishops of Colombo, Jaffna, Kandy, Galle and Trincomalee, whilst there are 173 foreign priests, 67 native priests, 26 foreign lay brothers, 64 native lay brothers, 186 foreign sisters and 324 native sisters. Among the congregations of women at work are the Sisters of the Good Shepherd, the Franciscan Missionaries of Mary, and the Sisters of the Holy Family. There are several native congregations including the St. Joseph's Society of lay brothers and the Societies of St. Peter and of St. Francis Xavier for women. The educational institutions include St. Joseph's College in Colombo, St. Patrick's College in Jaffna, St. Aloysius' College in Galle and the Papal General Seminary at Ampitiya near Kandy. The last named institution was founded by Pope Leo XIII in 1893 to provide a specially thorough theological education, of which all Indian dioceses might avail themselves.

The Church of England in Ceylon, according to the Government Census of 1911, numbered 41,095 members.

Ceylon, which had been added to the See of Calcutta in 1817, and to that of Madras in 1835 was erected into a separate Bishopric in 1845. The first Bishop of Calcutta, Dr. F. T. Middleton, was consecrated privately in Lambeth Palace on May 8, 1814, for 'fear of offending the natives' and the Dean of Winchester's sermon on the occasion was not allowed to be printed. His first episcopal visitation to Ceylon was in October 1816, when he arrived by the H.M. Cruiser, Aurora. His next visit was in 1821, when he consecrated St. Peter's Church in Colombo on May 22. Bishop Heber visited the island in 1825, followed by Bishop Turner in 1831, and Bishop Wilson in January 1843. The first Bishop of Colombo, Dr. James Chapman, was consecrated in Lambeth Palace Chapel on May 4, 1845, and landed in Colombo on All Saints' Day of that year, and after sixteen years of devoted service resigned in 1861. The C.M.S. Annual Report of 1845 said, 'The Committee anticipate much benefit to the Ceylon Mission from his spiritual direction and paternal superintendence over the Church in this interesting island.'

The second Bishop of Colombo, was Dr. Piers C. Claughton, who was translated from St. Helena in 1862, and after eight years' work resigned in 1870.

The third Bishop, Dr. Hugh W. Jermyn, was consecrated in 1871, but was forced by ill-health to resign in 1874, and afterwards was appointed Bishop of Brechin and Primus of Scotland.

In 1875, his successor, Dr. Reginald Stephen Copleston, was consecrated and worked assiduously for twenty-seven years, until his translation in 1902 to Calcutta. In 1892, was published his standard work on ' Buddhism, primitive and present, in Magadha and in Ceylon.' Dr. Copleston, owing to ill-health, resigned the See of Calcutta in 1912.

In 1903, his brother, Dr. Ernest A. Copleston who had been working in Ceylon for some years, was consecrated fifth Bishop of Colombo, in the Cathedral Church of Calcutta.

In 1881, the connection of the British Government with the endowment of religion by ecclesiastical votes from the general revenue to the Bishop and a number of Episcopal and Presbyterian Chaplains, was discontinued by ordinance, provision being made for existing incumbents. The Bishop thereupon summoned a Church assembly, comprising all the clergy in priests' orders, and lay delegates chosen by the various congregations, who elected a Committee to consider the future constitution of the Church. This Committee sat for nearly five years and ultimately drafted a complete constitution for 'the Church of England in Ceylon.' On July 6, 1886, the draft constitution was submitted to the Church assembly and approved, and recommended to the acceptance of the permanent Synod of the disestablished Church, which had already been elected by anticipation. The Synod met on the following day for the first time and solemnly accepted the constitution in the name of the whole Church in Ceylon. The proceedings closed with a joyful Te Deum.

The duty of self-organization and self-support which was thus forced upon the Church by the withdrawal of State aid, has served to quicken and to create corporate feeling, as well as the sense of unity, and has brought into it new life and liberality.

Under rule 8 of Chapter VII on the 'Revision and Formation of Parishes and Districts' of 'The Constitution and the Fundamental Provisions, and Regulations Non-Fundamental, of the Synod of the Church of England in Ceylon' it says 'nor shall any of the foregoing rules be so interpreted or understood as to hinder or prevent either the Society for the Propagation of the Gospel in Foreign parts or the Church

Missionary Society, or any other directly Mission Organization of the Church of England from carrying on as heretofore with the sanction and license of the Bishop, direct Evangelistic Missionary work amongst such heathen and Mohammedan populations,' and in Chapter VIII, on Patronage, Rule V, ' Nothing contained in this chapter shall interfere with the rights of the Society for the Propagation of the Gospel or of the Church Missionary Society or of any other Patrons, so long as they desire to exercise their Patronage independently of Synod.'

At the close of the year 1916 the number of clergy of the Church of England in Ceylon holding the Bishop's License was 108, viz. thirty-eight Europeans, five Burghers, twenty-nine Tamils and thirty-six Sinhalese.

The Church Missionary Society commenced work in 1818, and the Church of England Zenana Missionary Society in 1889, particulars of which will be found in Chapter VIII and the following pages of this volume.

In the Census of 1911 the population enumerated was 4,110,367. Of these 409,168 entered themselves as Christians, as follows:—

Roman Catholics	330,300
Church of England	41,095
Presbyterians	3,546
Wesleyans	17,323
Baptists	3,306
Congregationalists	2,978
Salvationists	1,042
Friends	120
Lutherans	142
Others	316

According to the Census of 1881 the Christians numbered 267,977, in 1891 they numbered 302,127, and in 1901 they numbered 349,239. The strength of the four principal religions in 1911 was, Buddhists, 60 per cent ; Hindus, 23 per cent ; Christians, 10 per cent ; and Mohammedans, 7 per cent, of the population.

One result of the World Missionary Conference held in Edinburgh in June 1910, was the appointment of a Continuation Committee of some forty leaders of the missionary forces. This Committee requested its Chairman, Dr. John R. Mott, to visit the mission fields, acquainting missionaries and native leaders with the work and plans of the Committee and assisting the work in such other ways as might be determined.

Dr. Mott accordingly spent from October 1912 to the following May in a tour through the principal mission fields of Asia, and held a series of twenty-one conferences. Never before have the great questions involved in the establishment of Christ's kingdom upon earth been discussed by so many recognized leaders of the Christian forces throughout the non-Christian world, nor has there ever been such an expression of united judgment and desire on the part of workers of the various Christian bodies.

Ceylon was the first centre visited and a Conference was held in Colombo, on November 11-13, 1912, at which sixty-six delegates chosen by the various religious bodies (excepting Roman Catholics) were present under the chairmanship of Dr. Mott. The following were chosen to represent the C.M.S., the Revs. G. S. Amarasekara, J. W. Balding, J. V. Daniel, A. E. Dibben, A. G. Fraser, W. E. Rowlands, W. G. Shorten, S. S. Somasundaram, Messrs. N. P. Campbell, N. Selvadurai, Mrs. A. G. Fraser and Miss L. E. Nixon.

The following is a summary of 'the findings' of the Conference, in regard to Ceylon.

Missionary work is located in the most populous and most accessible areas and is reaching the Sinhalese and Tamil speaking people. Very little, except through our schools, is being done for the Mohammedan men. The Parsis and the forest Veddahs are neglected. More direct evangelistic work among non-Christians needs to be done. A serious attempt should be made towards a better understanding of the religious standpoint of the people. Preachers and teachers should lay special stress by precept and example upon the truth that the task of the evangelization of this country is the task of every member of the Church. The Sinhalese and Tamil Churches connected with several missions support their own Ministry entirely in many places, partially in others. The community is strong enough in religious experience and intellectual attainment to supply an ordained ministry for its Church life, and is doing so. The progress made in self-government has resulted in greater generosity and in a deeper appreciation of independence, responsibility and power. The support of evangelistic efforts through indigenous Missionary Societies has been steadily increasing. Evangelistic effort in the immediate neighbourhood of independent churches and congregations is wholly inadequate. Leaders should be sought out and trained and every effort should be made to provide for them a ladder of responsibility, and to give freedom of initiative to such persons when discovered or trained. Mission schools should be concerned primarily in educating the Christian and social conscience of their pupils. Ceylonese workers should be accorded a powerful place in Church conferences and a full share in its consultations. Greater efforts should be made through the children attending schools to reach and influence their homes. As singular opportunities exist for the calling out and development of the missionary spirit in the various Christian schools and colleges, it would give encouragement to the missionary cause if the training of Ceylonese missionaries were placed in the forefront of the objects for which such colleges exist and if special scholarships were founded to help those who wish to qualify for missionary service. Greater attention should be given to the production and dissemination of Christian literature adapted to the needs of Ceylon Christians and non-Christians. There is a lack of leaders from among the Ceylonese women and a paucity of European women workers. Suitable Ceylonese women missionaries should receive exactly the same official and social status as the foreign workers. Simple inexpensive Anglo-vernacular Girls' Boarding Schools should be multiplied. The non-realization of many women and girls of the congregations of their duty to undertake voluntary church work is a defect. Simple medical work among women and children in backward districts is to be desired.

CHAPTER VII.

EDUCATION.

ABILITY to read and write at least one's own language, though not indispensable to the planting and development of Christianity, must be acknowledged to be a very importan aid to the work of the Christian Missionary. Christianity does not invite ignorance as an ally, but welcomes enlightenment as its co-adjutor. The total numbers able to read and write one language in all Ceylon in the last four decades were,

Census of	1881	...	...	404,441
,,	1891	...	...	603,047
,,	1901	...	...	773,196
,,	1911	...	...	1,082,828

The proportions of the above (in which males and females are included) are :—

	1881	1891	1901	1911
Percentage of Males	24·6	30·0	34·70	40·4
,, ,, Females	2·5	4·3	6·92	10·6

The total number of literates at the last Census was 878,766 males and 204,062 females. The total native population literate in English was 70,679. Of these 57,881 were males and 12,798 females, and of these 1,785 Sinhalese and 241 Ceylon Tamils, a total of 2,026 could not read and write their own language.

During the Dutch occupation of the Colony, schools were established and attendance was made compulsory. The teaching was largely religious and the girls had to show that they understood the catechism and creed before they could be married. In the Instructions from the Governor-General of India to the Governor of Ceylon in 1656,' it is laid down ' that the boys and girls should be made to attend schools, and be there received into Christianity. The observance of this point will cause some difficulty, because the natives think a great deal of their daughters, and the parents will not consent to their going to school after their eighth year. They may, perhaps, receive a little more instruction on the visits of the clergyman.'

That the education imparted was not of a very advanced type may be gathered from a quotation from Eschelskroon in his ' Description of Ceylon, 1782.' ' The schoolmasters are either chaplains, that come with the ships from Europe, or more usually still, broken mechanics, such as bakers, shoemakers, glaziers, etc., who have no more book learning than just to make a shift to sing the Psalms of David, and at the same time perhaps can say the Heidelberg catechism by heart, together with a few passages out of the Bible, and are able to read a sermon from some author, or else they are some wretched natives, that can scarce make a shift to read Dutch intelligibly, much less can they write a good hand, and in arithmetic are still more deficient.' When the British took possession in 1796, the question of education was neglected for some years, but with the advent of the missionary bodies, schools were established in various parts of the Island.

A School Commission was instituted by the Government on May 19, 1834, and the first Government Educational Institution, called the Colombo Academy, now known as the Royal College, was started on October 26, 1836. In January 1868, Sir Hercules Robinson's Education Scheme passed the Legislature, abolishing the School Commission, appointing a Director of Education, and regulating Grants-in-aid to all denominations and private schools in return for secular results only. This gave a great impetus to education, and the total number of scholars under the cognizance of the Department of Public Instruction has risen from 44,192 in 769 schools in 1873, to 384,533 in 4,303 schools in 1915. Of these 118,381 were girls, about 39 per cent of the girls of school-going age.

The total expenditure on 'Education' from the General Revenue in 1879 was Rs. 445,228 and for the year 1915 it amounted to Rs. 2,154,209.

The Cambridge Local Examinations were introduced in 1880, and for the first examination that year, were presented twenty-one boys and no girls; in 1915 there were 2,151 boys and 236 girls.

There are thirty-nine industrial schools, and carpentry among boys, and lace-making among girls, are the most popular industries.

The following extracts from Mr. E. B. Denham's 'Ceylon at the Census of 1911' are interesting. Under 'Instruction' he says, '67 per cent of the persons employed in this profession are males and 33 per cent females. In all it supports 15,500 persons. The number of persons depending on "Instruction" has increased by 5,000 during the decade. There were 4,690 school masters and teachers, as compared with 3,126 in 1901, and 2,269 school mistresses and teachers, as compared with 1,507 in 1901. Of the Kandyan Sinhalese, only 912 depend upon educational employment, as compared with 7,176 Low-country Sinhalese and 5,001 Ceylon Tamils.'

Again Mr. Denham writes under 'Education', 'The improved standard of comfort throughout the country, the growth of wealth, accompanied by considerable changes in manners and customs, have all produced an enormous demand—which may almost be described as a passion—for education. The older generation regard education as an investment for their children, which will enable them to take up positions to which their newly acquired wealth entitles them. The small landowner and cultivator who has prospered believes that education will make a clerk of his son or fit him for a learned profession, that the latter will then hold a better position in the world than his father, and that consequently the fortunes, and, what appeals to him equally strongly, the status of the family will be assured. The younger generations seek escape from rural life, from manual toil, from work which they begin to think degrading, in an education which will enable them to pass examinations, which will lead to posts in offices in the towns, and so to appointments which entitle the holders to the respect of the class from which they believe they have emancipated themselves.'

The Church Missionary Society, together with the other Christian Missions, has from the beginning been in the forefront in the matter of education, and has established some of the best schools in the Island. Consequently the Christians show the highest proportions of literates amongst all religions.

In 1911, the percentage of literates of each religion and sex was as follows:—

	Males.	Females.
Christians	60.3	38.8
Buddhists	41.8	9.1
Hindus	29.6	4.0
Mohammedans	36.2	3.2

During the last thirty years the Buddhists have taken a keener interest in education, and hundreds of vernacular schools have been opened in the villages for boys as well as for girls, and English schools in the towns. The Hindus are also now taking their share in the education of the young.

It is a cause for thankfulness that the education of girls has not been neglected, for the value of female education is so great that its importance cannot be exaggerated.

Sinhalese women have never been deliberately excluded from the acquisition of knowledge, and the old proverb of the Tamils, ' Though a woman may wear cloth upon cloth and is able to dance like a celestial, she is not to be desired if she can press a style on a palm leaf ' does not hold to-day.

Mr. John Ferguson in his review of ' Christian Missions in Ceylon ' says ' Education has made great strides . . . Perhaps the most unfailing and successful branch of mission work has been found in the boarding schools for girls as well as for boys, but especially for the girls. If a Christian philanthropist were to stipulate that his wealth had to be devoted solely to that branch of mission operations which had been found to give the most uniformly satisfactory results, we fancy the vote of the missionaries, as of Christian laymen in Ceylon, would go by a large majority in favour of Girls' Boarding Schools.'

CHAPTER VIII.

C.M.S. IN CEYLON.

ON February 16, 1796, Colombo was surrendered by the Dutch, with scarcely a blow being struck in its defence, and so the low country became a possession of the British crown.

Three years after, on Friday, April 12, 1799, in a first floor room in the 'Castle and Falcon Hotel' in Aldersgate Street, London, when sixteen clergymen and nine laymen were present, was founded 'The Church Missionary Society for Africa and the East.' In each year's annual report of the Society issued since, we are reminded that 'Ceylon was one of the first fields to which the fathers of the C.M.S. turned their eyes.'

The peculiar circumstances of Ceylon, its claims on British Christians, and the facilities it afforded for the prosecution of missionary work, led the Committee of the Society to determine on making an effort in its behalf as soon as they should find themselves in a position to do so. It was, however, not the heathenism of Ceylon, but its Christianity which led them to contemplate this step. In the first report of the Society's proceedings, published in 1801, we read, 'In the island of Ceylon, it appears that there are not less than 146 Christian schools; of these fifty-four are within the district of Colombo, and in that one district alone there are not less than 90,000 native Christians. The Christian religion having been thus successfully planted by the Portuguese and then further cultivated by the Dutch, it is hoped that it will not be suffered to decline now that the Island is subject to the Crown of England. This important subject has not escaped the attention of the Committee.'

With no actual experience of the real state of matters to guide them, the Island appeared to them as a field of labour 'white already to the harvest.' A clergyman stationed in Ceylon in a letter dated December, 1801, to one of the Governors of the Society, writes, ' From the time the English took possession, until the arrival of Mr. North, the Governor, the Christian schools and education of the inhabitants were entirely neglected, many Churches had fallen into ruins, and thousands of those who called themselves Christians had returned to their ancient paganism and idolatry. By the last returns in the Ecclesiastical department, there were nearly 170 schools and upwards of 342,000 Christians.'

Until 1813, the C.M.S. was unable, first from the want of funds, and then from the want of men, to take any direct step towards the opening of a mission. They, however, corresponded with men of influence in the island who took an interest in Christian work, in order to obtain information for future use, and further made an offer to Sir Alexander Johnston, the Chief Justice, to educate for the ministry any two native young men that he might select and send to England. Sir A. Johnson also caused the first number of the ' Missionary Register ' (January, 1813) to be translated into Sinhalese, Tamil and Portuguese, for circulation in the island. He also engaged two men to translate Bishop Porteus' work on the *Evidences of Christianity* into Sinhalese.

Two men, Thomas Norton and William Greenwood, had been accepted for training by the C.M.S. in 1809. Norton was a married shoemaker who had studied Greek, and Greenwood was a blanket manufacturer. After training, the Bishops declined to ordain men for work outside their own dioceses. Eventually they were ordained to curacies in England, and in 1814 appointed to Ceylon, being the first clergymen of the Church of England to go to Asia definitely as missionaries, the first two English men trained by the C.M.S. and the first two English clergymen sent out by the Society.

In the instructions delivered to them at the valedictory dismissal on January 7, 1814, the following passage occurs, ' You, Mr. Norton, and Mr. Greenwood, are destined to labour in the populous island of Ceylon. We feel great interest in the increase of true religion there, and in this desire our personal intercourse with Sir A. Johnston, has greatly confirmed the Committee. The war into which the ambitious violence of these days unwillingly forced Great Britain and Holland is now happily closed. This protracted war disabled the Dutch from maintaining in Ceylon that succession of clergymen which was necessary for the support of religion. We send you to lend your aid to the religious concerns of this important portion of the British colonial possessions, and in the persons in authority there, you will find willing protectors.' The two missionaries embarked in the same vessel for Ceylon, but she was obliged to put back for repairs, and before finally sailing, which was three weeks before the Battle of Waterloo in 1815, the Committee altered their destination to India.

In the autumn of 1817, the Committee appointed the Revs. Samuel Lambrick, Benjamin Ward, Robert Mayor and Joseph Knight, all of whom had been ordained by Bishop Ryder of Gloucester, as missionaries to Ceylon, and in their instructions we read, ' In few places are there more favourable opportunities of reviving and extending Christian truth. For want of religious instruction, numbers are fast degenerating into heathenism. The Chief Justice has prepared the way for our exertions, by diffusing information respecting the designs of our Society. There are two objects which you will ever keep in mind as forming the great design of your labours, the revival of true Christianity in the hearts of the natives who at present only nominally profess it, and the conversion of the heathen.'

On October 28, 1817, a valedictory dismissal under the presidency of Lord Gambier was held at the Freemason's Hall in the City of London, and a sermon was previously preached by the Rev. J. W. Cunningham, Vicar of Harrow, at St. Bride's Church, from Psalm lvi. 3, ' Though I am sometime afraid, yet put I my trust in Thee.'

The Rev. Charles Simon also gave an address to the departing missionaries. On December 20, 1817, the four men, with Mrs. Mayor and Mrs. Ward, embarked at Gravesend on board the *Vittoria*. They arrived at Teneriffe on January 5, leaving again on the 23rd, not reaching the Cape till April 14, in consequence of calms and contrary winds, arriving in Madras on June 17, and at Point de Galle on June 29, 1818, having taken two hundred days to accomplish the voyage. On disembarking at Galle, the missionaries were received with great kindness by the Rev. J. M. S. Glenie, the Chaplain at the station.

In the original plan of the Parent Committee it had been arranged that Mr. Lambrick should be stationed at Colombo, Mr. and Mrs. Mayor at Galle, Mr. Knight at Jaffna and Mr. and Mrs. Ward at Trincomalie, but on arrival representations were made to them which led to a change in the location of two of their number.

Messrs. Lambrick and Ward were stationed at Kandy and Calpentyn respectively, and Messrs. Mayor and Knight proceeded to the stations to which they were originally designated. After a few months Mr. Mayor thought it advisable to leave the town of Galle, so in 1819 moved twelve miles inland to Baddegama, and Mr. Ward finding Calpentyn unsuitable for a Mission station, removed to Jaffna and afterwards to Baddegama.

In 1822 the Cotta Mission was begun, Colombo was occupied in 1850 and the Kandyan Itinerancy and Tamil Cooly Mission were founded in 1853 and 1855 respectively. In 1827 the Cotta Institution to train workers was founded, but now for some years it has been carried on as an English school.

Early in 1850, Sir J. Emerson Tennent, Secretary to the Ceylon Government, and afterwards well known for his elaborate book on Ceylon, wrote a letter to Lord Chichester, the President of the C.M.S., in which he said, 'The mission of Christianity is not doomed to repulse, as has been improperly asserted. Its ministers are successfully carrying forward the work of enlightenment and civilization with an effect so remarkable, and a result so convincing, in Ceylon, as to afford every assurance of a wide and permanent triumph for the Gospel.'

An important high class boys' school was begun at Chundicully in 1851, which is now known as St. John's College, and the Copay Training Institution was opened in 1853. In 1857 the Kandy Collegiate School for boys was opened by the Rev. J. Ireland Jones and was closed after six years, but in 1872 was reopened under the name of Trinity College by the Rev. R. Collins.

Several boarding schools for girls were opened, the first at Nellore in 1842, another for Tamils at Borella by Mrs. W. E. Rowlands in 1869, the Cotta school in 1870 by Mrs. R. T. Dowbiggin, another at Baddegama in 1888 by Mrs. J. W. Balding, and one at Kegalle by Mrs. G. Liesching in 1895. Miss H. P. Phillips opened an industrial school at Dodanduwa in 1893 and a Girls' English High School was commenced at Chundicully in 1896 by Mrs. J. Carter.

The C.M.S. Ladies' College was opened in Colombo in 1900 by Miss L. E. Nixon and Miss E. Whitney, in 1903 a Girls' English School at Cotta by Mrs. J. W. Balding, and in 1904 a vernacular training school for Sinhalese women teachers was opened in Colombo which after a few months was transferred to Cotta and in 1916 to the newly instituted Training Colony at Peradeniya.

The Jubilee of the mission in Ceylon was celebrated in 1868 and an appeal was issued by the Rev. W. Oakley, the Secretary of the Mission in May 1868, for ' contributions to a Jubilee Fund, as a token that the utility of past efforts is recognized, and as a pledge of the desire that the work shall go still on.' The writer of the appeal also says, ' The amount of success has not perhaps been all that was at first anticipated, the number of satisfactory converts may have not been as great as in some more favoured missions, still the efforts made have not been without fruit, the prayers offered have not been without answer, and there is good reason to hope that in the midst of the great and countless multitude of the redeemed which shall hereafter surround God's throne, many shall appear whose first knowledge of the truth as it is in Jesus was conveyed to them by the workers of the C.M.S.' Meetings were held in various centres to celebrate the Jubilee, the chief one being held at the girls' school near the Kachcheri, in Colombo, on Friday evening, July 17, 1868. This was presided over by the Bishop, and the collection at the close amounted to £18.

The Rev. W. Oakley moved the first resolution, ' That this meeting feels bound to render hearty thanks to God for His goodness in having enabled the C.M.S. to continue uninterruptedly, its labours in Ceylon for a period of fifty years, and for the measure of success by which those labours have been crowned.' This was seconded by Dr. Willisford. Mr. R. V. Dunlop moved the second resolution which was seconded by the Hon'ble Colonel Layard, ' That this meeting desires to express its confidence in the soundness of those principles by which the C.M.S. has, from its commencement been guided, and to which it still firmly adheres.'

The Hon'ble R. F. Morgan moved the third resolution which was seconded by the Rev. J. Ireland Jones, ' That this meeting, while acknowledging with thankfulness the important results which have by God's blessing, followed from the Church Missionary Society's labours in Ceylon, feels deeply the urgent need which still exists for continued and extended efforts, and recognizes the duty of promoting by every possible means, the great ends which the Society has in view.'

Also to commemorate the Jubilee, the Rev J. Ireland Jones, wrote the small book already mentioned, entitled ' Jubilee Sketches.' In this review of the fifty years' work, the writer says, ' A more arduous task, a more trying field of labour, it would be difficult to imagine. It is a matter well understood by planters, that while the primeval forest land, if cleared and planted, will soon yield them a rich return, the chenas of the lower ranges, previously exhausted by native cultivation, though far more easy of access, and requiring far less outlay at the beginning, will too often mock their hopes, and can only be made to yield a return at last, by a long and expensive mode of cultivation. This fact has its counterpart in spiritual husbandry.'

In 1875, Dr. Reginald Stephen Copleston was consecrated fourth Bishop of Colombo, and arrived in the island early the following year. Soon after the Bishop's arrival, serious difficulties arose, owing to his seeking a more direct control than his predecessors had had, over the C.M.S. work. The Society conceived that its just liberties as an independent organization, and those of its missionaries as clergymen of the diocese, were at stake, and the controversy was rendered still more painful by theological differences. In 1880, the questions at issue were submitted to the Archbishop of Canterbury (Dr. Tait), the Archbishop of York (Dr. Thomson), the Bishops of London (Dr. Jackson), Durham (Dr. Lightfoot), and Winchester (Dr. Harold Browne), and the result was an 'Opinion' from these prelates which was accepted on both sides as satisfactory and under which the mission has been carried on ever since with little difficulty.

In 1881 the Bishop confirmed 520 candidates, including 174 Tamil coolies, in C.M.S. districts. In another tour in 1885, he confirmed eighty-three candidates, and wrote to a missionary magazine, *The Net*, 'I have lately seen much that was encouraging among the immigrant Tamil coolies and among the native Sinhalese respectively. The former set a very good example by the zeal and liberality with which they support their own Churches. In one planting district, while the English masters were waiting, and wishing, and considering how they should get a Church, their Tamil labourers built one.'

The Bishop was transferred to Calcutta in 1902, a gain to India but a corresponding loss to Ceylon. Whilst it is impossible to forget that the early years of his episcopate were a period of estrangement and conflict between the Bishop and the missionaries and the Committee, the alienation had long since disappeared and for many years the record had been one of unbroken and cordial co-operation. Differences indeed doubtless remained, theological, ecclesiastical and practical, but these have not prevented the discovery of a common ground on which all could work together for the glory of their common Lord. Clergy and laity alike, European and Ceylonese, learnt to revere the Bishop as a true Father in God.

In 1884 some questions arose upon which the missionaries and lay friends differed from the Home Committee, and the Revs. J. Barton and C. C. Fenn were sent out to adjust matters, which they accomplished to general satisfaction, and no further difficulty has occurred. In 1887 and again in 1889, 'Special Missions' were conducted by the Rev. G. C.

Grubb, assisted on the first occasion by Colonel Oldham. Much blessing was vouchsafed, many English planters were brought to Christ, and the Christian men among them stirred up to greater zeal, and the effect of this, both upon the Ceylonese Christians and upon the evangelistic work was very marked. It was afterwards marred by the antagonistic influence of the Exclusive Brethren. The Revs. E. N. Thwaites and Martin J. Hall also conducted special missions in 1894 and the Rev. E. Bacheler Russell in 1896 at Christ Church, Galle Face. Mrs. J. W. Balding, writing to the localized Gleaner in 1887 with reference to 'the missioners in the Baddegama District,' says, 'Blessed have been the messages, straight from the loving Saviour, through His instruments, messages of earnest, tender appeal for a full surrender of the heart to God, and perfect consecration to Him and to His service. The mission came, bringing to many a weary heart, rest, joy, and peace, and has gone, leaving behind a greater hungering and thirsting after righteousness. Some of our Christians have been stirred up to more active work. Every day there were good attendances. Backsliders were present whose faces had not been seen for many years. Buddhists also came. It was beautiful to note the earnest upturned faces, and the rapt attention with which the word was listened to, the word of God full of pardon, love and peace, melting to tears some of the hearers, imparting to others unspeakable joy.' The Rev. A. E. Dibben writing of the 1894 mission said, 'Europeans, Sinhalese and Tamils have been so stirred up that several have given in their names as wishing to engage directly in the Lord's work as He may lead.'

In 1886 the Rev. F. E. Wigram, the Honorary Clerical Secretary of the C.M.S. during his tour of the missions in the East, accompanied by his son, visited Ceylon.

In 1869 a system of Native Church organization was

brought into operation, with District Councils to manage all financial business, and a Central Council as a deliberative body. Large grants-in-aid which were received yearly from the Home Society were reduced by one-twentieth annually. These grants have now run out, and in 1911 the old system was superseded by the launching of a ' Scheme for the organization of Churches in Ceylon in connection with the C.M.S.' More responsibility is now thrown upon the Ceylonese clergy as they take independent charge of their pastorates. Several clergy have been accorded this position, and some have taken over the management of the schools and assumed responsibility for the evangelistic work in their respective areas. This new scheme has had the effect of developing the spirit of devotion and self-sacrifice, as well as of calling forth more prominently the co-operation of the laymen of the Church. Some of these independent pastorates also receive annual grants from the Synod of the diocese. In 1892 two teaplanters, Messrs. Ernest J. Carus Wilson and Sydney M. Simmons left their estates and commenced a Band of Associated Lay Evangelists in connection with the Sinhalese branch of the mission. Work was carried on in the villages with the assistance of catechists. The work was helped by the exhibition of large coloured Scripture pictures, hymn singing, lantern talks under the palm trees and work amongst children. The band was never really given a fair trial of steady and continued labour, as when any urgent vacancy occurred in the stations, one of the lay evangelists was at once sent to fill the gap. The evangelists went to England in 1896 and returned the following year. Mr. Simmons who had been ordained was appointed to take charge of Baddegama, and in 1899, Mr. Carus Wilson who had been engaged in evangelistic work at Bentota, was obliged to return to England.

In 1899 the Ceylon Mission commemorated the Centenary

of the Parent Society. On April 12 a public meeting was held in the school room at Galle Face Church, Colombo. The Bishop presided and the three speakers, all of whom have since passed to their rest, were the Revs. E. T. Higgens, J. D. Simmons and Sir W. W. Mitchell. Special services and meetings were held at all the stations. At Cotta, Rs. 315 was contributed as a birthday offering, at Baddegama Rs. 500 as a centenary thankoffering and at Holy Trinity Church, Kandy, Rs. 500 was given to meet the monthly liabilities of the pastorate. At Nellore a breakfast was given to five hundred persons. At Chundicully there was a social gathering and at 5.20 p.m. corresponding to noon in London, the Union Jack was unfurled, and the hymn 'Jesus shall reign' was sung. At Pallai, after the thanksgiving service, Sir W. Twynam entertained one hundred and fifty Christians at breakfast.

The C.M.S. Conference, which until quite recently met twice a year, now meets once a year in the month of August, with the Bishop as Chairman. All the European missionaries, four Ceylonese clergy and two Ceylonese laymen are members. The women missionaries have also a Conference which meets annually. The Conferences elect Standing Committees, Examination, Visiting and other sub-committees.[1]

The Finance Committee of the mission is composed of nine laymen, two missionaries and the Secretary of the mission. There have always been influential laymen willing to give their services, and one of these, Sir W. W. Mitchell, K.C.M.G., who died in Colombo on December 15, 1915, had been a valuable member for thirty-one years.

[1] A new constitution granted by the Parent Committee came into force at the August Conference, 1921. See Appendix.

In the year 1843 an Association, under the patronage of His Excellency, Sir Colin Campbell (then Governor), the Bishop of Madras and some of the principal members of the Civil Service, was established, in order to assist the evangelistic and educational work of the C.M.S. in Colombo and the Western Province. From the commencement 'the Ceylon Association of the C.M.S.' as it is now called, has contributed largely to the local funds of the mission, and for several years has made grants to the stations and has supported workers. The receipts of the Association for the twenty-five years, 1891—1915, amounted to no less than Rs. 126,804.

A few years ago a 'Home Branch of the Ceylon C.M.S. Association' was formed by Mr. Ernest J. Carus Wilson, Woodlea, Barnet, (formerly of the Ceylon Mission) in order to retain the prayerful sympathy and practical help of those interested in Ceylon and also of those who, when resident in the island, subscribed to the work. Gifts are forwarded to Ceylon and donors receive the monthly Gleaner and the annual report of the Association.

For some years the *Church Missionary Gleaner*, a monthly illustrated publication containing information of the work in various missions throughout the world, has been localized. The Ceylon portion furnishes details of local mission work and is edited by one of the missionaries.

During the hundred years, 108 European missionaries, clerical and lay, and sixty European women missionaries (not including wives) have worked in the mission with, during the same period, thirty-three Tamil clergy and twenty-nine Sinhalese.

As regards area, fully three-fourths of the island has been committed to the C.M.S. by diocesan authority, either for Sinhalese or Tamil work or for both, but it has to be acknowledged with regret that a great part of this area has never been effectively occupied. The following are the

Statistics of the Mission for 1918

	No.
1. *Mission Agents*—	
European Clergy	16
Ceylonese Clergy	27
Women Missionaries	14
Catechists and Readers	122
Biblewomen	37
School Masters	479
School Mistresses	319
2. *Congregations*—	
Communicants	6,041
Christians (adults and children) including the Communicants	14,796
Adult candidates for baptism	302
3. *Baptisms in* 1918—	
Adults	224
Children	487
4. Sunday Schools	253
Scholars	9,749
5. *Educational*—	
Training Schools	3
Students	52
High Schools	4
Students	1,357
Middle Schools	15
Students	1,342
Elementary Schools	290
Students	23,814
Industrial Schools	5
Students	141

STATISTICS OF THE MISSION FOR 1918—*continued.*

6. *Contributions in* 1918—

	Rs.
Grants by Parent Committee and contributions received through them	184,714:24
Contributions by Europeans and Burghers.	31,057:52
Contributions by Sinhalese and Tamils for their own Churches	42,346:10
Contributions for Tamil Cooly Mission	11,734:84
Ceylon Association	7,538:69
Total	92,677:15

It must be borne in mind that in dealing with the statistics the figures refer only to what are known as the C.M.S. districts, for instance, the number of Christians given above as 14,796, is the number living in the districts belonging to the congregations for that year. Many of our young people who by our means have been brought to the knowledge of the truth, move out into the world to obtain a livelihood, and attach themselves to other congregations. There is not a parish or district in the island in which will not be found those who have at one time or another, been connected with our districts or schools.

In 1918 the C.M.S. thus had in Ceylon 314 schools with 26,654 students.

Three hundred and ten of these schools received grants-in-aid from Government that year, amounting to Rs. 118,866 or nearly £7,924. The twenty-one English schools received of this amount, Rs. 36,300:50, the four Anglo-Vernacular schools, Rs. 4,375:21 and the 285 Vernacular schools, Rs. 78,190:61.

Again, the results of missionary work cannot be gauged by the number of converts living at any particular date. The real fruits of the work are the souls that have passed to the everlasting rest. Dr. Stock truly says in the *History of the C.M.S.* (vol. iii, p. 769) : ' Let it be repeated, that statistics fail to show the best fruits, the fruits already gathered into the heavenly garner, and no mission has given brighter examples of Christian deaths crowning Christian lives than the mission in Ceylon.'

Statistics of the Mission at various dates

	1818	1828	1838	1848	1858	1868
European Clergy	4	8	8	10	9	11
Ceylonese Clergy	...	...	8	3	2	7
Lay Workers	...	20	69	106	140	178
Christians	...	...	...	...	...	...
Communicants	...	28	133	306	440	724
Schools	1	48	52	72	87	104
Scholars	44	1,744	1,762	2,577	2,962	3,644

Statistics of the Mission at various dates—*contd.*

	1878	1888	1898	1908	1918
European Clergy	10	13	16	18	16
Ceylonese Clergy	10	14	17	21	27
Lay Workers	363	409	644	844	971
Christians	6,370	6,588	9,328	11,424	14,799
Communicants	1,512	2,191	3,383	4,294	6,041
Schools	222	190	293	339	314
Scholars	9,524	11,102	16,874	23,635	26,654

CHAPTER IX.

KANDY.

KANDY, beautifully situated in a valley amid the Kandyan hills, seventy-two miles from Colombo and 1,654 feet above sea-level, was founded about A.D. 1200 and from the year 1592 to 1815 was the Capital of the Sinhalese Kings. Kandy or Kande means the hill or hill country, but it is known to the people as ' Maha Nuwara,' the great city. Cruelty on the part of the last Sinhalese king had made his subjects regard him with hatred, and the execution of the wife and children of his prime minister, Ehelapola, led the people to compass his overthrow. The British were invited to help, and the arrest and death in exile of the tyrant, Sri Wickrama Raja Singha, terminated the line of Sinhalese kings. On March 2, 1815, the British flag was hoisted and the interior came under the dominion of the British Crown. At a Convention on the same day, between the Governor and the chiefs, it was agreed that the late sovereign had forfeited all claims to that title and that his descendants should be for ever excluded from the throne. It was also agreed that ' the religion of Buddha should be inviolable and its rites, ministers and places of worship maintained and protected.' The spirit of independence, however, still remained, the chiefs would not brook the restraints of the new government, and within three years a rebellion broke out the suppression of which cost the lives of a thousand British and many natives.

About this time the population of Kandy was about three thousand, whilst to-day it is over thirty thousand, and the low country people in the town out-number the Kandyans by nearly three thousand. A wonderful change has taken place in Kandy during the last hundred years. In the early days, the town consisted of mud huts thatched with straw, the streets being almost impassable, with open drains on each side, six or seven feet wide, which acted as receptacles for the filth of the town and over which were placed planks as approaches to the huts. Villagers brought in produce from the country, fowls could be bought at two pence each and one hundred and twenty eggs for a shilling. There were no proper roads and the first mail coach did not run till 1832. When the first C.M.S. missionaries arrived in Ceylon, the Governor strongly urged that one of their number should commence work in Kandy. There were many reasons which favoured this. Here was the temple, the Dalada Malagawa, containing the so-called tooth of Buddha, which was regarded with superstitious reverence by the Buddhists, also the viharas or colleges of the priests. The independence of the people was in itself a safeguard against hypocrisy and a pledge of their sincerity when they should be led to profess faith in Christ. So in 1818 the Rev. S. Lambrick entered on his work in Kandy. On October 27, 1818, he wrote 'I cannot be permitted at present to preach to the natives, but I have obtained authority to open schools, and have obtained two priests to be the masters of them. The children will be especially taught to read and write their own language as a step towards their receiving the words of eternal life.' Mr. Lambrick was for two years the only Church of England clergyman in Kandy and consequently gave much time to the spiritual care of the troops and other Europeans there. On the eve of the departure of the Governor, Sir R. Brownrigg, from the island, a levee was held at which the four C.M.S. missionaries were present and presented an address, to which the Governor replied, 'The whole island is now in a state of tranquillity, most favourable for the cultivation and improvement of the human mind. I cannot doubt but that under the guidance of providence, the progress of Christianity will be general, if the zeal for propagating the knowledge of Christianity be tempered with such a sound discretion as has been exhibited already by one of your mission (Mr. Lambrick) in the centre of the heathen population. It is my sincere wish that you may all follow that example, and that your success may justify my partial feelings of regard for the missionaries of the established Church.' On October 28, 1821, the Rev. and Mrs. Thomas Browning arrived to work with Mr. Lambrick. Owing to want of success among the Kandyans, there was some thought of abandoning the town and starting work in an interior village. The Government however would not sanction the removal on account of the unsettled state of the country. At the end of May, 1822, Mr. Lambrick removed to the low country. In June, 1822, Mr. Browning obtained from Government a grant of land, which still forms part of the Trinity College compound, on which he erected a bungalow and school room. Service was held in the school on Sundays, several Kaffir soldiers belonging to the Ceylon regiment were under instruction, and the Sinhalese prisoners in the jail were visited. At the end of 1823 there were 127 children attending the five schools which had been opened.

Bishop Heber, on his visit to Kandy in 1825, says 'We went up with the Governor, Sir E. Barnes, to Kandy, where I preached, administered the sacrament, and confirmed twenty-six young persons in the audience hall of the late King of Kandy, which now serves as a Church. Here, twelve years ago, this man, who was a dreadful tyrant, used to sit in state, to see those whom he had condemned, trodden to death by elephants trained for the purpose. Here he actually compelled the wife of one of his chief ministers, to bruise to death in a mortar, with a pestle, with her own hands, one of her children, before he put the other to death, and here at the time, no Englishman or Christian could have appeared, unless as a slave, or at the risk of being murdered. Now, in this very place, an English Governor and an English congregation, besides many converted natives of the island, were sitting peaceably to hear an English bishop preach.'

In 1826 a further piece of land was granted by Government for a burial ground. In 1827, 'there were eight communicants from the Portuguese and Sinhalese, whose moral conduct was consistent' and in 1830 'the state of things had not much altered for the better.' In March, 1831, Bishop Turner of Calcutta visited the station and confirmed thirty-six candidates, and in October of the same year the first Sunday school was opened.

The mission was strengthened in June, 1835, by the arrival of the Rev. William Oakley. Soon after, a house to house visitation of the Sinhalese Protestant Christians in Kandy was started, and in fifty families containing about three hundred persons, it was found that family worship was only kept up in ten, some were totally destitute of the word of God, some never attended divine worship, some were living in open sin, and others were found neglecting the baptism and education of their children. Another investigation of the number of Protestant families that were not Sinhalese was made, and it was found that out of five hundred and eighty souls in one hundred and twenty-three families, eighty children were unbaptized, and in between thirty and forty families, the parents were living together unmarried.

Mr. Oakley also visited the villages, the hospitals in the town and the Malay soldiers of the Ceylon Rifle regiment.

Mr. Browning died at sea in July, 1838, when only two days' sail from England. The Bishop of Madras visited the mission in November, 1839, and wrote 'My next visit was to a place very interesting to me, the Church Missionary premises in Kandy, where under the devoted care of Mr. Oakley the work grows and flourishes. His school room, which is also his Church, is becoming much too small for either purpose. He understands his work, and loves it, and is evidently doing good.' In 1840 there were at Kandy besides Mr. and Mrs. Oakley, eighteen native teachers, of whom two were women. There were twenty-two communicants and thirteen schools, containing three hundred and thirteen boys and fifty-six girls. Mrs. Oakley, who died on July 14, 1866, aged fifty-one years, was a remarkable woman, speaking both Tamil and Sinhalese, exercising great power for good and universally respected. A tablet to her memory was placed in Holy Trinity Church by the congregation.

For many years Mr. Oakley and the catechists visited the district of Yatanuwara, about twelve miles from Kandy, and during one of his early visits in 1837, a man who had been a prisoner in the Kandy jail expressed a wish to be baptized. On his release from prison, he returned to Ratmiwela, his village, taking with him some tracts and Scripture portions. He attended regularly the Sunday services in Kandy. He had been a devil dancer, and brought all his books connected with devil worship to the missionary saying, ' With these books I have for a long time deceived myself and the people. I shall use them no more. God has shown me that I must give up all these things, and I now give them to you, lest my family should get hold of them, and also be deceived.' His relations were greatly enraged with him for forsaking his old religion, and one of his brothers procured a gun intending to shoot him. He was baptized on Sunday, June 3, 1838, by the name of Abraham. The following August his eldest son was baptized by the name of Isaac, and his wife, who was at the first very much opposed to the step which her husband had taken, was on January 3, 1841, baptized by the name of Sarah.

Abraham was appointed school master in his native village,

and six years after his baptism, the brother who had threatened to shoot him was baptized by the name of Samuel. Samuel built a new school in the village and in 1849 a resident catechist was appointed. There were only three women in the whole district at that time who could read and write, and they were Mary, Martha and Rebecca, the daughters of Abraham. Two other women were also baptized by the names of Christina and Lydia, and the former became the wife of David, a son of Abraham. Samuel died in 1867, having lived a consistent life from the day of his conversion.

In 1860 died one, who had for forty years been a great strength and help to the Kandy mission, Cornelius Jayatilaka. From the very first he had connected himself with the mission, and aided in the erection of the buildings and the formation of schools and congregations. He was a Government officer of high rank, a Mudaliyar of the Governor's Gate, and a humble and consistent Christian. During a rebellion of the Kandyans, he obtained possession of the so-called ' tooth of Buddha.' The relic is, in the eyes of the Kandyans, of priceless value. For its surrender to the Buddhists, Jayatilaka might have made his own terms and named his own price. But true to his trust, he hid the relic in his long hair, made his way to the Commandant, and placed it in his hands. The fact of its capture broke the spirit of the rebels, and the rising was at once quelled. It was a striking sight to see this man of high family and rank kneeling at the Lord's Table close beside two half-naked Kandyan converts and with them partaking of the memorials of the death and passion of his Saviour and theirs.

During Mr. Oakley's time Trinity Church in the Mission compound and churches at Katukelle and Getambe were built. Trinity Church cost about £1,000 towards which the Sinhalese gave £500. Shortly before Mr. Oakley's retirement, Trinity Church was transferred to the care of the

Rev. Cornelius Jayasinha, and a council composed of Sinhalese gentlemen was formed for the management of the affairs of the three churches.

From the commencement of the Kandy Mission in 1818 to the year of Mr. Oakley's retirement in 1867, the number of adults baptized in connection with the congregations at Kandy was 128, viz. seventy-four men and fifty-four women. Of these thirty-six were Kandyans.

In 1872 the Rev. Henry Gunasekara (the son of the late Rev. A. Gunasekara of Baddegama) was appointed to Trinity Church, and for thirty-seven years till February 1909 when he retired, was the faithful pastor and friend of the congregations. The Christians in 1909 numbered 395, of whom 195 were communicants. Mr. Gunasekara died in 1916.

When the Missionary Conference assembled at Cotta on July 14, 1885, an incident occurred which was unique in the history of the mission. It was just over fifty years since Mr. Oakley had arrived in Ceylon, and with the exception of a short visit to India of three months, he had never been away from the island. Past and present missionaries had subscribed to a fund to provide a scholarship in connection with Trinity College, to bear his name, and this, which amounted to Rs. 800, was presented together with a copy of the Revised Version of the Bible and an illuminated address in the following words :—

'We, your fellow-labourers, and others who have worked with you in this mission, desire to offer you our warmest congratulations on the completion of your fiftieth year of missionary service in Ceylon. It is a matter of deep thankfulness to us all, that in God's mercy and love you have been allowed to spend so many years of continued labour in our Master's cause. During the long period you have been connected with this branch of the Church Missionary Society, it has been your earnest desire to glorify our Lord and Saviour

Jesus Christ, and as Secretary of this Mission, you have enjoyed the hearty, loving confidence of your brethren, over whose Conference you have so long presided. We have also a grateful remembrance of many personal kindnesses received at your hands. You have been glad with us in our joys, and in our troubles you have always sympathized, while the matured wisdom of your counsel and advice, your prudence, and forbearing gentleness, have been used by God in great measure, to secure that unity of feeling and of action which has characterized our mission for so many years.

We wish you to accept this volume—the Revised Version of the Bible—as a token of our esteem and affection, and to allow us to associate with your name a prize or exhibition, to be known as the 'Oakley' Prize or Exhibition, in connection with Trinity College, Kandy, the station where the greater part of your active missionary life was spent.

That our Heavenly Father may graciously spare you to us for many years to come, and, when your work on earth is finished, give you an abundant entrance into His eternal kingdom and glory, is the fervent desire and earnest prayer of your brethren of the Ceylon Mission.'

Just a year after, on July 11, 1886, Mr. Oakley entered into rest at Nuwara Eliya, aged seventy-nine years. To the last he was the active Secretary and revered counsellor and friend of the whole mission.

On February 13, 1909, the Rev. Gregory S. Amarasekara was appointed Incumbent of Trinity Church, the congregations connected therewith giving him a hearty welcome.

In 1918 the congregation of Trinity Church numbered 215 adults and eighty-three children, of whom 161 were communicants, whilst the average attendance at the Sunday morning service was 105 adults. The annual sale of work produces over Rs. 500 and one of the members of St. John's Church, Gatambe, bequeathed one thousand rupees to that Church.

TRINITY COLLEGE.

FOR some years the leading Sinhalese in Kandy had been urging on the C.M.S. the need of a superior school for the education of their sons, and had promised their support and help.

On October 16, 1857, the Rev. John Ireland Jones arrived from England and opened an establishment, under the name of the Kandy Collegiate School. Its primary object was to attract the sons of the Kandyan chiefs. In this it was not successful, although many of the principal residents of the town availed themselves of its advantages. The institution continued in operation for about six years, being during the latter half of the time under the charge of the Rev. R. B. Tonge.

On January 18, 1872, it was re-opened under the name of Trinity College and Collegiate School with the Rev. R. Collins as Principal, and Mr. Alfred Clark as Tutor, and quickly took an important position which it has since maintained. At the end of the same year there were 120 students on the roll.

Early in 1877 the latter half of the name was dropped and from thenceforth it became 'Trinity College,' and the Kandy Prince of Wales Reception Fund Committee presented the college with Rs. 2,000 in memory of his Royal Highness' visit to Kandy. In the following year the college was affiliated to the Calcutta University, and in 1879 the Acting Principal, Mr. Thomas Dunn, reported 'The Government examination was satisfactory, 90 per cent of passes being obtained. The Entrance and F.A. examinations were held in December. Six students went up for the first, and three for the second examination.'

In 1880 the Rev. J. G. Garrett was appointed Principal, and the following year there were 238 students, thirty of these being boarders. In 1883 the Rev. J. Field was appointed

Vice-Principal. In 1885 the Rev. E. Noel Hodges, formerly of the Noble High School in Masulipatam, became Principal, assisted by the Rev. J. Ilsley. In 1889 Mr. Hodges was appointed to the Bishopric of Travancore and Cochin, and his post at Kandy was taken by the Rev. E. J. Perry, who had been a master at Merchant Taylors' School. He threw himself into the work with a bright enthusiasm that augured great things, but on April 2, 1890, he was accidentally shot dead near Alut-nuwara, whilst on a visit to the Veddahs in the Bintenne country. As a memorial to him, a college mission, known as the ' Perry Memorial Mission ' was started in an outlying district. The Rev. J. W. Fall, the Vice-Principal, who had arrived in November 1889, carried on the work of the college, until the arrival of the new Principal, the Rev. H. P. Napier-Clavering, in June 1890. At that time there were 298 students, sixty-three of whom were boarders. Owing to the increased number of students two blocks of additional buildings were erected.

In November, 1891, the Rev. J. Carter arrived as Vice-Principal. The following year, Mr. Napier-Clavering reported that ' there were many boys hoping to be baptized as soon as they became their own masters ' and that ' on Advent Sunday seventeen of the students were confirmed.'

In 1895 the Rev. R. W. Ryde became Vice-Principal till August 1899, and the Rev. A. A. Pilson arrived to fill the vacancy in March 1900. Mr. Pilson died of typhoid fever at Nuwara Eliya on April 30, 1902, aged twenty-nine. The Rev. H. P. Napier-Clavering's resignation on account of home claims in August 1900, was universally regretted, as he was popular both with masters and boys, and the college had prospered under him. The period of his Principalship was emphatically one of progress, new buildings were erected, the number of students increased and the general status of the college raised. The Rev. R. W. Ryde succeeded to the

Principalship. The average daily attendance that year was 323 out of a roll of 410. The primary school, nurtured by the college, showed a daily attendance of fifty-four out of eighty-three, for the same period.

In 1902 the Rev. J. Carter became temporarily Principal and early the following year, the Rev. A. MacLulich MacLulich, Vice-Principal. During 1904 the college was carried on under the guidance of no less than four heads, succeeding each other. Mr. Carter was in charge until his departure for England on May 6, the Rev. H. P. Napier-Clavering till August 7, then the Rev. A. MacLulich, and, from November 5, Mr. A. G. Fraser. The annual report showed that in the 'highest things' the year had been one of prosperity and blessing. It says, 'The Te Deum has been swelling more and more as the months have rolled on. This year is in every sense an improvement on last, and has been continually improving on itself. Five lads have been baptized, and thirteen were confirmed by the Bishop.' Under Mr. Fraser's masterly direction the school has gone forward to a remarkable degree. The compound has been extended by the acquisition of new land; new buildings have been erected; a magnificent playing field of several acres has been hewn from a hillside; a strong staff including several Europeans has been built up, and the school has been further developed as a boarding school and has acquired a distinctive character and spirit. These things have involved a heavily increased expenditure and Mr. Fraser has worked successfully for the establishment of the Trinity College Extension Fund which has made these schemes of development possible.

In 1905 a bungalow and compound known as Woodlands, adjoining the college premises, were acquired by means of money collected by Mr. Fraser, thus giving a residence for the Principal and leaving the college bungalow for the Vice-Principal.

In August, 1906, Mr. Fraser was suddenly ordered home on account of ill-health. The Rev. W. S. Senior, who had recently arrived, assumed the office of Acting Principal, and was joined later in the year by the Rev. A. M. Walmsley.

Towards the end of the year 1908, Mr. Fraser returned with reinforcements of men, viz. the Rev. J. P. S. R. Gibson and Messrs. N. P. Campbell and K. J. Saunders, backed up by a wealth of prayer and sympathy. The aim of Mr. Fraser and the methods by which he proposed to achieve it may be best expressed in his own words.

The Aim.—We intend to make a serious effort—

First.—To train Christians in Ceylon so to present Christ that their hearers may realize Him not as a foreigner, but as the real and true fulfilment of all that is best and highest in their aspirations and in their past.

Second.—To make the pupils good citizens of their own land. (a) By carefully relating all that is taught them to the needs, problems and language of their own people. (b) By deliberately striving to foster and encourage their sense of responsibility and readiness to act and, so working, to produce leaders.

The Methods.—We propose (a) The appointment of three capable and accomplished students to devote themselves to the study of education in India and Ceylon, and of Hindu and Buddhist apologetics. (b) The establishment of a good training college for Christian teachers in the Vernacular and English and the creation of a ladder from the village school to the college with its possibilities of leadership. We hope by basing our education on the Vernaculars whilst teaching English thoroughly, to make the transition from village school to college easier, and to instruct pupils more readily and more intelligently from the basis of their own knowledge. (c) The efficient prosecution of higher education on the lines of the Japanese code or of the Arya Samaj in its national gurukulas, i.e. education in their own classics combined with that of the West, and modern science. (d) In all we hope to devolve responsibility more and more on the people themselves, to strictly limit the number of our pupils that each may have individual attention, and that there may be close contact between teachers and taught. *To sum up·* ' We are attempting to translate into carefully planned action the belief that the hope of the future lies with the native Christians, and our energies are most wisely exercised when not directly employed on Hindus, Mohammedans and Buddhists, but when building up a wise, eager and indigenous Church.'

In 1909 Mr. N. P. Campbell designed new buildings which were erected at the cost of £3000. These contain a chemical laboratory, a physical laboratory with gallery, a class room, quarters for two masters, a masters' common room, and a dormitory containing sixty beds. The compound was improved and two acres of land adjoining were leased from Government for ninety-nine years. In this year, Mr. G. K. Mulgrue, who had been on the teaching staff for some years, was taken into local connection.

The Rev. L. J. Gaster joined the staff in 1910. The following year Mr. Fraser left on a visit to England to plead for funds to carry out a Training Colony scheme and during his absence the Rev. H. P. Napier-Clavering was Honorary Acting Principal.

In 1914 Mr. K. J. Saunders who during his stay in Ceylon had written several books and pamphlets on Buddhism, left the College to take up Y.M.C.A. work in India. Mr. Campbell also left for England in the same year for training in connection with the war, and Mr. A. C. Houlder, who had previously been on the staff as a 'short service' man, rejoined the college as missionary in full connection.

At the close of 1915 the Rev. K. C. McPherson joined the teaching staff as a missionary of the C.M.S., and the Rev.

W. S. Senior who had been Vice-Principal for eight years, left to take charge of Christ Church, Galle Face, Colombo.

The 'Trinity College Annual for 1914' gives a wonderful account of the various activities and agencies of the college. It consists of nearly one hundred pages and many illustrations. The spiritual side is put well to the front as the following quotation will show: 'Trinity College, while a public school on the best lines, is before all a missionary school. Its success is not indeed to be measured by mere numbers of those baptized and confirmed or by the number of communicants. It is rather to be sought in the " atmosphere " and " tone," the outlook on life and the general product of the place. Yet if the general product never crystallized in particular results, our success would be questionable. It is with gratitude, then, that we are able to record a number of baptisms in 1913, and a few in the current year. No pressure save that of public preaching (and the " atmosphere " alluded to), no preferential treatment is ever brought to bear. Truth is our one weapon, and in several cases the candidates have very real obstacles of antecedents and circumstance to overcome. As to Confirmation, the numbers seem to increase yearly, and the annual Confirmation Service more and more becomes a red letter day of our calendar. No one can be present either on the Sunday evenings when public baptism is administered, or on the afternoons when the Bishop confirms, without being much moved and much inspired, with the thought of the reality and value of the educational missionary task.'

The students who are communicants have a 'Communicants' Union,' the Sunday School has twenty-eight classes and 210 students, there is also a 'Union for Social Service,' and in 1914 a 'College Hostel' was opened in Colombo, where so many Trinity boys go down for employment or to continue their studies. There is also a College Cadet Corps, and Cricket, Rugger, Boxing, Fives and Tennis are keenly supported. There are also Literary and Reading Associations, and a Masters' Guild.

In the report of the year's work read at the Prize-giving in 1915, the Rev. A. G. Fraser said, ' for the third year in succession we headed the Commercial examination, and in the Cambridge Senior Local four of our students won the first four places in the Empire in Book-keeping. In the Junior Local we passed twenty candidates, one obtaining first class honours, and we obtained four distinctions. In the Senior Local we passed thirty-five candidates, with two second class honours, five third class, and ten distinctions. In the Intermediate in Arts all our three candidates passed. In the Inter Science we presented four and all passed. In athletics, we won the Cricket Championship, and the Intercollegiate Shooting Cup for the ninth time in succession. We were the winners also of the Inter-collegiate Shields for Physical Drill, and for Military Drill, and we still retain the Boxing Shield. Our Rugby Football team was again without rivals, and the only Inter-collegiate competition we have not come first in is that for track running, and in that we were equal second.'

The Rev. L. J. Gaster went on furlough in 1915, and returned the following year. In his report as Acting Principal he says, ' I had the privilege of preparing twelve boys for confirmation, and a few for baptism. To see those boys coming forward in the face of opposition, ready to confess Christ in baptism, and to take up their cross and follow Him, is something which does not fail to leave its mark on oneself also. It can be said most emphatically that the Life and Person of Jesus Christ make a strong appeal, and an appeal not in vain to the young life of Ceylon.'

Mr. A. C. Houlder writes, ' The Social Service Union is, I believe, the strongest agency we have whereby the fulness of Christ, the life in Christ, may be demonstrated. The work is voluntary, the motto, " A patriot can serve his country only when he makes their sorrows and disabilities his own." There are about thirty members amongst the boys, and at least eight earnest workers amongst the masters. We have made frequent visits to villages, treating cases of sores and ulcers, and teaching games to the boys. We have also opened a school in an outcaste village. These people are mat-weavers by occupation. They are not allowed to attend school with any other caste people, and until we went there no Kandyan of good family had been near them at all. Our boys have visited them frequently, bicycling ten miles, or walking seven each way, to see the school, lecture to the boys, and help them in any way possible, also visiting their homes.'

The following with regard to the great war is an extract from the Report read at the Annual Prize Giving in December, 1918:

' The war ended almost as suddenly as it began. Trinity College is never a dull place, and has on occasions shown a wonderful energy of expression, but when the news came through that Germany had signed the armistice we surpassed all previous records in the irresponsible enthusiasm of our rejoicings.

There are sixty-two names on our Roll of Honour. Of this number ten were killed in action on the Western Front, one was drowned in the Mediterranean on his way to England to enlist, and one died of disease contracted on active service. In the midst of our rejoicings we think of these brave souls who will never return :—R. Aiyadurai, N. P. Campbell, F. Drieberg, H. C. Forster, C. F. H. Kent, J. Loos, K. Murray, A. G. F. Perera, A. Paramananthan, R. Skipp, P. Scott-Coates, and A. J. Wells. They went forth unafraid to defend the right, and they gave their lives that the right might triumph. We thank God for their courage, their vision, and their self-sacrifice.

One of the last to fall in the conflict was Herbert Forster, who left school for the Front early last year, and was killed in France in March of this year at the age of nineteen.

Besides those who gave their lives, eighteen of our number were wounded or gassed, and two were made prisoners. Those who received decorations are J. W. S. Bartholomeusz, who was awarded the French Croix de Guerre of the First Class, and Vere Modder, who won the Military Medal. Capt. E. C. Squire, who joined our staff and was about to sail for Ceylon when war broke out, has been awarded the Military Cross.

Three of our boys on the Western Front obtained Commissions, the last being Ajit Rudra, the son of the Principal of St. Stephen's College, Delhi, and five of our Old Boys recently obtained Commissions in the I. A. R. O.'

Mr. N. P. Campbell joined H. M. Forces at the end of 1914, obtaining a Commission as Captain in the Royal Engineers, and was killed in action on May 3, 1917. An *In Memoriam* notice in the *C.M.S. Gleaner* for the following month says, 'Not only in the school but outside it in Kandy were Mr. Campbell's energies spent. His work among the poor and needy and his keen efforts to help them, and to uplift them, are well known. Often was he seen alone on a roadside helping a lame man or binding up a sore foot. Even the poor in hospital knew him and were cheered by the concerts he organized for them. He did not spare himself in doing all he could for the needy, among whom he was much loved.

Early in the war he left us as he believed "no man had a right to keep away." Nothing could prevent him. He had dedicated his life to the cause of freedom.

>   As He died to make men holy
>   Let us live to make men free,

were the words he set before him. On his final mission he was called away to a Greater Freedom on High.'

THE TRAINING COLONY.

THIS institution takes its root in the first century of C.M.S. work and looks for its fruit in the second. It is the product of the past, and the prophet of the future. In main outline the plan was conceived by Mr. A. G. Fraser as far back as 1906. Into what it shall develop none can prophesy, for it faces the problems of the day in the dim though growing light of the future rather than in the still strong but waning twilight of the traditional past.

In the first place the Training Colony is co-denominational. The Church Missionary Society and the Wesleyan Methodist Missionary Society in Ceylon have federated as regards the governing of this institution which is in the hands of a special Council. The C.M.S. have at present the preponderating interest on the basis of larger capital invested, but there is nothing in the Constitution which in any way gives special rights or privileges to either Society.

Students from both Societies are admitted and the whole policy is that of the fullest combination possible for essentially similars, and not that of the mere juxtaposition of radically differents. Students eat and sleep, work and play, and also worship together except for the Sunday morning services, when as members of their respective Churches the students attend their own Church or Chapel. At the same time each Society has full rights and opportunities for teaching its own members such special doctrines or beliefs as it feels to be its sacred contribution to the Universal Church. Each Society has a Vice-Principal in residence to whom the supervision of the religious life of his flock is specially entrusted. Of these two, one is chosen Principal and as such impartially administers the joint interests of the Colony. Secondly, the

Colony is co-educational. Men and women are trained in joint classes, and Sinhalese women, as well as men, teach these classes. This is as real a step forward as is the wholehearted denominational federation, and is preparing the way for woman to take her right place in the East.

There are two main departments, the normal training of Sinhalese teachers for primary vernacular schools, and the training of evangelists. In the former there are about forty men and forty women. The course lasts three years and the objective is the Government Diploma. Government grants amounted last year to just over Rs. 7,000. The Evangelist Class is more irregular and so far no such class for women has been started.

The staff comprises three Europeans and seven Ceylonese.

The main policy of the work is summed up by the motto 'Victory through self-sacrifice,' self-expression attained through self-abnegation, Christ in me the hope of Glory. The vitalizing force in the Colony is the half-hour spent corporately in silent prayer each morning. From this observance flows power that gives meaning to the rest of the day.

In many ways, by special services for seed-sowing and harvesting, by a service of beating the bounds, by national music and art, by processions and illuminations, we seek to enable religious faith to express itself in national forms and the spontaneity of the expression makes one believe that the springs are deep. Apart from the daily half-hour of quiet, frequent times are taken when staff and students wait in silence upon God, with the mind receptive for the impress of the Divine. The medical side of the work enables the idea of Social Service to be developed and the elements of First-Aid to be acquired. The learning of pottery painting adds another form of beautiful self-expression. The elementary principles of agriculture which are taught send the men forth the better able to deal with rural problems.

Drill, games and mountaineering excursions develop the body and open the mind to the glories of Nature.

Such in outline is the ideal. In conclusion a few facts may be of interest. The Colony is on the site of the Rosehill Estate, Peradeniya Junction, and contains now about thirty acres planted in tea and rubber. The buildings comprise the Principal's Bungalow, the Women's Hostel (Laurie Hall), the Men's Hostel (Ashley Hall), and the main teaching school (Fraser Hall), the right wing of which is the Vice-Principal's house. There are also houses for the married staff, a dispensary, and buildings for the Evangelist Departments both men's and women's. The Colony was acquired and opened in 1914. Work began in Laurie Hall in 1916, in Ashley Hall in 1917, and in Fraser Hall in 1918. The total capital cost has been over Rs. 125,000.

CHAPTER X.

JAFFNA.

JAFFNA, in the extreme north, is a town of about 50,000 inhabitants, and the northern province, of which it is the capital, contains a population of 330,000, nearly all of whom are Tamils. Jaffna is 207 miles from Colombo, and, until the railway was opened in 1905, it seemed to be cut off from the rest of the island. A large fort still stands which was built by the Portuguese in 1624, and the massive Church in the form of a Greek cross, with the date 1706 over the main entrance, testifies to the importance of Jaffna in the Dutch period. Jaffna is supposed to have been founded in the year A.D. 101 and is thus described in Casie Chetty's Tamil Plutarch :—
'Yalpana was a minstrel who lived in the Chola country. Being blind, he depended on the earnings of his wife. One day his meals were not ready at the proper hour, so he quarrelled with his wife and left the house saying he was going to Ceylon. When he arrived there, he was refused admittance into the king's presence, but it was afterwards arranged that the king should stand behind a curtain and hear the blind minstrel's song. The king, being greatly pleased, honoured him with the gift of a tusked elephant, and by the donation of a piece of land in the northern extremity of the island in perpetuity. This was no other than the present peninsula of Jaffna. It was then uninhabited and covered with jungle, but he had it cleared, and, having induced a colony of Tamils from Southern India to settle in it, soon rendered it a rich country, which he called after his own professional name Yalpana Nadu, that is, the minstrel's country.'

Yalpana has been corrupted into the modern name of Jaffna. The climate and scenery differ from those of the other parts of the island. Agriculture is the main occupation of the people, palmyra palms and tobacco being the chief products. The C.M.S., the American Board of Foreign Missions, the Wesleyans and the Roman Catholics, have all strong missions in the district. The proportion per cent. of the adherents of each religion to the total population in 1911 was, Hindus 87·76, Mohammedans 1·11, Buddhists ·09, and Christians 11·04.

The Rev. Joseph Knight, the first C.M.S. missionary, arrived in Jaffna in July, 1818, and moved to Nellore in November. As soon as he commenced work he met with difficulties and opposition. The people thought it necessary to bathe themselves and purify their houses after the missionary's visit, and it was usual for the pundit to bathe at the tank on his way home after giving a lesson at the Mission House. The first printing press was set up by Mr. Knight, and thousands of tracts were printed and distributed. The extent of their distribution may be judged from the fact that 1,002,800 tracts were issued from the press in the years 1835 to 1838. This printing press was afterwards sold to the American Mission.

In 1820 there were 270 children in the schools, and much visiting was done. The Rev. and Mrs. Joseph Bailey arrived in March, 1822, but they were able to remain only twelve months, during which time Mr. Bailey took the English duties at the Dutch Church.

During this year Mr. Knight obtained from Government an old Dutch Church with a piece of land, adjoining the mission premises. Of this building, forty-two feet were taken from one end, for a dwelling house. Mr. Knight married Mrs. S. B. Richards and after her death, Mrs. E. S. Nichols, both widows of American missionaries. He died at Cotta and was buried there on October 11, 1840, aged fifty-three. In the preface to Winslow's 'Comprehensive Tamil and English Dictionary,' published at Madras in 1862, it is stated that 'it was commenced by the Rev. J. Knight, late of Jaffna.'

The Rev. W. Adley arrived in 1824 and continued till the death of Mrs. Adley in 1839, when he left for England, returning two years later, but being compelled owing to ill-health to relinquish his work in 1845. Mr. Adley died in England in 1889, aged ninety-seven years. In September 1826, Mr. Adley baptized four young Tamil men, pupils in the boarding school which had been established in Nellore in 1823. He wrote, 'I baptized the boys in the names of Edward Bickersteth, William Marsh, Josiah Pratt and John Raban, and afterwards described to them the characters of the persons whose names they bore, with a solemn exhortation that they would follow them as they followed Christ.'

The same year was baptized 'Samuel' who had been a leader of devil worship, practised incantations, given offerings to religious mendicants, given a cow to a temple, keeping it at his own house and giving the priests the milk daily, and had presented a silver sword and shield as an offering to St. James at a Roman Catholic Church. He became a most earnest Christian. He met his death one evening as he was returning from a missionary meeting, being bitten by a poisonous snake. His father, a heathen, said, 'Before, he was a devil, but after he gave himself up to Christ he put all evil away.' Shortly after his death his wife received baptism. The Rev. F. W. Taylor joined the mission in 1839 and remained till 1841, when the Rev. J. Talbot Johnston arrived and stayed eight years.

The same year the district of Chundicully was taken over. The old Portuguese Church of St. John the Baptist, with its congregation of ninety, had been handed over to the C.M.S. by their old Pastor, the Rev. Christian David, who was a convert of the missionary Schwartsz, in South India. Services were conducted in it till 1862, when the present church was erected and dedicated to St. John the Baptist.

The Rev. Robert Pargiter, who had come out as a Wesleyan missionary and had left that body and been ordained deacon in 1846 and priest in 1847 by Bishop Chapman, was added to the missionary band in 1846, spending the greater part of his time at Chundicully, till his retirement to England in 1864, where he died in 1915, aged ninety-eight years. The Rev. James O'Neil arrived also in 1846 at Nellore. Mrs. O'Neil under whose care the Girls' Boarding School, which had been opened in 1842, had grown and prospered, died on December 16, 1848, aged twenty-seven. A tablet to her memory in Nellore Church says, 'After the short space of two years and nine months, spent in mission labour, she exchanged earth for heaven.' Mr. O'Neil returned to England in 1856.

In July, 1847, Dr. Chapman, Bishop of Colombo, visited Jaffna, when one hundred and thirteen candidates were confirmed. In 1849 Copay was adopted as a separate mission district. The Mission House and Church were built on a piece of land given by Mr. P. A. Dyke, the Government Agent of the Province. The foundation stone of the church was laid on May 9, 1850, and the completed building opened on January 9, 1852, costing about £400. At the opening service three adults were baptized. The Rev. Robert Bren arrived at Copay in 1849 and returned to England in 1858. The Copay Training Institution for catechists, readers and teachers was opened in 1853. In 1855 so much hypocrisy and mercenary conduct appeared among the Christians in Jaffna, that it was proposed to close the stations and abandon the work, but a visit from Mr. Knight revived the spirits of the missionaries, and the work took a fresh start from that time. The Rev. C. C. MacArthur arrived in 1859 and extended the work till his retirement in 1867. The Rev. H. D. Buswell arrived in 1862, but was obliged to relinquish the work owing to ill-health in 1865. In February, 1867, the Rev. Thomas Good came, just as the schools had been closed and general work suspended in consequence of a visitation of cholera, and in January of the following year the Rev. David Wood arrived.

In September, 1863, the chief catechist, Mr. J. Hensman, was ordained deacon by the Bishop of Colombo, and was made priest two years later. The Rev. J. Hensman was a most energetic and enthusiastic worker till his death in 1884. Three other catechists, Messrs. T. P. Handy, G. Champion and E. Hoole were ordained deacons in 1865. In 1868 when the Jubilee of the Mission was celebrated, the statistics of the Mission were, two European missionaries, four Tamil clergy, ten catechists, three readers, thirty-four schoolmasters, ten school mistresses, one biblewoman, one colporteur, 677 Christians, 237 communicants, nineteen boys' schools with 961 pupils and seven girls' schools with 397 girls.

The following year, 8640 houses were visited by the pastors and catechists, 636 meetings held, the gospel preached to no less than 36,864 persons and work commenced in the Islands of Mundativu and Allypitty. A Church Council was formed and the amount contributed that year was £118-2-1.

In September, 1870, the Bishop, Dr. Piers Claughton, visited the Mission and the following account of the visit is given in the C. M. Record of January, 1871. ' We are seldom favoured with the visits of our Diocesan. The way of access to Jaffna, since the island steamer was discontinued, is so difficult and tedious that it requires no ordinary amount of courage and patience, first to undertake, and afterwards to endure the journey. It is almost as easy, and certainly more pleasant, to go to England from Colombo, than to come from

Colombo to Jaffna. Having received a telegram from Mr. Templer of Manaar, that the Bishop had left there at 6 a.m. for Jaffna, I drove to the beach at 3 p.m. to meet him, but in consequence of light winds, or no wind at all, there was no appearance of the boat. I waited till 8.30 p.m., and returned to Nellore. However I had the pleasure of welcoming his Lordship at 12 o'clock, midnight. The boat had grounded several times, and, in consequence of the darkness and shallow water, sailing in the large boat had become impossible, and his lordship wisely hailed a fishing " barrow," whose occupant was engaged in his nightly toil, and in this primitive craft came safely to shore.

On September 7, the Bishop held his visitation in St. John's Church, Chundicully. Four Tamil clergy, three English clergy and ten churchwardens were present. After this the Bishop visited the English Seminary, and in the afternoon a confirmation service was held at Nellore when twenty-seven candidates were presented. Next morning the Bishop examined the children of the schools of Chundicully under the mahogany trees, and afterwards held a confirmation in the church when twenty-eight candidates were confirmed. In the afternoon a confirmation was held at Copay where thirty candidates were presented, and the Bishop afterwards visited the English School and Training Institution. After sunset he attended a moonlight meeting two miles from Copay, and at 9 o'clock returned to Nellore. The following morning his lordship held a confirmation in the temporary church in the Pettah, when twenty-seven persons were confirmed, and the same afternoon laid the foundation stone of a church at Kokuvil.

On Saturday morning the Bishop visited the Girls' Boarding School after which he examined the three candidates for priests' orders, in the afternoon addressed the mission workers at Nellore, and in the evening laid the foundation stone of the Pettah Church. On Sunday morning at 9 o'clock, the Bishop preached in the Pettah, and at 11 o'clock conducted the ordination service at Nellore, preaching from the text, Titus, 1, 5, "That thou shouldest set in order the things that are wanting and ordain elders in every city." The Revs. Handy, Hoole and Champion were admitted to priests' orders, and the Revs. T. Good, D. Wood and J. Hensman assisted in the laying on of hands. There were 158 Tamil communicants. At four in the afternoon the Bishop preached at the Portuguese service in the Pettah, and at 5.30 in St. John's Church, Chundicully. The following day the Bishop held a confirmation in the Court House at Pallai, twenty-five miles from Jaffna.'

In 1871 the Rev. D. Wood removed to Colombo for a time and Mr. Hensman took the oversight of the Copay Training Institution. The following year, the missionary reports, 'The dowry system and caste are still great evils among the Christians. A man, professedly Christian, will not allow his children to marry those whom he considers of lower caste than his own, though everything else is in favour of such an alliance.'

Mission work was commenced this year, 1872, in Vavunia Valankullam, by the sending of a catechist and schoolmaster.

The Bishop, Dr. Jermyn, paid his first visit to Jaffna in June of that year. Much evangelistic work was carried on by the Jaffna clergy and hundreds of Scripture portions sold. One woman offered a quantity of thread for a gospel, another two leaves of tobacco, whilst a cooly woman on an estate begged her employer to pay a penny in advance out of her hire for the day, and bought a scripture portion with it. An interesting series of meetings was held in connection with a party of Christians from Tanjore, known as the 'Lyrical Preachers,' and blessing resulted.

On December 24, 1874, the Rev. J. D. Simmons, who had previously been fourteen years in the Tinnevelly Mission, arrived at Nellore. Mr. Wood returned to Jaffna in 1875, and in 1878 the Rev. E. Blackmore was stationed in Chundicully, taking the place of Mr. Wood who had been transferred to Colombo.

Mr. Blackmore died on October 24 of the following year. In 1878 there were thirty-eight schools for boys and fourteen for girls, with 2,152 boys and 420 girls, and three-fourths of the four pastors' stipends were paid by the Christians, of whom there were 485 adults and 285 children.

In December, 1880, the Rev. G. T. Fleming arrived, and the following year on July 17, the Rev. E. Hoole who had been a faithful and successful worker passed away in his fifty-second year. Mr. Hoole's father was the founder and proprietor of a temple dedicated to the goddess Amman, one of the wives of Siva. Every parental effort was directed towards the training of his three sons for their duties as temple-masters. The father's greatest ambition was to see his elder son growing in favour with the gods, but one day he received a great shock, when he had left him in charge of the household gods with strict injunctions as to the quantity of food and flowers to be offered. The boy prepared the offerings and presented them to the images, but after a time, seeing they had not partaken of the food, he expostulated, and threatened them. He then took a hammer and smashed the gods to pieces. He had once before seen an image of Pulliar, which had been sold for seven shillings and sixpence by a Brahman to a missionary who wanted to send the idol to England. This had also helped to undermine his faith. In 1837 he was baptized and became a Wesleyan minister. The mind of the younger brother was influenced by the example of the elder, and, renouncing his right to the temple, he openly professed Christianity and was baptized by the name of Elijah Hoole.

An In Memoriam notice in one of the papers referred to him as a model pastor, profound scholar and a speaker with few equals. Mrs. Hoole who had been a true helpmate died on August 26, 1906, in her seventieth year.

The Rev. E. M. Griffith was transferred to Jaffna in February, 1882. In 1884 the Rev. J. Hensman, and in May, 1885, the Rev. J. P. Handy, died, both faithful and good men. The Revs. J. Niles and J. Backus were ordained in 1885.

In 1888 during the month of March, Colonel Oldham and the Rev. G. C. Grubb conducted a Mission in Jaffna, when 'there were direct conversions, a great awakening among professing Christians and a great spiritual refreshing.'

On October 15, 1889, the foundation stone of the church at Pallai was laid, which was opened on November 30, 1895, and dedicated to St. Andrew.

On March 13, 1890, the Rev. E. M. Griffith died and the Rev. J. I. Pickford was appointed to succeed him.

On March 24, 1892, the Rev. J. Niles died. Few have realized more fully than he did the responsibilities of the pastor's office. The people and district committed to his charge were always uppermost in his thoughts.

The Nellore Girls' Boarding School continued to flourish and with 101 pupils it was necessary to erect additional buildings, whilst the English school at Copay had a hundred pupils, the fees and government grant meeting all expenses.

On Sunday, December 31, 1893, an ordination was held entirely in Tamil in Christ Church, when the Revs. G. Daniel, A. Matthias, S. Morse and C. T. Williams were admitted to deacons' orders. A confirmation was held the same day at Nellore when thirty-two candidates were confirmed.

Four women missionaries, Misses Heaney, Saul, Paul and Case were appointed to the district about this time. On January 15, 1896, a Girls' English High School was opened at Chundicully under the management of Mrs. J. Carter and during the first year there were thirty-nine pupils. Miss Spreat assisted in the school for a few months but returned to England and died there. Miss Goodchild became Principal in 1898 and Mrs. Carter, the founder, whose ability, earnest zeal and loving sympathy had won all hearts, died at Jaffna on June 8, 1899. Seventy-three girls were now in the school and Miss Payne arrived to assist. Eleven of the pupils were confirmed the following year. At the first government examination, forty-two girls out of the forty-six presented passed. In September 1904, Miss Goodchild went on furlough and her place was taken by Miss S. L. Page who had been helping in the work since May. Two Sivite pupils were baptized that year and there were 120 pupils, including fifty-three boarders. A Christian Endeavour Society and a monthly consecration meeting were started. Four years later there were 150 pupils, and new schoolrooms and dormitories were erected. Miss Whitney acted as Principal until Miss Page returned from furlough in December 1910. In 1914 there were 214 pupils, about half of whom were boarders. The government grant earned was six times as much as that earned at the first examination. Six girls passed the Junior and three the Senior Cambridge Locals. Fifteen girls were confirmed. On October 13, 1915, Bishop Copleston opened the new Kindergarten room, which had cost Rs. 2,100, the government contributing Rs. 600 of the amount. The school was also registered under the new government regulations as 'efficient' and entitled to receive a block grant yearly.

In 1896 a church was built at Pallai at a cost of Rs. 11,000. In 1868 Mr. John Backus, a catechist, who was afterwards ordained in 1885, had been sent to the district, his instructions from the missionaries being, ' Travel east and west, north and south, exercise your own discretion prayerfully and fix upon a centre.' He made Pallai his head-quarters, putting up a hut, twenty feet by twelve, one half of which served as a schoolroom, and the other half as a bed and dining room. Sir William Twynam gave a piece of land, and soon a better school and house were built. Mr. Backus continued his energetic work till 1903, during which time the church and eleven schools were opened.

In May, 1897, the Rev. Hugh Horsley took charge of the district work. There were at that time seven ordained pastors, three women missionaries, fifteen catechists and readers, seven biblewomen, 1,423 Christians, 637 communicants, sixty-seven schools and 3,234 scholars. Mr. Horsley in his report for the year says, ' If we may judge by the attendance at church and at the Holy Table, the spiritual life is certainly up to the average of that in England. Family prayer is the order of the day in many houses. Considerable interest has been shown in the restoration of some of the churches.'

A schoolmaster and catechist of many years standing, Mr. C. Bartlett, died this year. He and his brother being converted about the same time, vindicated their strong conviction of the truth of Christianity, by demolishing the heathen temple that was in their garden and was conducted under the management of their parents. They were the means also of leading their father, brother, and sisters, to Christ. The secretary of the Nellore Church Committee, Mr. Alexander Bailey, died this year. At his funeral, Sir William Twynam a former Government Agent of the Province, a friend and staunch supporter of mission work, said ' He was always a steady man and reliable.'

The Nellore Girls' Boarding School under Mrs. and Miss Horsley continued to be a bright spot. One of the girls gave a rupee to the church fund, saying that she had worked during the holidays at plaiting coconut leaves and had brought her earnings. The Rev. G. Daniel mentions ' an aged woman who had heard the Gospel for twenty-eight years, and had at last yielded herself to the power of the Word of God.' The Rev. J. Backus mentions the death of an old Christian, who was well known as 'the Bishop's good old man.' He was baptized late in life and at the confirmation service he was so ready with his answers to certain questions put by the Bishop, that the Bishop's curiosity was aroused, and he asked ' Who is that good old man, who was so ready with his answers?' Although he lived four miles from the nearest church, he was always among the first at the services.

In 1901 a church was erected in the heart of the Wanni at Vavunia, under the superintendence of the Rev. A. Matthias. The same year, Mr. Charles Wadsworth, whose name will be long remembered with affection and esteem, especially at Copay, where he worked for forty years as Headmaster of the Training Institution, was called to his rest. A large hall was built at Copay as a memorial to him and is known as the ' Wadsworth Memorial Hall.' The foundation stone was laid by the Bishop and, on July 10, 1912, the Hall was opened by him.

Miss E. G. Beeching, who had previously worked in the N.-W. America Mission, arrived at Copay this year. In February, 1902, Mr. Horsley was obliged to return to England owing to failure of health, and the Rev. J. I. Pickford filled the gap, until the appointment of Rev. W. J. Hanan in August. The Rev. G. Champion also retired from active service.

The following year the Rev. C. T. Williams left Copay to work at Anuradhapura, and the Rev. A. Matthias succeeded him. Mr. Matthias had spent thirty-one years in Vavunia. When he first went there, there were no Christians, schools nor church; when he left, there were seventy Christians, three schools and a church which was designed by him and built under his superintendence, partly with his own hands. Mrs. Hanan was now in charge of the Nellore Boarding School with ninety-two pupils. Miss Case reports that in 1903 ' the biblewomen paid 7,536 visits to houses and read the Bible, and taught twenty-two women to read.'

In August, 1905, Mr. Hanan went on furlough, Mr. Pickford took charge of the district and Miss A. T. Board of the Boarding School. The Rev. A. Matthias commenced branches of the Gleaners' Union and the Y. M. C. A. in his pastcrate, and Mr. Backus, who was now at Nellore, mentions sewing classes, prayer meetings, moonlight services and Sunday schools as being vigorously worked in his parish. The Rev. J. D. Sattianadhan was ordained priest on Trinity Sunday, 1906, and the same year Miss E. S. Young took charge of the women's work. Mr. and Mrs. Hanan returned in 1907, and the foundation stone of a new church was laid at Tanniuttu, a village in the Wanni, which was dedicated by the Bishop in 1913.

The Jaffna Missionary Association at this time was maintaining four workers in out-of-the-way places, the President of the Association being Mr. James Hensman, a son of the first Tamil ordained for C.M.S. work in Jaffna.

In 1909 Mr. Hanan moved to Copay in order better to supervise the Training Institution, Miss Young went to Nellore, and Miss Henrys arrived to superintend the Boarding School. The Rev. S. Morse died on September 8, after forty years' work, the Rev. T. D. Sattianadhan was transferred to the Tamil Cooly Mission, and Mr. S. Somasundaram was ordained to the diaconate on June 29, at Nellore. The Rev. G. T. Weston arrived to assist Mr. Hanan, and Mr. N. G. Nathaniel was ordained.

The following year, 1910, the Rev. George Champion died. He was one of the oldest Tamil Christians in Ceylon, having been born on October 1, 1824. In 1844 he became a teacher at Copay, in 1865 was ordained deacon, and in 1870 admitted to priests' orders. For twenty-five years he was in charge of Kokuvil, where he built the church. His record was one of fifty-eight years of active service for the Master.

Mr. Backus in his annual report of this year, mentions a sad case of apostasy of a mother and her three sons and three daughters, who openly denied Christ on Good Friday in a heathen temple. The mother many years before had become a Christian in order to be married, and apostatised in order to marry her daughters to heathen men.

The Rev. Jacob Thompson had charge of the Jaffna District throughout 1911 until the Rev. W. J. Hanan returned in May 1912. Miss Whitney towards the close of the year took charge of the Nellore school. About this time work was begun at Mankulam, a large convict settlement in the Wanni.

In 1913 the district had three superintending missionaries, namely, from January to March, the Rev. W. J. Hanan, from April to September, the Rev. J. Ilsley, and from September 25 to the end of the year, the Rev. A. E. Dibben.

It was decided this year to withdraw the European missionary and to hand over the greater part of the pastoral, evangelistic, and vernacular educational work to the various committees of the Tamil Churches.

In the Chundicully Pastorate, which includes work in the Island of Mandaitivu, the Incumbent was the Rev. S. S. Somasundaram. The Christians numbered 541, communicants, 246 and vernacular schools nine. The Nellore-Kokuvil Pastorate was in charge of the Rev. J. Backus. The Christians numbered 359, communicants 197, and vernacular schools 17 with 1,288 children.

On July 15, 1913, Mr. Backus celebrated his fiftieth year of service in connection with the C.M.S. The Bishop officiated at the Holy Communion, and eighty-two friends of the pastor partook of the Sacrament with him. There was a Thanksgiving Service in the afternoon, followed by a social gathering at which Sir William Twynam presided.

In 1915 the Rev. A. Matthias retired from the Incumbency of the Copay Pastorate, and in his last report says, 'The Christians number 374, communicants 161 and vernacular schools thirteen with 919 scholars. The starting of a 'Christian Union' greatly helped the congregation.'

The Rev. C. T. Williams was appointed pastor on the retirement of Mr. Matthias, thus returning to the scene of his former labours. At the beginning of the year Miss A. M. Tisdall took charge of the Nellore Boarding School receiving valuable help from Miss Findlay who volunteered to accompany her to Jaffna. There were then ninety-four pupils attending the school, of whom seven belonged to the training class and seventeen to the industrial class. Sixty-two were Christians and thirty-two Sivites.

The chief event in the year 1916, in the Jaffna mission, was the amalgamation of the Training Schools for vernacular teachers. Hitherto each of the three Protestant Missions had a training school of its own, the results from each being poor, yet each Mission was reluctant to give up its own school. The question reached a climax when the Government proposed to establish a well-equipped training school on secular lines, which would have ruined all three. It was then decided to amalgamate, and the Government agreeing that this should be done at the C.M.S. training school at Copay, necessary buildings and equipment were procured. It is believed that this combination will result in increased efficiency and economy, and at the same time form an outward and visible sign of the inward and spiritual unity which binds together the Missions of North Ceylon. As a part of the scheme sanctioned by Government, Hindu students also are admitted to a share in the secular parts of the teaching, but they are housed in a separate hostel of their own quite apart from the mission compound.

ST. JOHN'S COLLEGE.

In the year 1823, an English Seminary for the higher education of Tamil youths was opened at Nellore by the Rev. J. Knight and in 1825 was in charge of the Rev. W. Adley. The primary aim of the school was to bring forward agents for mission work. It had, on an average, thirty boys, selected from the day schools, who were boarded, clothed and educated free. The pupils were required to attend public worship and other religious services, the Bible was made the most prominent subject of study, and a good secular education was also given.

In 1841 the seminary was removed to Chundicully and in 1851 as a boarding establishment it was abolished. From its foundation to its close, upwards of two hundred lads passed through the regular course, and seventy became converts to Christianity. From 1851 it was called the 'Chundicully Seminary,' and carried on without a boarding department, the pupils paying fees from one shilling to eight shillings a quarter. A government grant-in-aid was received until 1862, when, because of the introduction of restrictions upon Scriptural teaching, the grant was relinquished. The school was divided into six classes, and the first of these was for boys preparing for Matriculation in the Madras University, to which the school was affiliated. In 1867 the only two Jaffna youths who were successful in this examination were pupils of the school. About this time the pupils numbered 230.

One day a Brahmin brought his son to be admitted. The Principal said to him, 'We teach the Bible and I shall make a Christian of him if I can.' The Brahmin replied, 'I know it, the Bible precepts are good for a son to learn, and as to his becoming a Christian, the Christian religion is good; it is better than Hinduism. If he wishes to become a Christian, he may, but I would rather he did not, at least before I die.'

The headmasters up to this date had been Mr. W. Santiagoe, 1841-48, Mr. J. Phillips, 1848-53, and Mr. R. Williams, 1853-66.

In a 'Retrospect of the Past,' written fifty years after by an old boy, Mr. F. R. Bartholomeusz, we read, 'The working of the Chundicully school was under the immediate eye of Mr. Robert Williams. His sternness was dreaded, but with a stout heart he possessed a winsome mind, tact, and ability.'

The Rev. R. Pargiter took charge of the school in 1846, built the old hall in 1861 and retired in 1866. In 1872 the number of pupils was 226 and the following year, the Governor of Ceylon, Sir W. H. Gregory, visited the school. It pursued the even tenor of its way and in 1885 the Principal, the Rev. G. T. Fleming, gave an encouraging report, showing that it had done well in scholastic work, and was the means of spiritual profit to many of the scholars. The following year the Headmaster, Mr. J. Ewarts, who was an able man and an earnest Christian, passed away. During the Michaelmas vacation about a dozen of the elder students, members of the Y.M.C.A., made an evangelistic tour in Mundativu, a large island in the lagoon.

The year 1891 was the Jubilee of the school and to mark the event the new name of St. John's College was given to the old Chundicully Seminary, the Rev. J. W. Fall being Principal at the time. The same year, three students passed the Calcutta Entrance examination and three the Cambridge Local. The Headmaster, the Rev. C. C. Handy, a son of the late Rev. J. P. Handy of Nellore, was ordained in May. The number of boarders increased from nine to forty, and an annexure was built to accommodate more. In 1894

Mr. Godwin Arulpragasam, who had served the College faithfully for fifteen years, died.

In 1895 the Rev. J. Carter, the Principal writes, ' Both as Chundiculty Seminary and as St. John's College, this school has done good work in Jaffna.' In 1899 the number of pupils had risen to 397, with a staff of fifteen Tamil masters assisting the Principal, the Rev. R. W. Ryde, who had arrived in August and continued till July, 1900, when he was succeeded by the Rev. Jacob Thompson.

Mr. Thompson a few months later writes, ' When I took charge, the College buildings were still in a state of picturesque ruin, while the walls of the boarding house were supported only by the rafters that had fallen from the roof of the other building. The students were being taught, some on the narrow verandah of the boarding house, some in the vestry of the church, others in the village girls' school, and even the shade of a large tree had been utilized.' By October of the following year, a new boarding house, a new hall with class-rooms and library, and a new dining hall had been built, and many other improvements effected. Above Rs. 10,000 were spent on the buildings. The Government Inspector of Schools for the province reported ' I have just been looking round the new buildings, which are now complete, not only externally but internally. In accommodation and furnishing they are models of taste, tidiness and comfort. The influence of beautiful surroundings, apart from positive training, will, I feel certain, tend to raise the tone of the school.'

In addition to the College, Mr. Thompson was responsible for a branch English school at Copay, with 150 boys (which was enlarged in 1903) and the Chaplaincy of Christ Church in the Pettah. Mr. Thompson went on furlough in September, 1904, and the Rev. W. J. Hanan took charge till August of the following year, when he handed over to the Rev. J. I. Pickford. Mr. Thompson returned at the end of the year, and in 1906 there were 539 scholars in the college and school.

Three men volunteered for training for Orders, one of these the son of the proprietor of one of the most popular temples. He had sacrificed his influential position in order to become a Christian and after taking his degree at Calcutta had been a master at the College. The government grant for the two schools had steadily increased from Rs. 1,300, in 1900, to Rs. 4,600 in 1907.

The following year the College lost by death the services of the Rev. C. C. Handy, who for nineteen years had worked with manifest unselfishness for the good of the students and people. During Mr. Handy's illness the Rev. and Mrs. A. M. Walmsley gave assistance in the College, and Mr. T. H. Crossette was appointed headmaster.

Twenty-two boys passed the Cambridge Locals, one of whom obtained honours, with distinction in Logic. This boy was a grandson of Mr. Phillips who sixty years before was headmaster of the school.

In 1909 the premises were further enlarged by an addition to the playground, the gift of the Old Boys' Association, in memory of the Rev. C. C. Handy. The Senior Mathematical master, Mr. S. S. Somasundaram, was also ordained this year. The number of pupils had now reached 600.

During 1910 the Rev. Jacob Thompson was absent from Ceylon for eight months, during which time the College was under the management of a Tamil, Mr. T. H. Crossette, and the number of students and the discipline were fully maintained. On June 21, 1911, the foundation stone of a new library was laid, the entire cost of erecting and furnishing having been given by Dr. J. M. Handy, in memory of his brother. In March, 1913, the library was opened by Mrs. J. M. Handy. The religious work of the College was being carried on quietly under the auspices of the College Y.M.C.A., Prayer meetings were conducted every Tuesday, Bible classes on Sunday mornings, Gospel meetings on Saturdays, and a Bible class on Sunday afternoons. A Scripture Union with ninety-six members had been started and a Communicants' Union met monthly.

In 1914 the Vice-Principal visited Singapore and Kuala Lumpur, and collected from the Tamil settlers about Rs. 9,000, with which a large hall and four airy class rooms were erected. The College was also re-organized into distinct schools, one providing a sound commercial education, and the other an education preparatory to University work. The staff was considerably strengthened and a laboratory added.

In 1915 the Director of Education recognized the uniformly excellent results of the Junior School by granting a first class certificate to Mr. Williams, the headmaster.

In 1916 there were over a thousand boys on the rolls of St. John's College and its branches, Copai, Urumparai and Kaithady, with fifty-five masters and one hundred and thirty boarders.

CHAPTER XI.

BADDEGAMA.

THE Rev. and Mrs. Robert Mayor landed at Galle on June 29, 1818, and were received with great kindness by the chaplain, the Rev. J. M. S. Glenie. Shortly after, Mr. Mayor writes to the C.M.S., ' It is not their readiness to welcome the light of the Gospel which must be your inducement to send out more labourers, but their great need of instruction, and the positive duty of a Christian nation to communicate the knowledge of the only Saviour to all its subjects. We have free access to the people, and their prejudices against Christianity are not deeply rooted; they are willing to have their children taught to read, and these children have an intellect capable of the highest cultivation.'

On October 20, Mr. Mayor visited several villages on the banks of the Gindara river by boat. At Telikada, six miles from Galle, the government schoolmaster with his scholars and the headmen, drew up in line and saluted him with three cheers.

The next place visited was Baddegama, twelve miles from Galle, where he was met by the Mudaliyar, the chief government officer, and the Government School boys. Mr. Mayor writes, ' The situation of Baddegama appears to be exceedingly convenient for the residence of a missionary. The people, though nominally Christians, are really Buddhists. The Mudaliyar is desirous that I should reside there, and offers to raise a subscription for the erection of a Church and School. The Archdeacon would, I believe, very much approve of my residing among the natives.'

The next day, Mr. Mayor proceeded up the river to Mapalagama, where about 800 people met him, and out of this number there were only ten who had not been baptized. Mr. Mayor again writes, ' The Dutch have done much injury to the cause of Christianity by disqualifying all persons from inheriting property who have not been baptized. In consequence of this law, every one, whether he worships Buddha or the devil, is eager to be baptized.' On his return journey, the headmen of Nagoda offered to build a school within six days and fill it with children. At Baddegama he again preached to about 150 people, on our Lord's feeding the five thousand.

On his return to Galle, after consultation with the other missionaries and with the approbation of Government, Mr. Mayor decided to settle in Baddegama. Accordingly on August 14, 1819, he took up his abode in a small house in Baddegama. Government gave a free grant of land and a substantial house was finished in November. The name Baddegama is derived from the Sinhalese ' Bat denna gamma,' or rice supplying village. It is recorded that the monks of Totagamuwa temple subsisted on the rice which was supplied from this village by order of the Sinhalese kings.

About the year A.D. 1240 a bridge of 120 cubits' span was in existence over the river at Baddegama, the same having been constructed by the minister Patiraja Deva, who was appointed Governor over the Southern provinces by King Parakrama II. The bridge was to connect the road from Bentota to Baddegama *via* Elpitiya. Near to Elpitiya Patiraja founded a college, and the ancient Sinhalese Grammar, Sidathsangarawa, was written there, and the locality is still known by the name of Patiraja Kanda.

The hill on which the mission house was built was named ' Church Hill.' It presents a delightful prospect of a winding river, a fruitful valley, well-watered fields and distant mountains. A large school-room of stone was next built, capable of holding 250 people, and was used for public worship till the church was built. Mr. Glenie having removed to Colombo, the Lieutenant Governor asked Mr. Mayor to undertake duty at Galle until another chaplain could be provided.

On October 26, 1819, the Rev. Benjamin Ward, on account of ill-health, moved from Calpentyn to Baddegama, and preached his first sermon in Sinhalese, ten months after arrival.

On February 14, 1821, the foundation stone of the church was laid by Don Abraham Dias Abeysinghe, Guard Mudaliyar of Galle, in the presence of a great concourse of people. The chief headman of the district, who had previously sent a donation of fifty-six dollars, was present and the collection amounted to £20. Sir Robert Brownrigg, the Governor, expressed his approbation by a public grant and a private donation. The Revs. Mayor, Ward and Glenie addressed the people. Rice and curry were provided for all who chose to partake and 350 children were feasted.

The difficulty of erecting the church may be judged from the fact that 700 lbs. of gunpowder were required to blast the rock for the foundation. The church is a substantial stone building, eighty-four feet by forty-three, with a square tower. The roof is supported by twelve round iron-wood pillars, thirty feet high, each cut out of a single tree. Most of the wood used was either iron-wood or teak. A deep verandah surrounds the church. Before the workmen commenced each morning, they assembled under a shed, and one of the missionaries offered a prayer and gave a short address. The church was opened on March 11, 1824, by the Archdeacon. In the large congregation were the chief government officials, and Sir Richard Ottley, the Chief Justice, who presented the Communion plate.

Mr. Mayor writes, ' The Church will remain, I doubt not, a monument to future ages of the day when the Sun of

Righteousness first rose upon this village. It is the first church which has ever been erected in the interior for the sole benefit of the Sinhalese.'

Before commencing the building of the church, Mr. Mayor asked to be relieved ot the garrison duty at Galle. The missionaries had also undertaken the superintendence of forty government schools in the Galle and Matara districts. Mr. Ward writes, 'These schools will give us access to many thousand natives; they will increase our influence, and will afford us opportunities of preaching the Gospel.'

Mr. Mayor, at one time when there was no medical officer in Galle, discharged the important functions of that post.

The following extract from Mr. Mayor's diary is interesting:

'August 6, 1822—Left for Belligama. Here preached to a large concourse. Seventy children present, twelve of whom read the New Testament. Fifty boys repeated their Catechism. Went to Denipitiya and married twenty-three couples.

August 7—Proceeded to Mirisse and preached upon the "fall of man." Married four couples.

August 8—Visited the Matara School after preaching; examined scholars. Married thirty-eight couples. Then on to Kottecagodde, where I preached and married eleven couples.'

Mr. Ward gives the following instance of the influence of caste. 'On Sunday, many came to have their banns of marriage published. By virtue of a late regulation of government, low-caste women are authorized to wear jackets, a privilege, which the system of caste had hitherto denied them. Three of these women appeared in the congregation, each decently clothed in a white cloth jacket. When I entered the church, I perceived the school-girls and other women in the utmost confusion, apparently resolved not to take their seats.

Some of them went out. The three women who had given so much offence sat at the opposite end of the building. I expostulated with the congregation on the impropriety of their conduct, explained to them the nature and tendency of our religion, and reasoned with them upon the childishness of taking offence at others, for wearing the same kind of clothing as themselves.'

Mr. Ward also writes, 'There exists prejudice even between individuals of the same caste, and these expect a distinction in seats. We have hitherto found it necessary not to indulge them with an elevated seat, but with a distinct one. A bench is placed either in the front or on one side, on which the headmen and higher families sit. The Mudaliyar is yet more distinguished by sitting on a chair.'

The missionaries resolutely set their faces against the prevalent abuse of the sacred ordinance of Baptism, which had led to the degradation of the Christian name, and Mr. Ward writes, 'The country is full of baptized persons, who worship Buddha and the devil. We have resolved to baptize the children of only those persons who attend the public worship of the true God.' Seven schools were commenced with an average attendance of 159 scholars. A school for girls was commenced in the verandah of the mission house, conducted by Mrs. Mayor, who writes 'The average number of girls is forty. They sit on mats, and are taught to read and sew. A portion of Scripture is read and explained. To encourage them to attend regularly, we give them clothes twice a year.'

Experience taught the missionaries to view appearances of success with caution. In the case of many apparently genuine seekers after truth, the hope of worldly honour and emolument appears to have been the real inducement. The missionaries received the following letter from the Secretary of the C.M.S., brother-in-law of Mr. Mayor:

C. M. House, London,
July 19, 1824.

'We anticipate much blessing on your work, because the Lord has so completely shown you your own helplessness, and is leading you to look more simply to His sufficiency. He will never disappoint those who trust in Him. We rejoice to see your zealous exertions in preaching the word. It is your grand weapon against the enemy. You probably somewhat under-rate education, but you do not under-rate preaching to the adults, and we pray God that there may be such a manifest blessing on your labours, as may be a great encouragement to your brethren everywhere. Go on in the strength of the Lord. We rejoice in your labours, and sympathize in your sorrows. You are our joy and comfort, and may the Divine Spirit be poured out more and more upon you and your work, and the Lord Jesus be constantly magnified in you.

E. Bickersteth.'

The church was consecrated by Bishop Reginald Heber of the occasion of his visit to Ceylon in 1825. The following is an extract from the Bishop's Indian Journal:—

'September 24, 1825. Long before day-break we were on our way to Baddegama. At Amlangoda we breakfasted, and at Kennery left the main road, and wound through very narrow paths and over broken bridges, till we had arrived at the river which we had first crossed on leaving Galle, but some miles higher up.

The country then improved into great beauty, and at the end of about two miles we came within sight of a church on the summit of a hill, with the house of one of the missionaries, Mr. Mayor, immediately adjoining it, and that of Mr. Ward on another eminence close to it, forming altogether a landscape of singular and interesting beauty. We ascended by a steep road to Mr. Mayor's where we found the families of the two missionaries and some of our friends from Galle, awaiting our arrival. At the foot of this hill, the river we had recently crossed winds through what has the appearance of a richly dressed lawn, while all around rise mountains, one above the other. On our right was the church, a very pretty building. The whole scene was peculiarly interesting. Here we found two very young men, with their wives and children, separated from all European society by many miles of country, impassable, save in two directions, even to palanquins, devoting themselves entirely to the service of their Maker, in spreading His religion among the heathen and in the education of their families. The two families, indeed, seem to form but one household living together in Christian fellowship, and with no other object but to serve God, and do their duty to their neighbour. I have seldom been more gratified, I may say, affected. Mr. Mayor who is son to our neighbour at Shawbury (Rev. John Mayor) was originally brought up in the medical line, his surgical and medical knowledge are invaluable to himself and his neighbours and even during the short time we were his guests, we found their use in a sudden attack our little girl had, brought on by fatigue and over-exertion.'

The Bishop consecrated the church and afterwards the burial ground on the morning of September 25. Almost all the European residents from Galle and a great number of natives were assembled to witness the ceremony. The Bishop preached from Genesis xxviii. 16 and 17 and in the afternoon confirmed thirteen persons, all of whom, save three, were Sinhalese. In the evening the Bishop examined some of the scholars.

'September 26, 1825. We left Baddegama in palanquins and made our way along the banks of the river, which was too much swollen by recent heavy rains to admit of our going in boats. Indeed, the track was in some parts covered with water so deep that it nearly entered my palanquin and was very fatiguing to the poor bearers. In the afternoon we arrived at Galle.'

The Bishop, writing to his mother on the following day from Galle, says, 'There are also some very meritorious missionaries in the Island. One of them, Mr. Mayor, together with another Shropshire man, Mr. Ward, has got together a very respectable congregation of natives as well as a large school. He has also built a pretty church, which I cousecrated last Sunday, in one of the wildest and most beautiful situations I ever saw.'

Writing to the Rev. J. Mayor, Vicar of Shawbury, Bishop Heber says 'Mrs. Heber and I had the pleasure of passing the best part of three days with Mr. and Mrs. Mayor, in their romantic home at Baddegama, where we also found his colleague Mr. Ward, with his wife and family, in perfect health and contented cheerfulness. They are active, zealous, well-informed and orderly clergymen, devoted to the instruction and help of their heathen neighbours, both enjoying a favourable report, I think I may say without exception, from the Governor, public functionaries, and in general, from all the English in the colony whom I have heard speak of them.'

Bishop Heber received his home call on April 3, 1826, at Trichinopoly, in South India.

Owing to failing health Messrs. Mayor and Ward left for England in April, 1828. Before they left, a joint report of their work was issued in which they say, 'The Sunday morning service is attended by about 100 children and seventy adults. The Litany is used in the native tongue. In the evening, prayers are read in English and an exposition interpreted into Sinhalese.'

A stone tablet in the church has the following inscription :—

'In memory of the Rev. Robert Mayor, the founder of this station, and by whose exertions this Church was built, who after nearly ten years of faithful labour in this country was compelled by the loss of his health to return to England where he afterwards became successively Rector of Coppenstall and Vicar of Acton in the county of Chester, at which last place he died in perfect peace on the 14th of July 1846, aged fifty-five. His friends in Ceylon have erected this tablet as a tribute of their affectionate remembrance of his character and labour.'

The Rev. George Conybeare Trimnell and Mrs. Trimnell took charge in September 1826 and soon afterwards the Rev. George Steers Faught and Mrs. Faught were associated with them. On Easter Sunday, 1830, the first adult convert from Buddhism in connection with the C.M.S. in the district was baptized, receiving the name of Edward Bickersteth.

In 1833 Mr. Trimnell reports, 'The schools are in a flourishing state, the girls' school having an attendance of 115. Where all or nearly all, a few years ago, were unlettered, there are now many who can read; where there was nothing to read but a few Buddhist books or foolish songs written on the leaf of a tree, there are now hundreds of printed copies of the word of God; where there was no sound of the Gospel it is now certainly preached and there are hundreds who hear it every Lord's day. Thus far all is well, but we who cannot be satisfied with a change in externals, or without an evidence of spiritual life among the people, and who have seen things almost in their present state for years, are often much discouraged.' He adds as a chief cause of sorrow 'there is scarcely any evidence of any one being really converted.'

On the return to England of Mr. and Mrs. Faught in 1836, the Rev. J. Selkirk took charge until the return of Mr. Trimnell. Mr. Selkirk again took up the work after Mr. Trimnell left for England in 1838, until set at liberty by the arrival of the Rev. and Mrs. H. Powell in January 1839.

Bishop Corrie of Madras visited Baddegama in 1840 and thus writes to the Earl of Chichester: ' Beautiful Baddegama, a Christian watchfire in a very dark night, a Christian lighthouse in a very dark place, a cradle of the gospel in a heathen land.'

In 1841 the Rev. and Mrs. Charles Greenwood took charge and for a few months in 1848 the Rev. and Mrs. Isaiah Wood were associated with them. Balapitimodera and Bentota, two towns of importance on the coast, were occupied as outstations.

In October, 1847, the first Bishop of Colombo, Dr. Chapman, visited Baddegama, and writing to the C.M.S. he says, ' My visit to Baddegama for the Confirmation was full of interest and encouragement. I was met on the banks of its beautiful river by Messrs. Greenwood and Gunasekara, your two valued missionaries, and all the catechists and the youths of the Seminary, and up the hill, close to the mission house, with its English-towered church and English scenery around, by Mrs. Greenwood and above sixty children of her native girls' school. No welcome could have been more characteristic or more pleasing. On the next day the church was filled for the Confirmation at eleven o'clock. Twenty-three were confirmed; one a poor cripple in limb but not in faith, was carried to the Holy Table, and I trust the fullness of the blessing conveyed to his heart by faith was not marred by the unworthiness of the channel through which it reached him.'

On June 21, 1850, the Rev. C. Greenwood, aged thirty-seven, was drowned while bathing in the river, and his sudden removal threw the charge of the station upon the Rev. George Parsons, who had been only six months in the Island.

A clock was placed in the church in memory of Mr. Greenwood. Mr. Parsons extended the work on the sea coast and for some time left Baddegama in charge of the Rev. Abraham Gunasekara, taking up his own residence at Bentota. Small congregations were collected at Bentota and Balapitimodera, but these were formed of nominal Christians, not of converts from heathenism; schools were opened, but the seed sown did not yield any visible fruit. At Dodanduwa, however, some enquirers presented themselves, and after several months of instruction, twelve adults were baptized.

The Rev. G. Pettitt, the Secretary of the Mission, visited Baddegama in April 1850, and thus writes ' The view from Palm Hill, the site of the second mission house, is peculiarly beautiful. The eye never rests upon a barren spot, or even upon a foot of soil or sandy ground, and all this loveliness is perpetual, for there is no winter in Ceylon. There are however disadvantages connected with this excellence; it is not Paradise after all. It is exceedingly damp, everything capable of it becomes mouldy in an incredibly short time, a little bodily exertion produces a disagreeable amount of perspiration, and the feeling of languor easily creeps over the frame, a short pointed grass takes advantage of your shortest walk to tease your legs and demands a considerable portion of time for its dislodgement, a small leech with a troublesome bite operates without medical prescription, while frequent rains either impede your plans of usefulness, or drench you in adhering to them. Snakes, centipedes, scorpions and other noxious insects abound.' From 1859 to 1862 during Mr. Parson's absence on furlough, the district was under the charge of the Rev. A. Gunasekara by whom the work was earnestly and faithfully carried on. Mr. Gunasekara was born in 1802 and died in 1862. His father Bastian Gunasekara who was born in 1773 and died in 1853, came to Baddegama from Galle, having been recommended to Mr. Mayor by the Galle Mudaliyar, for the post of overseer during the building of the church. A tablet to Mr. Gunasekara's memory was placed in the church, inscribed as follows :—

' He was the first Native Missionary of Baddegama where he laboured twenty-three years with zeal and fidelity in the Master's service. Deeply sensible of his unworthiness and firmly trusting in Jesus his Saviour he joyfully anticipated being present with the Lord.'

It is related of Mr. Gunasekara that once as a Buddhist boy he went into the temple to offer his evening flower. When he had done so, he looked into the idol's face, expecting to see a smile of approval, but he noticed that the great eyes stared on without any expression of pleasure in them. He thought therefore that so great a god would not condescend to accept a child's offering. Soon after a man came in, laid down his flower, turned his back and went carelessly away. The boy again looked in the idol's face and thought he would see an angry frown at this disrespect, but the eyes stared on as before. He then began to realize the fact that the image had no life in it, and was alike powerless to reward or punish.

In 1863 the vernacular institution for the training of catechists was removed from Cotta to Baddegama, and in the following year, an institution for the training of schoolmasters was opened under the Rev. S. Coles. These were carried on until 1868 when both were transferred to Cotta.

In November 1863, what is called the ' Baddegama Controversy ' began, and several public meetings were held till the following February, when they were stopped by order of the magistrates. Mr. Parsons writing to the C.M.S. says, ' The spirit of controversy broke out in November last, and though I was partly prepared for it, I was slow to believe it would become such a serious matter until urged by our people to prepare for a fierce contest. The result fully justified their anxieties, for never before in Ceylon was there such a marshalling of the enemy against Christianity. The one aim of the fifty priests and their two thousand followers who assembled here on February 8, was not to defend Buddhism but to overthrow Christianity. Encouraged by translations from Bishop Colenso's writings, they considered the utter defeat of Christianity easy and certain. Knowing the people we had to encounter, we felt that our victory would be more triumphant and complete, by attacking Buddhism, whilst we defended Christianity. It was not, however, till we were somewhat advanced in the controversy, that we could fairly estimate the difficulties of our position, and day by day, we had to commend ourselves in prayer to God and confide in Him for wisdom and direction at every step. On reviewing the whole controversy, I am thankful for what has taken place, and believe the effect upon this district has been healthy and encouraging.'

On November 24, 1864, Dr. Claughton, the Bishop, consecrated the new church at Balapitimodera, which was originally built by Dr. Clarke, a former Police Magistrate of the place. The Bishop also held a Confirmation at Baddegama when twenty-four candidates were confirmed. In April 1866, Mr. Parsons was suddenly removed, by death from fever, whilst on a visit to Colombo. Mrs. Parsons who had diligently worked among the girls and women, returned to England and died thirty years after in November 1896. A beautiful marble tablet was placed to his memory in the church by the Christians. The station then came under the superintendence of the Rev. E. T. Higgens. During his time the Church Council system came into operation, ahd Baddegama, Balapitiya and Dodanduwa were formed into separate pastorates under a district council.

In 1869 the Rev. John Allcock took charge, and although work had been carried on for fifty years, the Christians only numbered 240, of whom sixty-four were communicants, and in the eleven schools there were 457 children. Mr. Allcock in his first annual report writes, ' The Church here, like many other, is still deficient in apostolic simplicity, earnest conviction, zeal, faith, hope and charity; yet there are a few who earnestly desire to adorn the Gospel of our Lord Jesus Christ.'

In 1875 a church was erected at Dodanduwa costing Rs. 2,000, and dedicated to the Holy Trinity.

In 1881 two of the catechists Messrs. A. S. Amarasekara and G. B. Perera were ordained deacons and stationed at Dodanduwa and Balapitimodera.

Mr. Allcock was an earnest, simple-minded, good man, full of the Holy Ghost, enthusiasm and good works, whose one object was to preach the Gospel, in season and out of season. The greater part of his time was spent going from village to village, sowing the good seed. In one of his reports he writes, ' I do not expect very much good from girls' day schools.' In another, ' Schools are of little use, we must preach more,' and again, ' Preaching and sowing are the best means of winning the people.' In nearly all his letters he mourned over the apathy and indifference of the Sinhalese Christians, in not caring for the souls of others.

In 1881 Dr. Johnson, Metropolitan and Bishop of Calcutta, visited Baddegama, and before leaving wrote as follows, ' I visited Baddegama on Monday, February 7, 1881, driving out from Galle with the Bishop of Colombo. I addressed a large congregation, taking for my subject " The difficulty of getting free from bondage and the consequent liability to discouragement." A special service was held later in the day when I gave an address to the heathen, endeavouring to draw out the contrast between the morality of Buddhism and that of Christianity, the latter being based upon our relations with the One God, One Father. It seems that here, as in most parts of India, the progress is slow, the adult heathen being only brought out by ones and twos. The schools are gradually exercising an influence and by their means each generation must, it may be hoped, show increased results.'

When Mr. Allcock left for England in March 1883, the Christians numbered 481, of whom 137 were communicants, and the schools contained 1,353 children.

A few years after, on Mr. Allcock's death from fever in the Kandyan country, the sum of Rs. 250 was collected, and a large bell placed in the church tower with the inscription 'In memory of the Rev. John Allcock.'

In November, 1882, the Rev. J. W. Balding was transferred from the Kurunegala district to take charge of Baddegama. At the close of the following year he writes, 'What grieves me most is that in nearly every village, I find that of those who at one time or the other have professed Christ and been baptized, many now living carelessly are worse than the heathen around, whilst very few of the Christians make the slightest endeavour to bring others to a knowledge of the truth.'

In 1884 a stone school chapel was built at Kitulampitiya, and in 1885 a similar building at Elpitiya on a piece of land given by Mr. Elias Perera, the catechist there.

In 1886, an Ordination Service was held in Baddegama Church, when three deacons were admitted to the priesthood, by Dr. R. S. Copleston, Bishop of Colombo. Archdeacon Matthew and ten other clergy were present. This was the first time that an Ordination had been held in the Sinhalese language and in the midst of the people themselves.

On June 1, 1888, a Boarding School for Sinhalese girls was opened by Mrs. Balding, and from its commencement has been a success. Many of the pupils have become teachers in village schools. In addition to missionaries' wives, other European ladies, Miss Binfield, Miss Ursula Kriekenbeck, Miss Henry (all three since dead) and Miss C. Kerr have given valuable help in the school, whilst Mrs. Wirakoon, always called 'Mistress' by the girls and a daughter of the late Rev. H. Kannangara, has been the invaluable head mistress from the opening day to the present time. In May, 1893, a lady missionary, Miss Helen P. Philips, late Principal of the Clergy Daughters' School at Sydney and the first worker sent out by the New South Wales C.M.S. Association, was appointed to Dodanduwa, to be joined in the following November by Miss E. M. Josolyne. An industrial school for boys and girls, where printing, carpentry, wood-carving, tailoring and lacemaking were taught, was commenced.

On August 14, 1894, the seventy-fifth anniversary of the founding of the Baddegama mission was celebrated. Dr. Copleston, the Bishop, and fifteen clergy were present. At the morning service, a sermon was preached by the Rev. J. de Silva, on the Parable of the Mustard Seed, after which the Holy Communion was administered to 205 communicants. At mid-day the Rev. S. Coles addressed over 600 children in the church, and afterwards a public meeting presided over by the Bishop, was held in the English school. In the afternoon there was a garden party, and in the evening, a lantern address on the 'Holy Land,' by Archdeacon de Winton. The sum of Rs. 1,250 was given by the people towards the renovating of the church. A teak reading desk, lectern and pulpit were bought, and a brass offertory dish, alms bags, kneelers and an ebony Communion Table were presented. A stone tablet with the names of the missionaries who had worked in the district, with the text underneath ' Whose faith follow ' was also placed in the church.

In November, 1895, two more women missionaries, Miss C. N. Luxmoore and Miss M. S. Gedge arrived.

About this time the district was well supplied with Sinhalese clergy, the Rev. James Colombage in Baddegama, the Rev. G. B. Perera at Balapitimodera and the Rev. J. P. Kalpage at Dodanduwa.

In 1897 over 700 people attended the service in connection with the Diamond Jubilee of Queen Victoria. In the same year fifty girls were presented at the Government examination of the Girls' Boarding School, obtaining eighty-five per cent. of passes and in the Diocesan Religious Examination fourteen girls obtained prizes, and the school a second class certificate. One of the old girls who had gone to India as a mission worker, died of cholera this year. On the first page of her Bible was found written ' My mottoes for 1897. Holiness unto the Lord. First, suffering, then glory.'

In 1898 Mr. E. J. Carus Wilson, a lay missionary, was stationed at Bentota, Miss Townsend at Dodanduwa and Miss M. L. Young at Baddegama.

Miss L. M. Leslie Melville arrived in 1899, and the Rev. G. B. Perera, who had been in Balapitimodera for twenty-one years, moved to Baddegama.

About this period, the Rev. Professor Mayor of St. John's College, Cambridge, delivered a lecture on ' Antipathies of race and habit,' in which he said, ' In the Michaelmas term I had a proof, interesting to me at least, of the truth of that promise, " Cast thy bread upon the waters, and thou shalt find it after many days." A Sinhalese knocked at my door. He is in holy orders in the English Church, won a scholarship at Selwyn College and is reading for the theological tripos. His first words were " My father was a convert of your father." He must have been converted from devil-worship. Eighty-one years ago, my father founded a mission-station at Baddegama. To the ruin of his health, labouring under a tropical sun, he built church and school and parsonage. In that village my sister and I were born, in that church she and I were baptized. Seventy-one years ago we left Ceylon, where Reginald Heber, an old Shropshire friend of my father's had visited and blessed his work. My father would have hailed that one fruit of his labours as ample reward for shattered health and an early grave. My friend had taken part in the seventy-fifth anniversary of the mission.'

In December, 1900, Mr. G. A. Purser arrived to take charge of the Industrial School at Dodanduwa, and in October, 1901, the Rev. J. W. Balding, who had been connected with the district for twenty years, moved to Cotta to take charge of that station.

When Mr. Balding left, there were two Sinhalese clergy, five biblewomen, 653 Christians, 226 communicants, thirty-one schools and 2,110 scholars. The Rev. H. E. Heinekey took charge at the end of the year. In 1903 the district suffered severe losses in the home calls of the Rev. J. P. Kalpage, and of Mr. Baptist Karunaratne (a son-in-law of Rev. A. Gunasekara) who had been a mission worker for forty years. The Rev. G. B. Perera also left to become a pastor in the Cotta district. This year the Buddhists became very active in opposing Christian work, and establishing opposition schools.

The following year Mr. Heinekey reports ' Christianity cannot be said to be in a thriving condition here, converts are few, and the best of them seem glad to get away to other parts. Thus, there are now only 538 Christians against 653 in 1901, whilst there are 324 children less in the schools.'

The catechist, Mr. R. T. E. A. Gunatilake was ordained deacon in 1904. The same year the much-valued matron of the Girls' Boarding School, Mrs. Mary Perera, or ' old Mary ' as she called herself, passed away. For sixteen years she had faithfully filled her post, and for many years previously had been a valued school-teacher and biblewoman.

On the resignation of Mr. Heinekey in 1905 the Rev. S. M. Simmons was appointed. The Buddhists were now building schools of a far more substantial nature, which were thronged with children, and in charge of efficient teachers. Where there was no active opposition to Christianity, the attitude of the Christians was one of utter indifference. The Dodanduwa Industrial School continued to flourish, and at the Galle Agri-Horticultural Exhibition three prizes were won for carving.

In 1906 the School Chapel and two schools at Kitulampitiya were handed over to the incumbent of Galle.

The following year, Mrs. S. M. Simmons, who had thrown herself heart and soul into the work, and won the love and admiration of all, was called to higher service, and Mr. Simmons went on leave to England for a year, the Rev. R. H. Phair taking oversight of the work. Miss E. M. Josolyne was at this time in charge of the women's work in the district.

Miss Henry carried on the work of the school during the year 1908, Miss Walker then being located to Baddegama as Principal.

In 1909 the number of schools had fallen to 22 and the scholars to 1543.

Mr. G. A. Purser, who had been to England on furlough, returned to Baddegama in 1912, having been ordained, and with Mrs. Purser took charge. The following year, he laments the dearth of helpers, not a single Ceylonese clergyman or lady missionary being in the district. In 1914 the Rev. J. P. Ramanayake was stationed at Dodanduwa and in 1915, Mr. W. B. de Silva, the pastoral catechist, was ordained deacon. This year there were four adult and fourteen infant baptisms and several enquirers, and twenty-two candidates were presented for Confirmation. The Government grant to the schools had suffered considerably owing to the continued Buddhist opposition.

Mrs. Purser, who was Principal of the Girls' Boarding School, reports forty-six girls in the school, and the Inspector reported 'The results of the examination were satisfactory and reflect credit on the Lady Principal and her staff. The English recitation and writing were both above the average.'

At the Diocesan Scripture Examination the school obtained a first-class certificate. There is a branch of the Young People's Union in the school and a child is supported in a school at Dohnavur.

Mr. Robert de Silva, who has been connected with the Industrial School since its commencement, and is now in charge reports, 'We have sixty-three boys and at the last examination the Inspector wrote, "This is a very useful, school. The work done is really very good. I am much pleased with the work."' The Bishop and Mrs. Copleston visited the school, and wrote in the log-book 'We saw some very good carving, one boy shewing real talent. I saw some pages of the Gleaner being printed.' In September, 1916, Miss L. M. Leslie Melville and Miss Wardlaw Ramsay returned from England, and the former took up the post of Principal of the Girls' Boarding School, and the Rev. G. A. Purser removed to Dodanduwa, superintending the district from that centre.

In 1918 there were twenty-one schools in the district. There were two Sinhalese clergy, two catechists, two bible-women, twenty-two male teachers and twenty-three female teachers, 662 Christians, of whom 223 were communicants, and 1,112 boys and 568 girls in the schools.

CHAPTER XII.

COTTA.

COTTA, or Kotte, about six miles from Colombo, is a place famous in the annals of Ceylon as Jayawardhanapura, and at the time of the arrival of the Portuguese in A.D. 1505 was the capital and residence of the Sinhalese king. Sinhalese kings reigned there from A.D. 1378 to 1573. During the Dutch rule (1640 to 1796) the spiritual interests of Cotta and neighbourhood were not neglected. Cotta, with six adjacent villages, formed a parish, having its own pastor, supported by Government, and superintended by a Dutch Presbyterian clergyman. It had its large and substantial church in Etul Cotta, on the site where the C.M.S. girls' school now stands, well attended, for, with few exceptions, all the inhabitants had been baptized and many were communicants. There was also a school, with three teachers and a singing master, who also led the singing in church. The Dutch minister attended periodically from Colombo to perform religious rites and to examine the school.

The post of pastor was for a long time filled by a Mr. Philipsz, a Sinhalese gentleman, who had been educated and ordained in Holland. There was also a resident registrar whose duty was to collect the people for baptism and marriage on the periodical visits of a Proponent. On such occasions fathers and sons, who had been married for years, came to have their 'wedlock christianized' and their children and grandchildren baptized. Their names were then entered in the Thombuwa, or Register, and a fee of three fanams, or three pence, was levied for each entry, in payment

for the registrar's trouble. The following extract from the deed conveying the land to the Dutch minister is interesting :—
' On April 23, 1721, the Honourable Isaac Augustin Rumpf, ordinary Counseller of the Dutch Indies and Governor and Director of the Island of Ceylon, of his own free will and from motives of affection, resolved and thought proper to make a present of, for the service and benefit of the new-built native Reformed Church at Cotta, a certain garden, his property in the hamlet Etul Kotte, to the Rev. Wilhelmus Koning, the only officiating minister in Chingalee, through whose knowledge in the said Chingalee language accompanied by a great and good zeal to preach and propagate the true reformed religion amongst the Chingaleese and other natives, this Church was expressly commenced to be built about a year ago, for which reason also full power and authority is given by the said Honourable Donator to the said reverend gentleman to act and do with the said gardens as he should deem most proper for the service, greater airiness and embellishment of the said church and its compass.' The transfer of the Government to the British in 1796 produced a great change. Evangelization was laid aside. The churches and schools, including those of Cotta, were abandoned and allowed to fall into decay, and the people returned to Buddhism and its companions, kapuism and devil worship. The proponent system was soon abolished, having left, however, an almost indelible stamp on the religion of the country, handing down from generation to generation a nominal profession of a belief in Christianity where none was felt. The last of the proponents who officiated in Cotta was Don Abraham of Talangama.

The first English minister who exerted himself for the benefit of the people of Cotta was Mr. Chater of the Baptist Mission, but his efforts were attended with so little success that in the year 1820 he closed the school he had started, and retired from the place. In 1822 the Rev. Samuel Lambrick, who was one of the first four C.M.S. missionaries to Ceylon, and who on arrival had been stationed in Kandy, moved to Cotta. A piece of high and waste land, named Thotepallekannatte, on the border of the Cotta lake, Diwasnahwa or Juwannawa, was purchased from Government, and eight other pieces of land adjoining, from villagers, in order to build mission premises. The Government deed of conveyance is dated July 13, 1822, and signed by the Governor of Ceylon, Sir Edward Paget, K.G.C.B., and stipulates that the Rev. Samuel Lambrick 'shall and do take good care and preserve for the care and benefit of the Crown all the cinnamon trees which are now growing or which may hereafter grow on the said spot of ground.'

Soon after taking possession Mr. Lambrick wrote to the C.M.S., 'Cotta has a water communication with Colombo by means of a canal connecting the Calany with the Calpera and Pautura rivers; there is also a bridle road with wooden bridges over two branches of the canal, but in the rainy season this road is frequently impassable. It is sufficiently distant from Colombo to avoid the evils connected with a large town.'

The following year the Rev. Joseph Bailey was transferred to Cotta from Jaffna. Buildings were erected, and a printing press set up, from which 15,000 tracts were issued during the first year.

On November 8, 1827, Sir Edward Barnes, Governor of Ceylon, laid the foundation-stone of a theological college, called the Cotta Institution, to train Ceylonese for Christian work among their own people. Most of the civil and military residents from Colombo, the Archdeacon, the Chaplains and many others were present. On the opening of the Institution fifteen pupils were admitted 'who were to receive a good education in English, Science, Mathematics, Philology, Latin, Greek and Pali.'

The first student admitted was Abraham Gunasekara who was ordained in 1839 and worked at Baddegama till his death in 1862. The Rev. James Selkirk arrived in 1826, and, on his retirement in 1839, became Curate of Middleton Tyas, in Yorkshire, and in 1844 published his 'Recollections of Ceylon.'

In October, 1828, the first school for girls only was established under the superintendence of Mrs. Lambrick, who had arrived in the Island the previous year as Miss Stratford, and had been married to Mr. Lambrick. Great reluctance had always been shown by the mothers to send their daughters to 'learn letters' as they called it, and Mrs. Lambrick went to all the houses in the villages inviting the girls to attend. At the end of the year there were thirty-three girls attending.

In the same year, Mr. William Lambrick, a nephew of the Rev. S. Lambrick, was appointed classical teacher in the Institution and in 1831 the Rev. Joseph Marsh arrived from Madras to help.

The Cotta missionaries also prepared a translation of the Bible into colloquial Sinhalese, and on November 14, 1833, it was issued from the press and is known as the 'Cotta Bible.' To help in the printing of the Bible, a Mr. Riddesdale came out from England and had charge of the printing press for six years. It may be here stated that the first edition of the whole Bible in Sinhalese was published by the Bible Society in 1823, in three volumes, quarto, of 3,350 pages, the price per copy being £3-1-6, but as this edition was found to be too expensive and cumbersome for general use, and as the need of a glossary shewed that it required revision, a revised and more portable edition was, in November, 1830 published in one octavo volume of 1,212 pages, the price being only eleven shillings and sixpence.

The C.M.S. missionaries in 1824, considering that this edition 'contained so many words derived from the Sanscrit and Pali languages, words common in Sinhalese books and intelligible to persons of learning, but not to the great body of the people, and so many inflections of words, different from those in common use so as to render them difficult to be understood,' determined with the sanction of their Parent Society, to prepare and print at their own expense and at their press at Cotta a new version of the Bible in familiar Sinhalese. Thus there were two distinct versions of the Holy Scriptures in circulation, the older one, 'Tolfrey's,' prepared under the auspices of the Bible Society in Colombo, and the 'Cotta' version by the C.M.S. For some years it was found impossible to reconcile either of the respective translators to the use of the other version, although both parties felt that it was desirable that there should be but one standard version.

The controversy lasted until 1852, when, at a meeting held in the Dutch Church, Colombo, under the presidency of the Governor, Sir George Anderson, it was announced that all differences had terminated and that both sides would join to prepare one uniform Sinhalese version. The Rev. G. Pettitt of the C.M.S. and the Rev. D. J. Gogerly of the W.M.S. were elected joint Secretaries of the Bible Society, and the second period of translation and revision began. An *ad interim* version of the Bible was first prepared and a revised edition issued in 1857. A re-translation of the whole Bible was begun in 1858, by the Rev. D. J. Gogerly, but this translation was not altogether approved, so the re-translation was started again in 1887, with the Rev. S. Coles, C.M.S., as chief reviser. The work was performed with the most painstaking care, but when Mr. Coles suddenly died on September 13, 1901, whilst waiting for the assembling of the Revision Committee in the vestry of Galle Face Church, the revision had been completed only as far as the end of the Acts of the Apostles. Bishop R. S. Copleston took the place of Mr. Coles, and had completed Romans and Galatians, when he was appointed Metropolitan of India. It was not until 1911 that the whole work of re-translation was finished, and the new Bible published.

The first public examination of the Cotta Institution took place in 1831, and is thus noticed in the Government Gazette of December 17, 'A breakfast was given this morning by the Cotta Church missionaries to His Excellency the Governor (Sir R. J. Wilmot Horton) and Lady Wilmot Horton, at which all the civil and military authorities and a great number of the officers of the regiments stationed here were present. After breakfast the company adjourned to the Institution to hear the examination of the pupils in English reading, geography, geometry, arithmetic, Latin, and Greek. About two hours and a half were devoted to the examination. His Excellency expressed the pleasure and gratification that had been afforded him by an exhibition of so much talent, which did equal honour to those who taught and to those who received tuition. He could not express his own opinion more clearly than by referring to a passage that had just been construed by the Latin class: *Nullum munus reipublicae afferre majus meliusve possumus, quam si doceamus et erudiamus juventutem,*—we can confer no greater benefit upon the country than by the education of youth.' On November 11, 1834, the Bishop of Calcutta, Dr. Wilson, visited and with his chaplain spent two hours in examining the Institution students in geography, trigonometry, geometry, Latin, Greek and the Hebrew Bible.

In 1835 the Rev. S. Lambrick returned to England and became domestic chaplain to the Marquis of Cholmondeley, and died in 1854, aged 85.

On the retirement of Messrs. Lambrick and Selkirk, the Revs. J. Bailey and F. W. Taylor carried on the work of the various departments of the district with the assistance of the Rev. Cornelius Jayasinha, who had been ordained by Bishop

Spencer of Madras. After twenty years' trial it was found that the object for which the Institution was established had not been fully effected, as many of the students, after having completed their course, made choice of the more lucrative and popular employments at the disposal of the Government.

In 1851 the Rev. C. C. Fenn (who died in 1913 in England at the age of 90) was appointed and it was decided to make the Institution more comprehensive by changing it into a kind of Grammar School. It was thought that in this way many more than formerly would be brought under Christian influence and instruction. In 1853 there were 106 pupils on the list with an average attendance of seventy. Of these twenty were boarders, one paid nine shillings, nine paid seven shillings and sixpence, and four paid four and sixpence monthly, three were pupil teachers receiving food and four shillings each monthly, and three were free students.

After ten years of trial of the plans worked out by Mr. Fenn, it was manifest that although greater numbers were under instruction, there was no better supply of mission workers, and owing to the opening of the Government Academy, afterwards the Royal College, in Colombo, and other Colleges, boys stayed a much shorter time in the Institution than formerly. It was, therefore, decided not to keep up an expensive institution, and the present English school took its place. The total number of students educated in the Institution amounted to nearly two thousand. Of these, seventeen became ordained ministers, forty-one catechists, six Scripture readers, sixty-seven school masters, two advocates, one magistrate, eight proctors, six mudaliyars, sixty-eight government employees, and many others merchants, clerks, etc.

In 1841 Mr. Bailey was suddenly removed by death, and the Rev. H. Powell was transferred from Baddegama to Cotta. Two years later no less than sixty-nine adults and

128 children were baptized during the year and 110 candidates were confirmed by the Bishop, and the accounts of the work were so encouraging that the annual report of the Parent Society for that year speaks of Cotta as 'the heart of the Ceylon Mission.'

From 1848 till 1861 the Rev. Isaiah Wood was in charge. During this period the printing establishment was closed and the press sold. In 1861 the Rev. J. H. Clowes arrived, and the Rev. J. Ireland Jones was the Superintending Missionary.

During the eighteen months that followed, mission work throughout the entire low-country underwent a severe sifting process, which brought to light an amount of heathenism and hypocrisy among those who called themselves and were regarded as Christians, which was hardly credible. A Buddhist revival took place during which public lectures were given for the avowed purpose of overthrowing Christianity, and leading the converts back to their original faith. The result was that hundreds of those, whose names had stood on the congregational lists of the various missionary societies, forsook all connection with the Christian church. The one bright feature of all this was that the revival of Buddhism seemed to accomplish what missionaries for years had been labouring in vain to effect. It taught many that it was utterly inconsistent to call themselves Christians while they were Buddhists in heart.

In 1863 the Rev. E. T. Higgens removed from Kandy and took charge. The unsatisfactory character of many of the people he felt deeply, and in order to discover how many there were who were really Christian, and to draw a line of demarcation between them and the heathen, he instituted a test which he required the Christians to sign. It was a declaration that they believed Christianity to be the only true religion, that they regarded Buddhism as false, and that they had renounced all connection with heathenism and all practice of its ceremonies. Out of one thousand professing Christians, only 342 persons signed this test, and of these many were in the employ of the Mission.

In 1865 Mr. Clowes was in charge and had a zealous helper in the Rev. J. de Livera. The following year the Rev. J. Ireland Jones returned with instructions ' to pursue vigorously the work of reorganization. ' The Rev. Cornelius Jayasinghe who had been in charge of Talangama removed to Kandy.

Three years later, when the Mission Jubilee was celebrated, there were 440 adults who professed to have given up all faith in Buddhism. The schools numbered twenty, with seven hundred children attending, the number on the lists being about one-half more. The communicants numbered 175.

In 1869 the Rev. R. T. Dowbiggin was appointed and remained in charge for the next thirty years.

In June, 1871, Mrs. Dowbiggin (who was a daughter of Sir C. P. Layard, Government Agent of the Western Province) opened a Girls' Anglo-Vernacular Boarding School which continues to flourish to the present day, and has been a benefit and blessing to many. Up to the end of the year 1916, 860 girls had passed through the school. In 1886 the Rev. S. Coles had charge of a class for training catechists, with seven students.

Two years later the Rev. H. de Silva, the Pastor of Talangama and Welikada, the Rev. G. S. Amarasekara, the Pastor of Cotta and Nugegoda, and the Rev. W. L. Botejue, the Pastor of Mampe, gave cheering and encouraging accounts of the work in their Pastorates.

In 1897 Miss A. Dowbiggin was working as a missionary among the women and girls.

In the same year the Revs. Joseph Perera, Theodore Perera and W. E. Botejue were appointed to Colombo, Talangama and Mampe respectively. At the close of 1900 Mr. Dowbiggin gave a survey of the work of the district during his thirty years' superintendence with the following statistics:—

	1870	1900
Christians	874	1,361
Communicants	144	412
Contributions	Rs. 750	3,230
Girls in G. B. S.	29	76
Boys in English School	60	268
Vernacular School Pupils	1,082	3,300

Early in the following year the missionary was called to higher service after a painful illness patiently borne and a memorial brass in the Cotta Church bears these words—

IN LOVING MEMORY OF THE

REV. RICHARD THOMAS DOWBIGGIN,
C.M.S.

WHO FOR THIRTY YEARS
PREACHED CHRIST IN THE COTTA DISTRICT.

DIED AT SEA NEAR SUEZ

MARCH 8TH 1901. AGED 63 YEARS.

TO ME TO LIVE IS CHRIST, AND TO DIE IS GAIN.

THIS TABLET WAS ERECTED BY MANY FRIENDS.

On March 1 the Rev. J. Ireland Jones was appointed to Cotta, but the death of the Rev. S. Coles in September necessitated his return to Colombo, when the superintendence of the district was handed over to the Rev. J. W. Balding who had been for many years in Baddegama.

A portion of the district was cut off in 1909 and placed in the independent charge of the Rev. G. S. Amarasekara, and called the Nugegoda Pastorate. This consisted of St. John's Church, Nugegoda, Christ Church, Mirihana, and six vernacular schools. During his incumbency, Mr. Amarasekara collected funds and built a parsonage. On the appointment of Mr. Amarasekara to Kandy in 1908, the Rev. J. H. Wikramayake of Mampe succeeded him.

The following year the Rev. G. B. Perera moved to Cotta and the same year a long-felt want was met by the starting of a girls' English day school by Mrs. Balding.

In 1905 the Sinhalese Women Teachers' Vernacular Training School, which had been started in a hired house in Colombo by Miss H. P. Phillips, was moved to Cotta under the superintendence of Miss K. Gedge. Mr. Balding went on furlough this year and the Rev. R. W. Ryde took charge. In 1908 the re-built Church of St. Matthias, Boralesgamuwa, was opened, and a new church, dedicated to St. John, was built at Homagama through the liberality of Mr. J. C. Ebert.

In 1909 Mr. Balding writes, ' The Buddhist opposition to Christian work is severe and intense, and our means to combat it are limited.'

The Men Teachers' Training School, established some years previously, was this year transferred to Colombo, where a hostel was opened and the students attended the Government Training College. After the marriage of Miss K. Gedge to the Rev. H. P. Napier-Clavering in 1909, Mrs. Balding had charge of the Women Teachers' Training School for some months till the appointment of Miss Leslie Melville.

In 1910 Mrs. Dowbiggin went to England, and Miss Leslie Melville with the help of Miss G. Hutchinson managed the Girls' Boarding School. Mrs. Dowbiggin was missed by all. She had a remarkable way of keeping in touch with the old girls and a wonderful power of winning and retaining the love of her pupils.

In 1911 there passed away in one week two of the best and oldest workers of the district, both good men, full of the Holy Spirit and good works, whose praise was in all the churches, William de Silva, son of Thomas de Silva, a former catechist, who for fifty-two years had been Headmaster of the Cotta English School, and Hendrick de Silva, a catechist for fifty-one years.

At the end of the same year the Rev. and Mrs. A. M. Walmsley took charge of the Girls' Boarding School, the staff was strengthened, the buildings renovated, and some necessary equipment added. The spiritual side of the work was not neglected as the following letter to the missionary's wife will shew, ' I regret very much to let you know that I have made out from the letters sent by my two girls that you have infused into their childish brains the teachings of your religion, and have nearly succeeded in attempting to revert their minds to same. We sent the girls to your school to get them educated only. We never expect that our children become Christians. Therefore I hereby give you notice with thanks that I am going to withdraw said two girls by the end of March.'

The last visit of the Metropolitan, Dr. R. S. Copleston, took place in 1912, when about 400 people met in the Mission compound for a garden party and assembled for Evening Service in church when His Lordship gave an address.

One of the best catechists, Peter de Silva, a man of little education and no training, but whose life was a living witness, was called Home during this year.

The following year, Miss Wardlaw Ramsay, who had been a missionary in Palestine for some years, came to reside with Miss Leslie Melville in Cotta, and gave much voluntary help in every good work. The Rev. G. B. Perera moved to Colombo, and was succeeded by the Rev. R. T. E. A. Gunatilaka. The Talangama Pastorate, consisting of St. Matthew's Church, Talangama, St. Mark's Church, Kotewegoda, and St. Stephen's Church, Upper Welikada, with nine vernacular schools, was cut off from the Cotta district, and became an independent incumbency under the Rev. D. L. Welikala.

When Mrs. Dowbiggin returned from England in 1911 she made her home in Liyanwala, a corner of the district where a good work, inaugurated by her husband, had been carried on for some years. With the help of a companion and a staff of Biblewomen, she still carries on her self-denying labours, going in and out among the people carrying the Word of Life, tending them in their sicknesses and encouraging the teachers, working independently but in close co-operation with the Superintending Missionary.

The Buddhist opposition continued active throughout the district, and not only had they their day schools, but all Christian methods were adopted, such as Sunday schools, fancy bazaars, Scripture examinations, prize givings, etc. A Buddhist priest, writing to a local Buddhist paper, said, 'Christianity is an epidemic which is spreading far and wide.'

In June, 1914, the Rev. J. W. Balding left on furlough and the Rev. A. M. Walmsley took charge until the arrival of the Rev. S. M. Simmons in July. Unfortunately Mr. Simmons was invalided home in September, when the Rev. A. E. Dibben took the oversight until the arrival of the Rev. J. W. Ferrier in 1915.

Mr. Ferrier in his first report, referring to the Boys' School, writes, 'Here is an Institution the glories of the past of which are without parallel in the annals of the Mission. It has made an indelible mark in the civil and ecclesiastical life of the Island. Nearly every C.M.S. Pastor, Catechist, and Teacher prior to the year 1900 has been helped in it.'

COTTA   141

Of Liyanwala he writes, 'A very earnest congregation worship at St. Paul's Church, which is the centre of an efficient group of schools. One great advantage to the work is the residence there of Mrs. Dowbiggin and her helper, Miss Hutchinson. Both itinerate in the villages, visiting the schools and cheering the teachers, and in the house-to-house visiting are assisted by several Biblewomen.' From April, 1915 to September, 1916, Mr. Ferrier motor-cycled 6,000 miles in connection with his work.

The 'Baptismal Register' of the Cotta district records the baptism of nearly six thousand persons since the commencement of the Mission. This does not include the baptisms in the churches of the separate incumbencies which have been made in recent years. The first entry is the following, 'Samuel, an adult Jew, on the credible profession of faith in Christ. He was known before by the name of Joseph Judah Misrabi, and is a native of Cochin on the Malabar Coast. Baptized on November 4, 1827, by me, Samuel Lambrick.'

The first entry in the Register of Marriages is 'James Ford, late a Private in H.M.'s 16th Regiment, and Anachy Anna Kangany married at Cotta on December 22, 1827, by me, James Selkirk, Church Missionary.' The 'Register of Burials' records the burial of 212 persons, in the little churchyard in Cotta. In the graveyard there are only sixteen stones to mark their resting-places, and four of these are in memory of two European missionaries and two English children, so 196 Sinhalese have no memorial stones.

The burials during the first twenty years of the Mission do not seem to have been recorded. The first entry is 'Anna Maria, wife of Maddamahallinnaygay Juan de Silva, aged 34 years, buried December 8, 1844, by me, Henry Powell, Church Missionary.'

One of the first four C.M.S. missionaries to Ceylon lies buried in the churchyard, and the following is the inscription on the tomb-stone, 'Sacred to the memory of the Rev. Joseph Knight—born October 17, 1787, died October 11, 1840—he laboured as a missionary in connection with the C.M. Society at Jaffna for more than twenty years. Was wrecked off the Cape on his way Home in 1838, when he is thought to have contracted an affection of the lungs, of which he died shortly after his return to Ceylon. His end was peace.'

Although work was commenced in 1822 and ten churches have been built in the out-stations, at the headquarters in Cotta there has never been a proper church building, and the services have been held in the large hall of the Boys' English School. In August, 1904, the Rev. J. W. Balding determined to raise money to build a church and issued an appeal supported by the Metropolitan and the Bishop of the Diocese. A sum of about Rs. 20,000 has been received from about 2,500 contributors, and a further Rs. 10,000 is needed for the work.

On December 31, 1918, there were in the whole Cotta District four Ceylonese clergy; 109 lay workers; thirty-four schools with 1,412 boys and 1,156 girls, making a total of 2,568 pupils; 1,687 Christians, of whom 680 were communicants. Of these Christians 397 were in the Talangama Pastorate and 590 in the Nugegoda Pastorate.

CHAPTER XIII.

THE KANDYAN ITINERANCIES.

WORK in the Kandyan Sinhalese Itinerancies was commenced in the year 1853, and now covers the greater part of the Central, North-Central and North-Western Provinces and a portion of the Sabaragamuwa Province. For the previous thirty-five years the work carried on at the Kandy Station had been almost entirely confined to the Low-country Sinhalese resident in the town and neighbourhood. Very few Kandyan families resided in the town itself, and the object of this new effort was to convey the Gospel to the Kandyans in their villages. The Rev. E. T. Higgens commenced the work in July, 1853, in the district of Harispattu, as being the most populous for its size of the Kandyan districts. The name Harispattu means the 'country of the four hundred.'

According to tradition it received its name from its having been originally peopled by four hundred captives brought from the Coromandel Coast by King Gaja Bahu (113–125 A.D.) in lieu of those whom the sovereign of that country had carried off from Ceylon during the reign of his father. The country of the 'four hundred' is now a division with 44,000 inhabitants.

Mr. Higgens entered on the work single-handed, but in the first year, repeated attacks of jungle-fever compelled him to take a sea voyage to the Cape. On his return he found that his wife had passed away during his absence, but he vigorously resumed his preaching in Harispattu, visiting every village in turn. Permanent outstations were commenced in Kurunegala in 1854 and at Hanguranketa in 1855, and the

Itineration was extended to other parts of the country, including the populous districts of Uda Nuwara and Yata Nuwara.

Robert Knox, who was a prisoner in the interior of Ceylon from 1659 to 1679, on his escape from captivity, wrote the first account we have of Ceylon in the English language, in which he says of Uda Nuwara and Yata Nuwara, ' These two counties have the pre-eminence of all the rest in the land. They are most populous and fruitful. The inhabitants thereof are the chief and principal men, insomuch that it is a usual saying among them that, if they want a king, they may take any man, of either of these two counties from the plough, and wash the dust off him and he by reason of his quality and descent is fit to be a king. And they have this peculiar privilege, that none may be their Governor but one born in their own country.'

The great body of the people, when the Mission was commenced, were entirely ignorant of Christianity.

In 1854 Mr. E. R. Clarke joined the Mission and worked in Yata and Uda Nuwara for a couple of years.

At Hanguranketa and Maturata small congregations had been collected, and at the former place was built a little church, by a Sinhalese gentleman, Mr. C. H. de Soysa.

In 1861 the Rev. J. Ireland Jones joined in the work, living on an abandoned coffee estate in Harispattu. Mr. Higgens, owing to repeated attacks of fever, removed to the low-country, and the Rev. J. H. Clowes took his place. The Kandyans of Harispattu were not responsive to the Gospel, so Mr. Jones removed to Kurunegala, about twenty-seven miles from Kandy, and made it his centre.

The congregation at Kurunegala assumed a more settled character and a small church was erected where Europeans and Sinhalese united in worship. The Rev. J. A. de Livera was appointed Pastor, and by his diligence the congregation made further advance.

On Mr. de Livera's removal in 1862, Mr. Jones again took up his residence there and visited the villages around.

In one of these, Talampitiya, some five years previously, a New Testament had been left, which had been read by the villagers. The Holy Spirit had blessed the reading, and when the missionary visited them again, a crowd, attentive and earnest, listened to the glad tidings. Within a few months thirteen men were baptized, one of them formerly a Buddhist priest. These converts became missionaries to their own people, with the result that fourteen more adults were baptized. About this time Mr. Jones was compelled to return to England and the Rev. E. T. Higgens again took charge. The Rev. John Allcock also arrived. The Church at Talampitiya continued to prosper, and up to 1867 fifty converts from Buddhism had been baptized, some of them men of much intellect as well as deep spirituality. One of the first converts was Elandege Abraham, whose Christian life and character showed the reality of his faith. He became an earnest evangelist and in later years often accompanied the missionaries in their preaching tours. He passed to his rest on December 13, 1891, and was buried in the Talampitiya churchyard. In 1866 Mr. Higgens was transferred to another district, and Mr. Allcock became Superintendent.

In 1870 Mr. Jones was again in charge and the work was extended to Anuradhapura, the ancient capital of the Island. Two catechists visited it and the country round for a considerable distance, preaching and distributing tracts. The journey was undertaken at the request of Mr. Louis Liesching, a Government official there, who collected the money to pay the travelling expenses of the workers. Mr. Jones also spent the month of April visiting the villages. At the close of the same year a Girls' Boarding School was begun in Kandy by Mrs. Jones with seven boarders; the following year there were thirteen. Catechists were stationed at Ruanwela, Kegalle and Nawalapitiya. A church committee was formed at Gampola, and efforts were made to pay the salary and house-rent of the catechist.

In July, 1872, the Rev. S. Coles took charge, at which time there were eight catechists and six readers and a number of village schools. In 1877 the Rev. G. F. Unwin, who had been for a short time in Kegalle, moved to Anuradhapura, but owing to ill-health had to return to England the following year. Mr. Coles was now left single-handed in the district with twenty-seven congregations, forty day schools and 1,200 Christians. In 1880 Mr. Coles broke down, and Mr. Jones again took charge, residing at Kurunegala. The Holy Emmanuel Church was built and opened in 1881. The Rev. G. L. P. Liesching arrived in 1882, and worked in the Kegalle and Kurunegala districts for nearly nineteen years. During his time a Mission House was purchased at Kegalle, and a Girls' Boarding School opened on June 1, 1895. The Rev. J. Allcock had charge of the Central District from 1884 till his death in Kandy in March, 1887. In the year 1886 sixty-five adults and twenty-two children were baptized by Mr. Allcock and eleven adults and nineteen children by Mr. Liesching. The following year the invasion of the district by the Salvation Army caused a division among the Talampitiya Christians.

In 1888 the Rev. J. G. Garrett took charge of the Central District, residing in Kandy, and for twenty-three years with enthusiasm and earnestness threw his very best into the work. Early in 1911 he returned to Dublin to undergo an operation and shortly after was called to his eternal rest.

The centre of women's work in the Central District is the Mowbray Home. This embodies a development of the village work begun by Miss Denyer, who first came out in 1889 with Miss Bellerby and Miss James of the C.E.Z.M.S., but afterwards attached herself to the C.M.S. as an honorary worker.

After some years of itinerating work with Kandy as her centre, she was joined in 1897 by Miss A. L. Earp from the parish of Mowbray, S. Africa. During their village work they became convinced that it was necessary to get enquirers away from their heathen surroundings, at any rate until their faith was established, and to this end they obtained help from Miss Earp's home parish and took up their quarters in various rented houses one after another. Here they gathered round them various grades of enquirers, some with their families, and also received village women sent on from the C.E.Z. Mission in Gampola to be tested and taught. There were some real conversions, and some converts of that day are still Christian workers, as are also their children. Rescue work was attempted, but experience showed that it could not be carried on with the other work and accordingly it was handed over to the Salvation Army. The work found a permanent home in 1906 after the purchase and adaptation of the bungalow and grounds now known as Mowbray. Here enquirers from many villages were taken in and taught, not only Christianity, but elementary secular subjects and lace-making.

Miss Hargrove came out in 1908 and was located to Mowbray for language study. In 1910 Miss Earp writes:— 'Sixteen have been admitted into the Home this year, and two of the girls baptized. These two are the first fruits of an old girl's work in a village school. Five of the girls confirmed at Kegalle were sent to school there from Mowbray, and another girl, confirmed at Gampola, is a probationary Biblewoman there. Three of the old girls are now employed as teachers in the Home. There have been no less than six Christian marriages this year, five of them with C.M.S. workers. The new Maternity Home and Biblewomen's House are nearing completion and the Mission House in Hurikaduwa is finished.'

In 1911 Miss Earp mentions the opening of a Training Home for Biblewomen and the admission of four women for training. She also reports the baptism of seven converts. Miss Earp resigned in 1914 and Miss Denyer, with the help of Miss Findlay, an honorary worker from S. Africa, carried on the work, the Biblewomen's Training Class being given up. Miss Hargrove returned from furlough early in 1915 and was put in charge of the ' Home " work, Miss Josolyne also living at Mowbray and doing evangelistic work among the women and girls of the district. Miss Denyer left for England in 1915 after sixteen years of faithful and devoted honorary service in the Mission.

In his last annual report at the close of 1910 Mr. Garrett gives the following statistics: ' Sixteen catechists and lay readers, two Biblewomen, 712 Christians, 312 communicants, fifty-three men teachers, twenty-seven women teachers, forty-four schools and 4,878 scholars.' In another part he writes, ' The schools are crowded out with the very children we want to reach.' '.But till a Spirit-filled Sinhalese evangelistic agency is raised up the work will not grow.' ' The whole community in a village gathered to witness the first two baptisms ever seen in the place. Two young men, aged eighteen and fifteen, answered most satisfactorily, showing a grasp of the teaching as to the Holy Spirit. The scene was most impressive, a schoolroom, i.e., a shed on rough posts, with mud walls four feet high, a clay bench all along three sides, a sloping board nailed on two posts for a school desk, the village fathers all in a long line along one mud bench which forms half our school furniture ; the children, twenty-seven in number, along the opposite side behind the desk ; several little ones on the floor looking up at the bowl of water on my white table cloth ; the mothers all lining the wall outside, looking over the children's heads ; the catechist and school master on our two school chairs, the only ones in the village, behind the little children, facing the table. My Christian servant and Mark, a new convert from a neighbouring village, formed the Christian congregation. I read all the service carefully and explained almost every clause, after which my two brothers, Richard and Thomas, came and knelt on a mat before the table, and, pouring a handful of water over them, I admitted them into the fellowship of the people of Him who died for them, and I believe they are indeed living members of His body.'

In September, 1891, the Rev. and Mrs. G. Liesching left and the Rev. A. E. Dibben took charge of the Western Itinerancy until June, 1893, when Mr. Coles became responsible until Mr. Liesching's return. In January, 1895, the Itinerancy which had hitherto been divided into two districts, the Central and the Western, was further divided, and a new one called the Northern Itinerancy was formed and placed in charge of the Rev. H. E. Heinekey.

In July, 1898, Major Mathison, an honorary lay missionary, was appointed to evangelistic work in the Dumbara portion of the Northern Itinerancy, while the Rev. J. Colombage was working in Anuradhapura and the Rev. F. W. Daundesekara in Kegalle.

Mr. Liesching returned to England in July, 1899, and the Rev. S. M. Simmons took his place in January, 1900, and shortly afterwards Miss S. C. Lloyd and Miss M. S. Gedge were appointed to work in the district. In 1903 the Rev. C. T. Williams became Pastor at Anuradhapura, and Major Mathison had charge of the evangelistic and school work. During his superintendence a new mission house costing about Rs. 12,000 was built. The same year Mr. Simmons was invalided home and the Rev. W. G. Shorten took up his residence in Kegalle.

Mr. Heinekey whilst in Anuradhapura was instrumental in collecting a large proportion of the money for the building of a church, the foundation-stone of which was laid by the Bishop on August 26, 1905. On St. Andrew's Day of the following year the building, which had cost over Rs. 16,000, was consecrated as St. Andrew's Church. When Major Mathison left on furlough in 1908, there were 191 Christians, fifty-seven communicants, twenty-eight enquirers, five catechists and four schools with 196 scholars.

The Rev. R. W. Ryde succeeded Major Mathison, and had just prepared the mission house for the residence of himself and family, when he passed away after a short illness in Colombo.

In 1907 Miss A. K. Deering and Miss Bennett were working in Kegalle, whilst the following year Miss M. S. Gedge and Miss S.H.M. Townshend had charge of the women's work. In June, 1909, the Rev. R. H. Phair made Kurunegala his headquarters, and the Rev. C. Wijesinghe was appointed Pastor, but on the return of Mr. Shorten, Mr. Phair moved to Anuradhapura and took over the Northern Itinerancy. The Rev. A. M. Walmsley for eight months had been spending a week each month in the district in addition to his work at Trinity College.

In 1911 the Rev. J. P. S. R. Gibson paid periodical visits and the Rev. J. D. Welcome was Pastor in Anuradhapura.

On the death of Mr. Garrett, the Rev. W. G. Shorten was appointed to the Central Itineration and Miss M. S. Gedge took charge of the Kegalle Girls' Boarding School.

The following year Mr. Walmsley was in charge of the Northern Itineration for six months, after which the Rev. and Mrs. T. S. Johnson took up their residence in Anuradhapura.

In the annual report for 1913 the Rev. T. S. Johnson says, ' Anuradhapura may be regarded as the most interesting town in the Island. Here is a buried city of ancient fame and splendour, where Sinhalese kings reigned at the zenith of Sinhalese history and where to-day ruins, rivalled only by those of Egypt, lift themselves skyward from the mass of jungle and scrub with which thousands of square miles of country is covered.'

The Rev. R. H. Phair was again back as Superintendent of the Western Itinerancy, and in 1913 writes:—' The Buddhist opposition has been bitter and persistent. Those who are at variance in every other matter are united in opposition to the cause of Christ. False stories backed by false witnesses and fabrications of all sorts are alleged against us and our teaching. The Jesuits in some places add their rivalry to Buddhist opposition and in face of all this there is a lack of workers.'

In 1915 the Kegalle Girls' Boarding School was again in charge of Miss M. S. Gedge with the assistance of Miss de Vos, and Miss E. M. Josolyne was released for work at Mowbray.

Mr. Shorten went on furlough in May, 1915, the Rev. A. M. Walmsley taking charge of the Central Itinerancy. At the close of the year he gives the following statistics:—'One Sinhalese clergyman, four catechists, three readers, three Biblewomen, 141 teachers, 830 Christians, 335 communicants, nineteen adults and forty-two children baptized, fifty-seven catechumens, forty confirmed, forty-four schools and 5,378 scholars.'

In the early days of the Itinerancy the missionary had to tramp from village to village or use a springless bullock cart as his means of locomotion. The present-day missionary has his motor cycle and Mr. Walmsley writes:—' In rain and shine, up hill and down dale, by day and by night, it has been my constant companion and scarcely ever-failing friend. It hardly ever grows weary, and still more rarely grumbles. We have travelled together, during the past year, over seven thousand miles, and have never yet broken an engagement.'

On October 6, 1916, Mr. Phair, then in charge of the Northern Itinerancy, met with a serious accident whilst riding his motor cycle. He collided with a bullock cart and his injuries were so serious that his right leg had to be amputated. From the shock of this operation he never fully recovered. In January, 1917, he left for England and returned to his work in February, 1918, before physically fit to resume it.

Several of the old mud-and-thatch school buildings have been replaced by more substantial ones during the last few years. Just before leaving Mr. Shorten made the following entry in the log-book of Gonagama School which was re-opened in June, 1915 :—' This building has an interesting history. The site is our own property. The zinc for the roof was given by Mr. L. W. A. de Soysa. The sawing expenses were paid by Mr. Williams, a planter. The trees were given by Government, except for one jak tree which was given by Mr. Soysa. The teacher got the villagers to transport all the timber—some 2,000 square feet—free, from a jungle four miles away, the best bit of work I have ever got done through a teacher. The zinc—1 ton, 4 cwts—was brought by the school children, three miles away over a mountain pass, without costing me a cent. Mr. R. E. S. de Soysa transported it from Kandy to Hanguranketa at the same rate. When I visited this place on March 5 three or four coolies were leisurely clearing the ground or site for the new building. All the timber was then growing, except two trees, which had been cut down the previous week. The dressed stones for the pillars were still solid rock, and neither sand nor lime were collected. This is May 7, and the building is now practically finished. The success of the effort is largely due to the zeal and hard work of the head teacher.'

Mr. Walmsley writes :—' We can say, in all humility and thankfulness to God, that the work is progressing. I am sure that the men and women working away quietly in scores of villages are testifying by word and life, and that we shall continue steadily to reap the fruits of their labours in the

Lord. In one village I found a bright sweet-faced woman with eight children, who gave evidence of an earnest desire to become a Christian. She is learning regularly, and seems to drink in what one says. I remember what a joy it was to watch her face, as I told her recently of Christ's sacrifice for her sins. We have as many enquirers, catechumens and candidates for confirmation as we can well deal with, considering the amount of time available for that side of our work, and so we thank God and take courage.

If one were determined to look on the dark side of things there is always enough to break one's heart. Indeed, Ceylon has always been a heart-breaking place, from a missionary point of view. Why it should be so, I have been trying for nearly ten years to find out, but so far unsuccessfully. Doubtless a great deal of the difficulty is accounted for by the inexpressible inertia of Buddhism. It seems impossible to get a move on, to make the dry bones live. Men who come to face Ceylon Buddhism must realize that God only wants men who can do the impossible, men who can do all things through Christ, Who strengtheneth them.'

In 1916 the Rev. T. S. Johnson, who had for three and a half years ministered in three languages, was transferred from Anuradhapura to the Tamil Cooly Mission, while still remaining in charge of the Anuradhapura district.

The Rev. J. N. Seneviratne, who as curate to the incumbent of Gampola, has the pastoral oversight of the work of that town and in addition is in charge of St. Andrew's, Nawalapitiya, in his report for 1916, says :—' The Pastorate consists of three congregations, English and Sinhalese at Gampola, and Sinhalese at Nawalapitiya. The membership is as follows :— English—sixty adults, twenty communicants; Sinhalese (Gampola)—eighty-five adults, sixty-four communicants; Sinhalese (Nawalapitiya)—forty-six adults, eighteen communicants. The contributions to the pastorate amounted to

Rs. 1,561 during the year. A Confirmation Service was held at Nawalapitiya in three languages, when thirty-eight candidates were presented. From 1906 to the present date the attendance at St. Andrew's Church has been steadily increasing, and the building is not large enough to accommodate the congregation. A Building Committee has been appointed and it is hoped to raise Rs. 25,000 during the next three years in order to build a new church.'

CHAPTER XIV.

COLOMBO.

THERE are several theories of the derivation of the name Colombo. Some connect it with the Kelani River, which enters the sea near Colombo, by others it is said to be derived from Calamba, a seaport or fortified place. The derivation most generally received is that the village and port were originally known as Colontota, from the Sinhalese words Cola—amba—tota, ' mango leaves port.' The Portuguese, finding a name so like that of their famous navigator Christopher Columbus, called the city Colombo.

There is a tradition that the Khalif of Baghdad, in the tenth century, hearing that the Moorish traders settled in Colombo were not very orthodox Mohammedans, sent a priest to instruct them, who also built a mosque for their use.

A writer in 1344 described Kalambu as the finest town in Serendib.

At the first census of the people of Ceylon, of which there is any record, in 1824, the population of Colombo is given as 31,188; in 1871 the population had increased to 95,843; and in 1911 to 211,274.

Percival, writing in 1803 of Colombo, says :—' There is no part of the world where so many different languages are spoken, or which contains such a mixture of nations, manners and religions.' This description remains true to-day.

At the census of 1911, persons of seventy-eight different races were enumerated in Colombo; these included 2,374 British, 110 French, 97 Germans, 13,485 Burghers and Eurasians, 2,495 Kandyan Sinhalese, 91,590 low-country

Sinhalese, 15,252 Ceylon Tamils, 36,717 Indian Tamils, 24,481 Ceylon Moors, 13,688 Indian Moors and 5,364 Malays. Among the other races represented were Americans, Australians, Arabs, Boers, Chinese, Canadians, Japanese, Egyptians, Parsees, Kaffirs, Zulus, Maldivians, Burmese and Maoris.

The proportion per cent of the adherents of the four chief religions to the total population in Colombo in 1911 was Buddhists 30.89, Christians 28.31, Mohammedans, 21.56 and Hindus 19.07. The Church Missionary Society did not commence a settled work in Colombo until the year 1850, although it was their intention that one of the four missionaries first appointed to Ceylon should be stationed there. The first missionaries thought it more desirable to occupy villages near large towns than the towns themselves. In 1828 the Rev. A. Armour, Chaplain of St. Paul's Church in Colombo, addressed a letter to the Conference assembled at Cotta urging them to begin work in Colombo, but the invitation was not accepted. In 1843 a C. M. S. Association was formed under the patronage of Sir Colin Campbell, the Governor, in Colombo, to help the Mission with funds.

In 1850 the Parent Society reviewed their missions and said :—' While most of the missions have enlarged themselves, the Ceylon Mission has remained almost stationary. Extension in a mission must be looked for, and in this respect at least, the Ceylon Mission has proved unsatisfactory. Inviting fields present themselves continually in other parts of the world, and when these are put in contrast with the Ceylon Mission, a temptation to withdraw its forces for employment under brighter prospects arises.

The Home Committee could not entertain the idea of withdrawal until their best efforts should have been made for its improvement. For this purpose they have adopted a new system of management for the mission. A Central Committee, with the Bishop of the Diocese as its President, has been appointed, and its permanent Secretary will reside in Colombo.'

The Secretary here referred to was the Rev. G. Pettitt, who arrived from Tinnevelly in April, 1850, and visited the stations before taking up his residence in Colombo in November of the same year.

He found a few Sinhalese catechists at work in Colombo and a few converts, and these were organized under the Rev. C. Jayasinghe. Tamil work was commenced and a catechist employed. The duties of Mr. Pettitt, as Secretary to the Central Committee, did not include any ministerial work, and he suggested that a church should be built, where the Secretary might take regular English duty. A sub-committee was appointed to enquire whether there was room in Colombo for another church, and the facts ascertained were such as to lead to the conclusion that the building of another church was a great desideratum.

The Parent Committee agreed and gave £700 on condition that local assistance should also be given. An appeal was issued in September, 1851, and on January 21, 1853, the foundation-stone was laid. The land was purchased for £225 ' on the Esplanade of the Fort called the Galle Face, near to the bridge which passes from it into Slave Island, and on the edge of the lake. With the sea at a distance of about three hundred yards in front and the lake close behind it, the situation is both cool and pleasant.'

On October 13, of the same year, the church was opened for Divine Service by Bishop Chapman, who preached a sermon from Malachi i. 11, ' From the rising of the sun even unto the going down of the same, My name shall be great among the Gentiles.'

In the next annual report of the C.M.S. the Rev. Henry Venn, the Secretary, referred to this service as ' affording a happy illustration of one of the main objects of the erection of the church—the union of races in the Church of Christ.'

The total expenditure for the site, the church with its fittings, and the churchyard wall was £1,566.

The Rev. G. Pettitt ministered to the English and Tamil congregations of Christ Church until January, 1855, when he left for England, and the Rev. H. Whitley, Curate of Sapcote, Leicester, was appointed to succeed him.

In 1857 a piece of land was acquired adjoining the church premises upon which a parsonage was built. The Parent Committee made a grant of £600 which was supplemented by local funds and subscriptions of £450 towards this purpose. The house was completed by the end of September, 1860. Mr. and Mrs. Whitley took possession in October, but on November 10 Mr. Whitley received fatal injuries through the falling of a wall in the church premises. Bishop Chapman wrote to the C.M.S.:—' The last sad offices were solemnized by myself on the following evening amid more universal sorrow than I have witnessed on any previous occasion. The pall was borne by persons of the highest position in the Colony.' A tablet in the Church records that ' Mr. Whitley ministered to congregations worshipping in three different languages' and that ' he was also a faithful and earnest preacher of the Gospel to the heathen population of the town.' A memorial stone set in the floor of the schoolroom at Galle Face records the circumstances of his death. Early in 1861 the Rev. C. C. Fenn removed from Cotta to Colombo, and carried on the work until the end of the year, when he was joined by the Rev. W. E. Rowlands. Mr. Rowlands was directed to give his attention to the study of Tamil and to assist Mr. Fenn in the English services, which he did until October, 1862, when he was transferred to the Tamil Cooly Mission. The following year Mr. Fenn left for England, the Rev. J. H. Clowes was appointed to Christ

Church and in January, 1864, Mr. Rowlands returned to Colombo.

In 1866 Mr. Clowes left and the Rev. J. Ireland Jones, while residing at Cotta, assisted in the work. In 1867 the Rev. J. C. Mill was appointed to Colombo and with Mr. Rowlands worked among the Tamil-speaking population.

In February, 1865, the Government made a grant of land situated in the Cinnamon Gardens near the Borella Road for the erection of a mission house and school. To erect these buildings the Parent Committee made a grant of £600, the Local Fund £50, while £133 raised some years before for a Sinhalese Boarding School was appropriated, a Sale of Work in the Colombo Racquet Court produced £246 and nearly £700 was received by subscriptions. The mission house and school were soon built and on December, 1867, the first pupils were admitted to the Tamil Girls' Boarding School, Borella, the foundation of which had been laid by Mrs. Temple on the previous June 14.

In his report of the following year Mr. Rowlands (who had been mainly instrumental by his own efforts and liberality in procuring the Borella land and buildings) writes :—' There cannot be a doubt that if we are enabled to carry on the school as we desire, and if the Divine blessing follow our efforts, the school will tend very much to improve the condition of the young women of the upper classes, and thereby confer a benefit which cannot easily be over-estimated upon the Tamil people generally.'

In July, 1870, the Rev. E. T. Higgens took charge of the English work at Christ Church, the evangelistic work among the Sinhalese and the management of the Sinhalese schools, and the Rev. H. Gunasekara was appointed Pastor of the Sinhalese congregations.

Preaching was carried on in the streets and lanes, in the coffee-curing establishments and at the Police Court, and the hospitals and jails were visited. Services were held by Mr. Gunasekara in school-rooms at Maradana, Hunupitiya and Borella, whilst the Sunday afternoon service at Christ Church had an average attendance of fifty-three Sinhalese.

The Tamil work was vigorously carried on by Mr. Rowlands; work was started on the coconut and cinnamon estates in the Negombo district, and a congregation of fifty Christians living at Thiverlei was taken over. Preaching was carried on in the streets and coffee stores. There were also four congregations of Tamil Christians, numbering 478 persons.

In September, 1871, Mr. Rowlands sailed for England and the Rev. D. Wood took charge. This year the Rev. C. Jayasinghe was the Pastor of the Christ Church Sinhalese congregation.

The Rev. H. Newton became Incumbent of Christ Church in February, 1877, and the following year the Rev. J. I. Pickford arrived to strengthen the Tamil Mission.

Both the Boys' and Girls' Boarding Schools at Borella were full of children, and the number of Christians on the congregational lists was 1,092. Their subscriptions in 1879 amounted to Rs. 1,189·02. Miss M. Young arrived in 1879 to take charge of the Girls' Boarding School, and was married in 1880 to the Rev. J. I. Pickford. The same year the average number present at Christ Church English service was 144 in the morning and 130 in the evening on Sundays, and 49 at the Wednesday evening service. The Rev. J. Gabb was assisting at the Tamil services.

In 1881 Miss M. Hall arrived to help in the Girls' Boarding School. She was not only the youngest missionary ever sent out by the C.M.S. but the only lady worker sent out that year to any mission field. Three years later she was married to the Rev. J. W. Balding.

On June 30, 1881, St. Luke's Church, Borella, was opened, when the Rev. J. I. Jones, who had also laid the foundation-stone in the previous year, preached the sermon. Services are now held there in Sinhalese, Tamil and English.

The Rev. H. Newton on his retirement from Ceylon suggested to the Parent Committee the holding of 'Missionary Missions' or 'Special Missionary Weeks,' and he was appointed one of the first missioners. The first 'Special Missionary Week' was held in England in December, 1883, when the Rev. S. Coles of Ceylon, who was at home on furlough, was one of the missioners.

In 1883 the Rev. E. T. Higgens again took charge of Christ Church and the Rev. S. Samuel assisted with the Tamil work.

During the year 1886 over four thousand persons visited the mission room in the Pettah to converse on the subject of Christianity. This room, to quote the words of a Tamil Christian, was 'like a good well of water cut in a dry plain.'

The Rev. J. I. Pickford left for England in 1887 and the Rev. D. Wood early in 1888, when the Rev. J. Ilsley took charge of the Colombo Tamil work.

Miss Eva Young, who arrived in 1884, began work among the Hindu and Mohammedan women assisted by five Biblewomen.

In 1890 the Tamil work was in charge of the Rev. J. D. Thomas. Miss Thomas superintended the Biblewomen and was assisted by Miss B. Child who arrived in 1891.

A house and garden for the Slave Island pastor was bought by the Tamil Christians, and at Wellawatte a school chapel and residence for a Tamil worker erected. A piece of land was also purchased at Maradana, on which were erected a school and a house.

It is interesting to mention here that the month of December, 1893, marked a great epoch in the history of the Uganda mission in Africa. Pilkington, one of the missionaries there, received into his soul a message from God through a little book written by V. D. David, a Tamil evangelist, which led to a great spiritual revival in Uganda. David was for some years a worker in the Tamil mission in Colombo.

In 1895 the Tamil clergymen, the Revs. S. Samuel and P. Peter, died within six weeks of each other. The Rev. G. T. Fleming took over part of the Tamil work, but in the following year both he and the Rev. J. D. Thomas were called to higher service. Mrs. Thomas remained in Ceylon, continuing in missionary work. The school hall adjoining St. Luke's Church, Borella, was erected as a memorial to Mr. Fleming.

In 1895 the Rev. A. E. Dibben took charge of Christ Church and the work among the Portuguese. A branch of the Boys' Brigade was started and also a branch of the Gleaners' Union.

In 1897, owing to the fall of part of the west wall and the generally unsatisfactory state of the fabric of Christ Church, it was pulled down, entirely re-built, and re-opened on March 18, 1899.

In 1899 the English work was in charge of the Rev. J. Thompson and the Tamil work in charge of the Rev. J. I. Pickford. In the following May the Rev. E. T. Higgens, who first came to Ceylon in 1851, retired.

Mr. John Daniel, the Headmaster of the Tamil Boys' Boarding School, was ordained this year, and the mission suffered a serious loss by the death of Lieut.-Colonel Meaden, who was honorary treasurer of the mission, a member of the Finance Committee, and treasurer of the C.M.S. Colombo Association.

The pastorates of the Sinhalese congregations of Christ Church and St. Luke's Church were separated from the Cotta district and placed under the Rev. D. J. Perera as pastor.

It had been felt for some years that the work in Colombo needed supplementing by the establishment of a high-class educational institution for girls, and therefore in February,

1900, the Ladies' College was opened in a large bungalow in Union Place, with Miss L. E. Nixon as Principal, and Miss E. Whitney as Superintendent. Progress was at first slow, and only twelve pupils were in the school at the end of the first year, representing Tamil, Sinhalese, Jewish and English homes.

In 1901 the Rev. E. T. Higgens, who had been mainly instrumental in starting the Ladies' College, died in England on June 11. For the last few years of his life, before his retirement, he had resided at the Galle Face Mission House, undertaking the duties of the Secretariat. But the old love of evangelization remained and constantly he was to be seen in the streets and public places with the catechists, preaching and inviting the heathen to come to Christ.

The Rev. S. Coles, who was in charge of the Sinhalese station in addition to the work of revising the Sinhalese Bible, also received his Home call this year. One more diligent in business, fervent in Spirit, and earnest in serving the Lord, it would be difficult to name. A brother missionary, after spending some time in his company, remarked, ' How that fellow does work. I never saw anything like it.'

And that work continued to the last moment of his life. On the morning of September 23 he spent some two hours preparing for the meeting of the Revision Committee appointed to take place on that day. At the hour appointed he walked from the mission house to the vestry of Christ Church, declining proffered help, and saying in his bright way that he ' felt like a young man.' These were his last words. He took his seat in the vestry, and had only just done so, when with hardly a sigh or a sound he was gone. Mr. Coles came out to Ceylon in 1861. His chief, if not his only recreation was to get for a time among children. His appearance among a crowd of young people, enjoying the freedom of play hour, was greeted with shouts of welcome.

For the children's benefit he used to good purpose his remarkable gift of versification in Sinhalese. The Rev. J. I. Jones returned to Ceylon and took over the Sinhalese work in May, 1900, Miss A. Higgens and Miss E. M. Josolyne were working among the women, and the Rev. W. J. Hanan among the Tamils, assisted by Mrs. J. D. Thomas, Miss E. S. Young and Miss E. J. Howes.

The Rev. A. R. Virasinghe having resigned, the Rev. J. V. Daniel was appointed to succeed him as Tamil pastor.

The following year Mr. Pickford returned to superintend the Colombo Tamil work.

This year the Government acquired for railway extension purposes the land on which St. John's Church, Maradana, had been erected a few years before, thus necessitating the demolition of the little church. Mr. Chellappah, who had been head master of the Girls' Boarding School for about twenty-eight years, died this year. He was, as he once said, 'a Christian from conviction,' and he had to suffer for his conviction.

In June, 1903, Mr. J. W. Ferrier arrived from Australia as mission accountant. He also took charge of a Sunday School in the Kew Police Barracks, re-started the Gleaners' Union, and gave help in taking services in and around Colombo.

On November 12 the Rev. J. Ireland Jones, who had been connected with Ceylon since 1857, was called to his eternal rest. Mr. Jones had acted on three separate occasions as Bishop's Commissary, and also taken a leading part in the ecclesiastical settlement made at the time of the disestablishment of the Church in Ceylon. His 'Handbook of Sinhalese' has been useful to many a student of the language, and his booklet, 'The Wonderful Garden,' a story designed to convince Buddhists of the existence of a Creator, has been a blessing to many. Of a very gentle and loving disposition, he yet never made any compromise where he considered the honour of the Lord or the truth of His word to be concerned. This year the Tamil work in Galle was strengthened by the appointment of Miss E. C. Vines and Miss H. E. Payne.

In January, 1904, the Rev. R. W. Ryde took charge of the Sinhalese work and the Rev. W. Booth, who had come out in 1901, of the Tamil work. At the end of the same year Miss Young and Miss A. E. Thomas were working among the women. The following extract from a letter written by the latter will give some idea of the nature of the work and of the blessing that rested upon it:—' I had between 200 and 300 houses on my list to visit. In addition to the pupils many men, women and children have heard the Gospel. In the course of the work I have realized the truth of the promise, " Cast thy bread upon the waters and thou shalt find it after many days." Taken by one of the Biblewomen to see a young Christian women, I was told that some years ago she was a learner. After a time she expressed a wish to become a Christian, but her parents strongly opposed, and prevented her learning with the Biblewoman by leaving that neighbourhood. But she had learnt to read and had a Scripture portion which she used to read secretly. Then the mother married her to a man who had been baptized in his infancy, but apparently was not a Christian except in name. These two went back to the man's native village in Tinnevelly. There she had more opportunity of learning, so, getting her husband's consent, she became a candidate for baptism, and was baptized by my brother-in-law, the Rev. E. A. Douglas. When they returned to Colombo, she begged the Biblewoman to come and read the Scriptures and pray with her. Her father was dead, but her mother was living with her. Her mother is still opposed to Christianity, and would not stay in the room when I read. Two days afterwards the Biblewoman asked if I remembered seeing another heathen woman there, who listened most attentively while I was speaking. She said, after I had left, that woman exclaimed, "Oh, why was I never told this before? Why did no one ever teach me about these things? You must come and teach me, I want to hear more." '

In 1906 the Rev. A. MacLulich was appointed to assist at Christ Church, the Rev. G. T. Weston and Miss A. M. Tisdall to Tamil work, Miss Sparrow to Sinhalese work and Miss Henrys to work in Galle. The Rev. G. M. Arulanantham was also appointed to the Tamil mission.

A special mission was held at Christ Church in October by the Rev. H. Pakenham Walsh (afterwards Bishop of Assam) assisted by the Rev. C. R. Burnett. The services were well attended and deep interest was manifested, especially by European men, whose hearts were so stirred that a number of them forthwith organized a weekly meeting at the house of each in turn for Bible study and prayer. These meetings were continued with much success till they were broken up by the interference of military duties consequent on the outbreak of the Great War in 1914.

The following year (1907) the Rev. H. P. Napier-Clavering was Incumbent of Christ Church and Secretary of the Mission, and Miss L. M. Leslie Melville was superintending the Biblewomen.

In September, 1908, Mr. MacLulich resigned and accepted the Incumbency of Holy Trinity Church, Colombo, and on Mr. Dibben's return from furlough Mr. Napier-Clavering took up his new sphere of work as Planters' Chaplain at Pussellawa. The Rev. J. Ilsley took over the Tamil work in May. In August, 1909, the Rev. R. W. Ryde died in Colombo. His knowledge of Sinhalese, his literary ability, and varied experience, added to his gifts of character and charm of manner, had made him a most valuable missionary and caused his loss to be greatly felt.

The Rev. A. K. Finnimore arrived in August to take charge of Christ Church having been in his early days a Ceylon planter and afterwards a C.M.S. missionary, first in South India and then in Mauritius.

In 1910 Mr. J. W. Ferrier returned to Australia and Miss M. A. Ledward joined the Tamil Mission.

This year the Rev. D. J. Perera was given a more independent position by being placed in full charge of the Sinhalese congregations of Christ Church and St. Luke's. He had 360 Christians under his care, 160 of whom were communicants.

The Rev. G. M. Arulanantham was in charge of what had now come to be called the Tamil Northern Pastorate, which included the congregations of Hultsdorf, Mutwal and Maradana.

The Rev. J. V. Daniel was in charge of the Tamil Southern Pastorate, which included the congregations of Slave Island and Wellawatte. The Slave Island congregation worshipping in Christ Church numbered 319 persons, of whom 112 were communicants.

The three ladies, Mrs. Thomas, Miss Tisdall and Miss Ledward, working among the Tamils, were living at ' The Lodge,' whilst Miss A. Higgens and Miss H. E. Hobson were working among the Sinhalese. The Ladies' College had been growing yearly, and as the work was hindered by cramped accommodation and noisy surroundings, it was deemed essential that more suitable premises should be secured. In addition to Miss Nixon and Miss Whitney, Miss Hall, Miss C. E. Browne, Miss Clarke, Miss A. Horsley and others had helped to make the school a success. So in 1910 the College was established in its own new quarters in Flower Road.

The money for the purchase of the land and bungalow was largely obtained through the exertions of Miss Nixon, also funds for the erection of class-rooms, drill-hall, assembly-hall, kindergarten rooms and dormitory accommodation. The late Rev. C. L. Burrows, when on a visit to Ceylon with Bishop Ingham, gave £1,000 towards the extension in memory of his wife. At the time of the transfer there were eighteen teachers and 237 pupils. These included fifty little boys between the ages of four and ten in the school for young boys attached to the College, a class for the training of kindergarten teachers, and about twenty boarders. A class for 'Old Boys' on Sundays, and a monthly 'At Home' for 'Old Girls,' a 'Students' Union' and a prayer meeting for girls were also inaugurated. The students also supported a catechist in the Tamil Cooly Mission.

In 1913 in the Cambridge Local Examinations, nine students passed, four in the Senior, one with honours, and five in the Junior. Sixty-four girls entered for the Trinity College of Music Examination, all of whom passed, twenty-four with honours.

In April of the following year Miss Nixon resigned after fourteen years of devoted work and building up of the College.

Miss Wardlaw-Ramsay kindly consented to act as Principal, and with the help of Miss A. E. Kent, who had arrived from England, the College continued to prosper. It was this year placed under Government as a grant-in-aid institution and, subsequently, classed as a 'fully organized secondary school.' Miss Kent resigned on her marriage in December, 1915, Miss G. L. F. Opie arrived as prospective Principal from New Zealand and Miss E. Morgan arrived from England about the same time. Miss Whitney returned from Nellore to the College early in 1916 as acting-Principal, afterwards becoming Warden of the Hostel.

A library of reference books, mainly collected through the efforts of Miss Nixon, numbers over a thousand volumes.

In 1917 only four girl-students in the whole of Colombo passed the Senior School Certificate Examination, and two of these were pupils of the Ladies' College.

In 1910 the men teachers who had been in training in the school at Cotta were removed to Colombo, and resided in the Teachers' Hostel at Bambalapitiya whilst attending lectures at the Government Training College. The hostel was given up when the training of men teachers was commenced at the Training Colony. On September 19, 1912, the new Holy Emmanuel Memorial Church at Maradana was consecrated by the Bishop in the presence of a large gathering of Tamil Christians. The Rev. W. E. Rowlands preached from Psalm 32, v. 7-8, and 133 communicants partook of the Holy Communion. The church has accommodation for about six hundred people, and is the gift of Mr. Rowlands to the Tamil Christians as a memorial to his wife who died in Colombo in 1877.

On September 17, 1912, the Rev. D. J. Perera, who for some years had been pastor of the Sinhalese congregations, died.

In 1914 the Rev. W. J. Hanan was appointed acting-Incumbent of Christ Church, the Rev. A. E. Dibben, the Secretary of the Mission, left on furlough for Australia in March, and the Rev. J. W. Balding was acting-Secretary till the end of the year, when Mr. Dibben, who had returned from Australia in September, resumed office. The Rev. G. B. Perera was appointed Incumbent of the Sinhalese congregations, and Miss Townshend took charge of the Sinhalese women's work.

This year the Tamil catechist stationed at the Ragama Camp, where coolies from India on their way to tea and rubber estates are detained for a few days by the medical authorities, discovered 869 Christians and reported their arrival to their future pastors. This work was commenced through the liberality of a Colombo lady, who gave Rs. 5,000 in memory of her husband, towards the salary of a Christian worker, who should seek out the Christian coolies who came from India, shepherd them while in the Camp, and send their names and addresses to the clergyman who lived nearest the estate they were bound for.

A few years ago work was commenced among the Malayali people who come over from Travancore to find work. There are about 5,000 of these people in Colombo alone. A congregation of over sixty has been gathered together, who hold their services in Holy Emmanuel Church, and a Malayalam catechist works among them. Open-air services are also held for the Malayali coolies working on the railway.

Much of the progress in this work is due to the devoted service of the catechist, Mr. K. E. Ephen, who suddenly died in 1915 from an attack of cholera, whilst on a visit to his relatives in India.

The Rev. W. J. Hanan in his report for 1915 says, ' I must give one illustration of modern persecution. My Tamil congregation at Mutwal consists largely of road and rickshaw coolies. Not far from Mutwal school is a rickshaw stand, where about twenty coolies wait for customers. Three of these are Christians. On a Hindu festival day the others decided that a present must be sent from that rickshaw stand to a Hindu temple, and that all must subscribe. The three Christians refused saying that their religion did not allow them. They were threatened that they would be driven from the stand, and that complaints would be made to the Police constable near, who would soon find an excuse for locking them up. They remained firm, so the aid of the constable was invoked. He, being a Hindu, entered into the spirit of the thing, and told the Christians that if they did not subscribe he would have them in jail before a week. The Christians then appealed to me to help them, and sent a petition with an account of their difficulties and the number of the constable. I sent it to the Inspector-General of Police and asked for an enquiry. That very day one of the Christians was arrested by the constable on a false charge and put in prison. I engaged a Christian proctor to defend him and went with a copy of the petition to the Police Court. It was proved to the satisfaction of the Magistrate that the charge was a false one, and the man was acquitted. The Christian coolies are poor ignorant men, unable to read or write, unable perhaps to give a reason for the faith that is in them that would satisfy many of the modern professors of Christianity, but willing to suffer loss and imprisonment for the sake of Christ.'

The Rev. W. J. Hanan, who had been acting-Incumbent of Christ Church for two years, relinquished this position in May, 1915, and the Rev. A. E. Dibben took charge until the appointment of the Rev. W. S. Senior in September of that year.

Miss Margaret Keith, who had been the organist for twenty-five years, left for England in November, whilst in December, by the death of Sir William Mitchell, the Church lost one of its oldest and most influential members.

The Rev. G. B. Perera, the Incumbent of the Sinhalese Churches, retired on account of old age in June, 1916, and the Rev. D. L. Welikala was appointed. Mr. Perera was one of a Buddhist family who lived in Talangama in the Cotta district and had four brothers and four sisters. It was their custom to relate stories as they lay on their mats in the evening. One night the mother told the children a story which she had heard from an old woman in the village who was a Christian. The mother also told them that it was a story from the Bible. Next morning Mr. Perera, who was then a boy of eight, on going to school, tried to find the story, which was the parable of Dives and Lazarus. His teacher found it for him, and the Holy Spirit so blessed the boy's reading that he became a Christian. Soon after this he had an attack of fever, and the mother brought in a devil priest to perform a ceremony over him, but the boy threatened to jump from the bed and make himself worse if any ceremony was performed. The mother was angry and scolded him, but to her surprise he recovered without the ceremony.

Mr. Perera's wife, who was a true helpmeet and earnest Christian, died in 1915, after fifty-one years of married life. She had a similar story to tell of her early days. She became a Christian whilst a pupil in the C.M.S. school at Baddegama, and her parents and three brothers and five sisters were all Buddhists. On one occasion when she had an attack of fever, her people got some charmed oil to be rubbed on her forehead, but, knowing that she did not believe in such things, put the charmed oil on one side in order to rub it on when she fell asleep. The girl, overhearing their plans, got out of her bed quietly, took the cup and poured the oil on the ground. Mr. and Mrs. Perera were able by God's grace to lead their parents and many other members of their families to Christ; and many of their children and children's children are now Christians.

The Sinhalese evangelistic and school work was handed over to the charge of the Rev. D. L. Welikala at the end of 1917, his Church Committee not seeing their way to shouldering this responsibility.

CHAPTER XV.

THE TAMIL COOLY MISSION.

THE existence of the Tamil Cooly Mission is very closely connected with the fame which Ceylon acquired as a coffee-producing country soon after the British took possession.

Coffee planting was first commenced in the Kandyan country in the year 1820, and the first regular plantation was opened in 1827. The export of coffee that year was 16,000 cwts. Ten years later in 1837 the exports reached 34,600 cwts., in 1849 they had reached 373,368 cwts., and the Government had sold 287,360 acres of forest land, suitable for the cultivation of coffee. Many speculators suffered from their inexperience. But still, Coffee became King, and in 1870 the annual export had risen to 974,333 cwts., valued at £5,000,000.

In 1840 Major Skinner from the top of Adam's Peak looked down on a dense pathless forest and foretold that this region was destined to become the garden of Ceylon and peopled with Europeans as well as Asiatics. His prophecy has been largely fulfilled.

We now come to the people by whom the labour market is supplied and on whom the planters are dependent for the cultivation of the estates.

Mr. C. R. Rigg, in an article in the *Journal of the Indian Archipelago and Eastern Asia*, Vol. VI, No. 3, writes:—
' When planting first came into vogue, the Kandyans flocked in hundreds to the great distribution of rupees, but this source of labour was soon found to be insufficient, and of too precarious a nature to be relied on. The Kandyan has such

a reverence for his patrimonial lands, that, were his gain to be quadrupled, he would not abandon their culture. It was only during a portion of the year that he could be induced even by the new stimulus—money—to exert himself. Next came the Sinhalese from the maritime provinces, who have a stronger love of gain, a liking for arrack, and a rooted propensity for gambling. In 1841-3 thousands of these people were employed on estates; they generally left their homes for six months at a time, and then returned with their earnings. The sudden access of wealth amongst them soon engendered as much independence as was to be found in the Kandyans. This source of labour became dried up, and the lowlanders were only known in the central provinces as domestics, artificers, traders and carters. Southern India stepped forward to fill up the vacancy occasioned by the cessation from labour of the sons of the soil.'

The arrivals of Tamil coolies at Ceylon ports from South India for the years 1841 to 1846 were 190,074 men, 3,083 women and 1,614 children, a total of 194,771, whilst the departures were 110,704 men, 2,331 women and 1,421 children, a total of 114,456. During that period the coolies remitted to their country about £400,000, whilst the value of rice imported during the same period was valued at £2,116,189. In the year 1900, the immigrants numbered 207,995. For their enterprise in migrating, the Tamils have been called the Scotchmen of the East. The coolies live on the estates in long rows of buildings called 'lines'. They have plenty to eat, their doctors, houses, and teachers cost them nothing, and their other wants are few. At early dawn they are summoned by tom-tom or horn to the muster-ground and then proceed to work. At about four in the afternoon they finish for the day, first having their names entered on the check-roll. In the evening the women prepare the evening meal of curry and rice, and all retire early.

THE TAMIL COOLY MISSION

Missionary work had been carried on for many years among the Tamils of Southern India, and had been most productive, so that among those who came over to Ceylon there were many Christians. In the year 1851 the Rev. J. T. Tucker, a missionary in Tinnevelly, wrote:—'In July last, finding no means of getting a living, twenty-seven of our Christians went to Ceylon, but previously appointed one of themselves to act as their reader, and took a Testament and Prayer Book with them. Twenty-five of them returned at the end of the year. They had maintained, as far as I can learn, their Christian character, notwithstanding they were absent from almost all means of grace.' In 1846 two of the South Indian missionaries, Messrs. Pettitt and Thomas, visited Ceylon to ascertain if there were any means of reaching the coolies when away from their homes. But no opening at that time presented itself.

In 1854 the Rev. W. Knight, one of the C.M.S. Secretaries, visited Ceylon, and was invited by the proprietors of some estates in the district of Matale, in company with Dr. John Murdoch, who was interested in the spiritual welfare of the coolies, to consider the subject. The result was, that some of the planters agreed to support and bring over from Tinnevelly trained catechists and arranged that the C.M.S. should supply a missionary to superintend the work. Pending the appointment of a superintending missionary, the Rev. E. T. Higgens, who was then engaged in the Kandyan Sinhalese Itineration, consented to do what was necessary.

Dr. Murdoch went over to Tinnevelly and laid the subject before the missionaries and Christians, and invited catechists to volunteer for the work. Eight men offered themselves and at the close of the year six came over to Ceylon. The Rev. J. Thomas thus describes their departure:—'We had an interesting dismissal of the catechists to Ceylon, when instructions were delivered to them as to the mode of pursuing their work. Each departing catechist addressed the meeting.'

They arrived in Kandy in November, 1854, and were located as follows:—Annathan to Cabragalla, Joseph to Kinrara, Gnanamuttu to Pitikanda, Arumanayagam to Hoolankanda, Vethanayagam to Elkaduwa, Gnanapragasam to Rajawela. The owners of these estates kindly undertook to pay their salaries of £2-10-0 per month.

The following March the catechists went over to Tinnevelly and brought back with them their families in July.

In November, 1855, the Rev. Septimus Hobbs, who had for thirteen years been a missionary in Tinnevelly, arrived with Mrs. Hobbs, and became Superintendent of the Tamil Cooly Mission.

The C.M.S. took charge of the work, a local committee of planters, comprising men of various denominations, undertaking to defray all expenses, except the stipends and allowances of the European missionaries.

The Committee met quarterly, all matters of importance were freely discussed, and much practical good resulted from this system of management. It was also decided that instead of being confined to single estates, the catechists should itinerate, according to a regular cycle, through all the districts within a reasonable distance. This plan was adopted only as a temporary measure, and in later years the number of stationed catechists has been steadily increasing. The catechist is now appointed to take charge of some thirty estates, and lives in the centre of the district.

He is able, therefore, to visit each estate at least once a month, and has opportunities for becoming much more intimately acquainted with each individual Christian, and for instructing each one more thoroughly.

The catechist only preaches on those estates where he has the permission of the Superintendent, and generally at six o'clock in the morning for about twenty minutes when the coolies assemble at 'muster.' He also visits the 'lines,' reading and speaking to the sick, or any other people he may find there, visits the schools and gives addresses to the children, distributes tracts and portions of Scripture, visits and instructs the Christians, and prepares catechumens for baptism, and in the absence of a missionary or pastor conducts the Sunday Services.

Mr. Hobbs remained in charge for seven years, until the close of the year 1862, when the Rev. W. E. Rowlands became responsible until the arrival of the Rev. and Mrs. J. Pickford in January, 1864. Mrs. Pickford soon made her influence felt upon the women and girls who came within her reach, regularly met the wives of the catechists, established a Tamil girls' school in the Kandy bazaar, and 'did what she could' until her death on May 6, 1866.

The Rev. D. Fenn was in charge for a few months in 1867, and Mr. Pickford had finally to retire in March, 1868, owing to ill-health. The Rev. W. Clark, who had been eighteen years in the Tinnevelly Mission, took charge in November, 1868, assisted by the Rev. E. M. Griffith, who had been appointed in consequence of an appeal made by the local committee for a second European missionary and who was the first T.C.M. missionary to take up his residence in the Uva district.

This year, the twelfth since the commencement of the work, there were eighteen workers and 600 estates under visitation, whilst there had been 394 baptisms during the twelve years.

About this time, in May, 1869, orange-coloured spots appeared on the coffee leaves—a disease called *Hemeleia vastatrix*—which rapidly spread over the whole coffee region, whilst grubs attacked the roots, and brown bugs sapped the life-blood of the trees. In a few years King Coffee fell and was a thing of the past. With the grit and gold of the British, other products, cinchona, cocoa, cardamoms, vanilla, camphor and tea were planted experimentally, and in a few years, tea—*Camelia Theifera*—had the supremacy and became Queen over the fair fields of Ceylon. In 1873 only 23 lbs. of tea were exported, in 1911 about 184 million pounds, 380,000 acres of land being under tea cultivation. Four years later, in 1915, the export of tea had risen to over 211 million pounds.

The tea shrubs are planted in rows, and owing to constant pruning never grow to a great height. The tender leaves or shoots are called the ' flush,' and women and children working in gangs under ' kanganies ' or overseers pick the flush and carry it in baskets to the factories. It is there withered, rolled, fermented and fired, and is graded as broken orange pekoe, orange pekoe, pekoe, pekoe souchong, souchong, congou and dust. It is then packed and forwarded to Colombo, where it is shipped to all countries of the globe, as it has won universal favour as the ' best tea in the world.'

The Tamil Cooly Mission continued to prosper, and in 1878 there were 42 catechists, 34 school masters, 955 adult Christians, 442 Christian children, 378 communicants and 32 schools with 354 pupils. A church had also been built in Hill Street in Kandy, which was in charge of a Tamil pastor, and two Tamil clergy, the Revs. P. Peter and G. Gnanamuttu, were stationed at Pelmadulla and Dickoya.

During the next ten years the Mission was divided into three districts under the superintendence of the Revs. J. D. Simmons, J. D. Thomas and H. Horsley. The Christians had increased to 1,705, the communicants to 418, and the school children to 867. During part of this period, the Revs. A. R. Cavalier, W. P. Schaffter, V. W. Harcourt and F. Glanvill had worked in the Mission. Mrs. Glanvill died and was buried in Haputale after a few months of married life in 1882, and the following year Mr. Glanvill, after two years' work, retired, and died in Bristol in 1914, after doing good work as an Organizing Secretary and Vicar. Dr. Stock, in his C.M.S. History, writes :—' Glanvill was a most lovable character and a model Organizing Secretary. It was said that he had more real personal influence in Durham and Northumberland than bishops, deans, archdeacons or canons, and when he was brought to London, he quickly won the hearts of the clergy with whom he came in contact.'

In 1898 the Revs. J. D. Simmons, J. Ilsley and W. Welchman were the Superintending Missionaries. Mr. Welchman had worked in the T.C.M. for five years and writes as follows :—

' The number of the Christians on the estates is constantly increasing. There are, of course, amongst them not only the earnest, but the lukewarm and the backsliders. The missionaries are often wonderfully encouraged by the consistency of the great mass of Christians. Many planters will come forward and give the highest testimony as to their lives, and there are many ways by which the sincerity of their faith may be tested. Not only do the Christians give liberally to the Church Fund and to the building and maintenance of churches, but are themselves supporting several catechists who are working amongst the heathen on the estates. One man, a conductor, spent Rs. 100 in purchasing a magic lantern, and Rs. 900 on slides representing the life of Christ, and now goes about the estates preaching to the coolies. It is no easy matter for a cooly to get up and walk ten miles to church and ten back in the burning sun, and yet this is what very many of them do. Nor is it a trifling matter for the catechists and schoolmasters to give up their time and all to the work when they could get much more remunerative employment elsewhere, or for the Christians, as they often do to stand up in the open air and testify for Christ. An overseer on an estate built a small room. Day by day he gathered coolies together and read God's word to them. On being asked his reason for so doing, he replied, " God has taken six of my little children to Himself, now I want to win six souls for Him." Not long ago a youth who had learnt about Christ in one of the schools was turned out of his father's house for refusing to take an offering to the little idol-house, and another man was beaten very severely for going to the schoolmaster's house to read the Bible and learn about Christ.'

The Christians in 1898 numbered 2,932, the communicants 1,070, the schools 48, the scholars 1,893, whilst the income from all sources amounted to Rs. 10,934. During this last decade the Revs. W. J. Hanan, J. W. Fall and H. C. Townsend were workers for different periods, whilst in 1899 the Rev. J. I. Pickford and in 1904 the Rev. A. N. C. Storrs gave valuable help. The Rev. W. Booth joined the Mission in 1901.

The Rev. J. D. Simmons retired in 1903 and died in 1914, and an ' In Memoriam notice ' in the *C. M. Review* for June, 1914, said:—' Few men have more decidedly left their mark upon the Tamil Cooly Mission than he has. His sterling character and entire devotion to the work he had in hand were highly appreciated by the European planters, even by those who were not in a position to estimate his spiritual qualifications at their true value, while his gentlemanly bearing and kindly disposition won for him the affectionate esteem of many of them. The catechists and schoolmasters could not fail to realize that in him they had a teacher and guide of no ordinary spiritual power.'

In 1904 the Rev. J. Ilsley was in charge of the Central Division and part of the Southern Division, residing at Nanuoya, and the Rev. R. P. Butterfield, who arrived in Ceylon in 1900 and had rendered help in Haputale, St. John's

College, Jaffna, and Colombo, assumed charge of the Northern Division, together with the Sabaragamuwa portion of the Southern Division. Working in Kandy among the Tamil and Mohammedan women were Miss Franklin, Miss Howes and Miss Finney. On the departure of the latter to England, Miss Poole (who afterwards became Mrs. W. S. Senior) was associated with Miss Howes in the same work.

Until 1895 this work had been carried on under the superintendence of the wives of the missionaries stationed in Kandy. It was greatly handicapped for many years by having no 'Home,' to which enquirers and others could be brought for instruction or protection. In 1906 the need was supplied by the renting of the 'Snuggery' as the headquarters of the Women's Work, and the 'Home' thus provided has proved the means of much blessing. Miss Howes in one of her annual letters speaks of it as being the most fruitful part of her work. In the early days, lace-making was taught as a means of livelihood for the converts, and was brought to a high degree of perfection, but of later years the 'Home' has gradually assumed the character of a school, thus showing that there is in Kandy an opening for a boarding school for Tamil girls. Several converts have gone from the 'Snuggery' to be trained as nurses in the American Mission Hospital for Women at Uduvil, Jaffna, and in all 140 girls have passed through the 'Home,' 54 of whom were Hindus and 12 Mohammedans.

The visiting in the slums of Kandy has gone on regularly and many Mohammedan women have learnt to read the Bible. Definite results have not been obtained, but the way of Life has been opened to many. As Miss Howes writes: 'It is difficult for the women to make any stand for Christ as they are so much in the power of their relations' and again 'definite results are precluded largely because the men, their husbands, are untouched.' In 1910, 150 Mohammedan women were being taught regularly. Visiting has been done in Gampola, Nawalapitiya, Matale, Peradeniya, but when, as has frequently occurred, one missionary has had to carry on alone, the outstation work has had to be dropped. Miss Case, Miss Henrys, Miss Tisdall and Miss Ledward have all worked in Kandy at different times. The lace school in Brownrigg Street, carried on for many years as part of the women's work and attended mainly by Hindu and Mohammedan girls, was handed over to the Kandy Tamil Pastorate in 1913.

The numerical weakness of the staff of missionaries in the T.C.M. became very marked in 1905 when the Rev. J. Ilsley having left for England, the burden of the whole work fell on the Rev. R. P. Butterfield and the Rev. T. S. Johnson, who later in the year took charge of the Southern Division. On the return of the Rev. J. Ilsley the T.C.M. had once more its normal complement of three missionaries. This state of things however only lasted for a brief while, for in March, 1906, the Rev. J. Ilsley left the mission and the work again devolved on his two younger colleagues.

But in 1907 the T.C.M. received a very welcome accession to its staff in the person of the Rev. W. E. Rowlands, who had had so much to do with its earlier development and who, after a lengthy spell of 23 years in parish work in England, now returned to the land and the people he loved so well.

The Rev. and Mrs. R. P. Butterfield left on furlough in 1908 and for two years the T.C.M. was managed by the Rev. W. E. Rowlands and the Rev. T. S. Johnson. During this period however a marked advance was made in the organization of the Tamil congregations into nine definite pastorates. In 1907 the Kelani Valley had become a vigorous pastorate under the Rev. J. G. Doss. This was a comparatively new district having been first opened for evangelistic work among the coolies in 1884 by the Rev. J. D. Simmons, when there were reported to be 45 Christians, whose contributions amounted to Rs. 13·40. In 1917 there were 813 Christians, and their contributions amounted to Rs. 2,129·59. We also find the Rev. A. Sathianathan at Dickoya, the Rev. A. Pakkianathan in Dimbula and the Rev. C. T. Williams in Kandy.

In 1908 the Christians in the whole T.C.M. had increased to 3,934, the communicants to 1,400, the schools to 107 and the scholars to 5,551. The statistics of the mission do not always fully represent the year's work, as sometimes it happens that a larger number of Christians than usual return to 'the coast,' or a larger number arrive. During recent years the cultivation of para rubber (*Hevea Brasiliensis*) has been taken up by the planters. In 1898 only ten tons of rubber were exported ; thirteen years after in 1911, six million pounds weight, valued at over 28 million rupees, left the country. Four years later, in 1915, the exports in rubber had reached the enormous amount of forty-six million pounds weight.

'Rubber is obtained from the trees by what is called tapping. Spiral or herringbone cuts are made in the tree to the height of about six feet, and the milk or latex then runs down, is collected in tins, removed to the factory, mixed with creosote and acetic acid, and clotted into sheets of rubber, which are placed in the hydraulic press and compressed into blocks about two inches thick. The wounds on the tree are re-opened at the next tapping by shaving off a small slice.' (Dr. Willis.)

Rubber will grow almost anywhere in Ceylon below an elevation of 3,000 feet, and Sinhalese villagers seem to be attracted to work on rubber estates.

The Rev. T. S. Johnson left on furlough in 1909, and his place in Kandy was filled by the Rev. W. Booth, who had also returned from furlough, while the Rev. R. P. Butterfield assumed charge of the Central Division.

The *Ceylon Observer*, established in 1834, and since 1859 owned by the Ferguson family (Messrs. A. M. and J. Ferguson) has from its commencement been a warm supporter of all Christian work. It had a leading article on the Tamil Cooly Mission in its issue of April 24, 1911, from which the following is an extract :—' The report of the Tamil Cooly Mission constitutes a very effective reply to that diminishing number of people, who are still sceptical or doubtful of the use and value of Christian work in the planting districts of the island. There are still some who think that the Tamil cooly was a better labourer and a more contented man in the good old days before any attempt had been made to bring him that Message to which his employer owed more than he was frequently willing to confess. That attitude completely ignores the vast changes which have taken place in the labour problem in the period in question. The planter of fifty years ago was in most cases a proprietor with a closer personal interest in his workers than the average servant of a company can possibly have. Moreover, the moral status of the cooly when compared with that of fifty years ago is immensely higher. That is not to say that it is as high as it should be, or that it is impossible to find grounds for cheap sneers at—or even sincere criticism of— the cooly's character. But if we begin to mark iniquity in that fashion, who shall be able to stand? When a fair estimate is made of the generations of soul-destroying heathenism which lie behind the cooly, it is surprising that his level is not lower than we find it.

And the most hopeful feature of the case is, that the cooly is so susceptible to civilizing and evangelizing influences, that he responds so readily to the truth that is taught when it is brought in clear and guileless methods before him, that, speaking generally, he proves to be a consistent Christian according to the light that he has. We do not forget that even now an occasional facetious advertiser declines to consider applications from Christians for employment. But the most casual examination of such cases usually shows that the irate employer has been deceived by a smart scoundrel using Christianity for financial profit, which could easily have been detected by the simple method of writing to the man's alleged pastor, or that there has been a good deal to say on both sides, and the employer is by no means the only injured party in the affair. The Christian Church in Ceylon can point to numerous cases, perfectly genuine and open to the most rigid scrutiny, of coolies who have embraced the Christian faith, and are as a result living up to a standard that would not disgrace a Christian of any nation. There are authentic records of direct evangelistic efforts made by coolies who were not satisfied that they alone should remain in possession of a manner of life, that they had learned to value so highly, and that had made so great a difference to them. Thus the conversion of one or two members of the labour force of an estate sets in motion forces for good, the results of which it is difficult to calculate.'

In 1912 the Rev. A. K. Finnimore, who had joined the Ceylon Mission in 1909, succeeded the Rev. W. E. Rowlands in the charge of the Southern Division and in the Secretaryship of the Mission, and in the same year a new pastorate was formed in Sabaragamuwa under the charge of the Rev. P. A. Paukiam, son of an old catechist connected with the Tamil Cooly Mission.

In the report for 1915 we find there was an income of Rs. 13,949. The 5,500 adults and children also contributed Rs. 17,361. The Rev. W. Booth writes:—' The grace of liberality, efforts to win others for Christ, and the honouring of God's word by reading it privately and at family prayers show that some of the Christians have got hold of the real thing. A tea maker is giving by instalments a sum sufficient for the purchase of a set of communion vessels.

At a Confirmation an overseer brought two sovereigns as a thank-offering for his recovery from a serious illness. In one district, on Good Friday, when a collection was made for the Jews, a woman in the congregation brought Rs. 12 as her offering.

The catechists, who are our messengers to the people, greatly deserve the prayerful sympathy of all who wish their work to prosper, for their task is not an easy one, and the discouragements they meet with from those who ought to help them are many.'

One of these catechists writes in his journal, ' The estates are not near to each other. I have to pass through forests, cross rivers and climb up and down the steep hills. On some estates I have no place to sleep, and sometimes I can get nothing to eat before I lie down. Yet I take much pleasure in visiting the estates, and telling the Hindus about Christ.' Another writes, ' I walk in sunshine and rain. On some estates I find no place to stop for the night. On one occasion I had to sleep in a cattle shed.'

A noteworthy point, gleaned from the statistics for the year 1916, is that the contributions of the Tamil Christians themselves—Rs. 16,879·29—exceed the European and general contributions—Rs. 13,990·35—by Rs. 2,888·94. When one considers the circumstances of the coolies who form the greater part of the congregations, one realizes with thankfulness and feelings of shame that the lesson of self-support and the duty of every church to be from its commencement a missionary church, are being learnt and put into practice by these new Christians in a way that sets an example to Christians and Churches of an older growth.

In 1917 the staff of the Mission was the normal one of four superintending missionaries—the Revs. W. E. Rowlands, A. K. Finnimore, R. P. Butterfield and T. S. Johnson. At the same time there were eight Tamil clergy associated with them in the pastoral oversight of the congregations. These were the Rev. T. D. Sathianathan at Badulla, the Rev. P. A. Paukiam at Rakwana, the Rev. J. Yorke at Avisawella, the Rev. A. Pakkianathan at Lindula, the Rev. J. G. Doss at Dickoya, the Rev. S. M. Thomas at Gampola, the Rev. N. G. Nathaniel at Matale, while the Rev. G. M. Arulanantham was expected to take charge of the Kandy Tamil congregations.

The Christians connected with the T.C.M. have increased from 3,140 in 1900 to 4,711 in 1918 and their contributions from Rs. 5,314·93 to Rs. 14,728·48.

The work sustained a severe loss in 1918 by the death in England of the Rev. W. Booth, and a further one by the well-earned retirement of the Rev. W. E. Rowlands, which was the occasion for the unique honour of an appreciative minute being passed by the Ceylon Planters' Association and for the request that an enlarged portrait of the veteran missionary should be placed in the Planters' Hall, Kandy.

The minute is as follows:—

'This Association desires to express the deep sense of planters of Ceylon of their appreciation of the long and valuable services rendered to the community in general and to planters and their coolies in particular by the Rev. W. E. Rowlands, Secretary of the Tamil Cooly Mission.'

CHAPTER XVI.

CHURCH OF ENGLAND ZENANA MISSIONARY SOCIETY IN CEYLON.

AN effort to bring Christian education to the Kandyan girls of rank first led the C.E.Z.M.S. into Ceylon. The high-class Buddhists of the Kandyan country had seemed as inaccessible to ordinary methods of foreign missions as the rocky height of Adam's Peak, which only enthusiastic pilgrims scale in search of salvation. The Rev. and Mrs. J. Ireland Jones believed, in spite of every discouragement and adverse opinion, that it would be possible to induce the parents to entrust their daughters to the care of English ladies. The Rev. J. G. Garrett (C.M.S.) also had the project at heart and when speaking in Birmingham in 1888, appealed for ladies to start the work.

Miss Bellerby and Miss James responded to the appeal and the Church of England Zenana Missionary Society sent them out in 1889, the expense of the venture being largely met by a few warm supporters of the Society.

On arrival in Ceylon, Miss Bellerby and Miss James went to Cotta to learn the language. Miss Denyer, who went out as an unattached and honorary worker, joined them and worked amongst the villages around Kandy. Later on she transferred to the C.M.S., as that Society was responsible for the evangelistic work in the Kandy district.

In 1890 a suitable bungalow, Hillwood, was found, in which to begin the proposed boarding-school in Kandy, and Miss Bellerby and Miss James removed there. A prospectus was issued bearing the names of three Kandyan Chiefs. Miss R. Gooneratna of Cotta was associated with the missionaries in the work during these early years and her wise and untiring efforts did much to build up the school.

Hillwood was originally called the 'Clarence Memorial School' in memory of the infant son of the Rev. and Mrs. J. Ireland Jones, but owing to the confusion that constantly arose through having two names to the same institution, the Society decided in 1900 to drop the name 'Clarence Memorial.' Such progress was made that in 1892 there were altogether twenty girls in the boarding school, and Miss Malden was sent out to help Miss Bellerby in the work as Miss James had married the Rev. E. Bellerby.

Miss Scovell accompanied Miss Malden and, after learning the language at Hillwood, went to Gampola to start the village mission work there.

In 1892 the Government Agent, Mr. P. A. Temple, in the Administrative Report writes, ' I should not pass unnoticed an admirable institution conducted in Kandy by some English ladies for the education of the daughters of Kandyan Chiefs. It is no small thing to have made an attempt, even partially successful, to bring out into the sunshine of knowledge and womanly accomplishments a class which native prejudice has hitherto consigned to the gloomy and uncultured life of a Kandyan Walauwa.'

In 1893 three of the pupils were confirmed—one being the first convert to Christianity.

In 1894 the work was reported of as successful, though the spadework done in those early years by Miss Bellerby had been exceedingly difficult. For many years, owing to the inaccessibility of the Walauwas—before the days of train and of motors—the children only went home once a year, during Sinhalese New Year in April.

The numbers soon outgrew the capacity of the bungalow,

and in 1895 a dormitory to accommodate thirty girls was added. In 1897 Miss Alice Naish arrived to help in the school and carried on bravely with Miss Malden during Miss Bellerby's furlough, but she died at Home in 1901, the strain of the work having too great for her.

In January, 1901, Miss Lena Chapman, who had been invalided home from Bengal, was sent to Kandy. During this year, the arrangement by which the Principal of Trinity College was manager of the school, the Rev. J. G. Garrett, Clerical Secretary and Mr. (afterwards Sir) William Duff Gibbon, Financial Secretary, came to an end. Miss Bellerby was appointed Manager as well as Principal, and the Rev. A. E. Dibben became Corresponding Secretary with the Home Society.

In 1902 Miss Menage came out to help in the care of the girls. She was transferred to the Deaf School in Palamcottah, South India in the following year, and returned to help in the Deaf and Blind School in 1912.

In 1903 Miss Scovell and Miss Malden retired. The latter had been invalided home in 1901 having done good work in the school, and was not allowed to return. The first success in a public examination—Junior Cambridge—was obtained in 1903, one result of this being that girls were allowed to stay longer at school; thus a blow was struck at the prevalent practice of too early marriage.

In 1904 Miss Eva Heather, B.A., came to Hillwood, and from 1904–1907 Miss Lena Chapman was acting-Principal, while Miss Bellerby was on furlough. Miss E. Curtis joined Hillwood in 1905 as a local worker, and in 1907 'Middlewood,' a bungalow near Hillwood, was opened as a school for little boys from four to eight years of age, the boys' schools in Kandy not catering for such young children and the parents being desirous of having their small boys at 'Hillwood' with their sisters. Miss F. Naish took charge of Middlewood.

In 1908 Miss Rose Overton (Somerville College, Oxford) joined the Hillwood staff and Miss M. F. and Miss B. E. Brutton came out to give voluntary help for a year. In this year, Hillwood was enlarged to accommodate over a hundred girls. This was done by blasting away a large portion of the hillside and filling up a deep ravine with the débris. Thus a two-storied school building, play-ground, and tennis court were evolved.

In 1909 seven girls were baptized and five confirmed—fruits of the faithful work of the past years in breaking up the soil. In 1910 Miss Cave, M.A., formerly Editorial Superintendent of the C.E.Z.M.S. and Miss J. Oakley arrived to help at Hillwood and Middlewood.

Miss Lena Chapman returned from furlough in 1910 and opened Peradeniya School for girls ineligible for Hillwood, but in the following year Miss Bellerby was invalided home and retired from the work, and Miss Lena Chapman was asked to close Peradeniya School and return to Hillwood as Principal bringing some of her girls and all her school plant with her.

Miss Heather, who had been in England for some little time, retired from the C.E.Z.M.S. in 1911. The 'Annexe' was built on the hillside in 1912 and it has served as a valuable isolation block in cases of infectious illness. In 1913 the first day pupils were admitted to 'Hillwood.' Miss Hall, B.SC., joined the staff in 1915 and a Science Room was built. Miss Rose Overton, having learnt the vernacular (Sinhalese), was lent to the C.M.S. Training School, and she has since been in charge of the Women's Department of the 'Training Colony,' Peradeniya. In 1915 the first 'Middlewood' old boy was baptized at Trinity College.

In 1916 class rooms and a 'covered way' connecting the 'Annexe' with the school were added. Several baptisms had taken place during these years, and this year saw the first Christian marriage from Hillwood. Miss Dorothy Gunston arrived during the year and took charge of the Kindergarten. Other Christian marriages followed in 1917, and thus the goal of the work, the foundation of the Christian Home, having been now reached, the school was abundantly justifying its existence.

In 1917 Miss Oakley returned from furlough and brought Miss Cragg with her as an honorary worker. As Miss Oakley broke down a few months after her arrival, Miss Cragg gave invaluable help for over three years at Middlewood by taking over the charge of the small boys.

The Kandyans are a rapidly changing community and are coming abreast of the other races in their national life. Perhaps not the least potent force in this modern forward movement is the influence of its educated and enlightened womanhood.

The School for the Deaf and Blind

In 1910 Miss M. F. Chapman joined her sister at the Peradeniya School for a year and whilst there wrote an article in a Sinhalese newspaper, ' The Rivikirana,' calling attention to the fact that nothing was being done for the deaf and dumb of the Island and appealing for funds to start the work. The census returns for 1911 showed that there were 3,233 deaf and dumb persons in the Island and 3,957 blind, 947 of these being under fifteen. Mr. K. J. Saunders, of Trinity College, took up Miss Chapman's appeal and commended it to the public through the press. Mr. T. Gracie, Secretary of the Ceylon branch of the Bible Society, also wrote supporting the appeal and suggesting the formation of a scheme which would include the blind also. As a result, an Appeal Fund Committee was formed with the Bishop of Colombo as Chairman, Mr. Saunders as Honorary Secretary and Mr. Gracie as Honorary Treasurer, with the object of raising Rs. 37,500. Meanwhile, Miss Chapman went to England and succeeded in collecting over a thousand pounds. She also secured the services of Miss Bausor, a trained teacher of the blind, and induced the C.E.Z. M.S. to enter upon this new work in Ceylon. Miss G. Bergg offered herself to the Society specially for work amongst the deaf of Ceylon and went into training. Miss Mase, a trained teacher of the deaf, came out to help in the work until Miss Bergg had completed her course, and Miss Menage, who had previously worked at Palamcottah, joined the staff as matron. The Appeal Committee collected about Rs. 48,600, the Hon. Mr. A. J. R. de Soysa, M.L.C., gave a site of six acres near Mt. Lavinia, and on this land the school was built. The work itself was begun in 1912 in a rented bungalow in Dehiwala, the new building not being ready for occupation until 1914, when the Appeal Fund Committee, having completed its work, handed over to the C.E.Z.M.S. A serious outbreak of illness occurred immediately after the removal and as it was seen that further drainage was necessary, Icicle Hall in Colombo was rented and the school carried on there for a time. Miss Bausor returned to England in 1914 owing to illhealth and Miss G. Bergg, having completed her training, arrived in Colombo in February, 1915, Miss Mase leaving shortly afterwards. In September, 1915, Miss Chapman left on medical advice and the school was re-transferred to the new buildings. Miss S. C. Lloyd, of the C.M.S., was asked to undertake the oversight of the work temporarily, and, after five months, Miss Bergg became Principal, and shortly afterwards, Manager also. During the years 1916 and 1917 steady progress was made, several new buildings were added, the numbers increased and new industries were started. A training class was opened for girls who wished to become teachers of the deaf or blind, and most encouraging reports were received as a result of the Government examination, the annual Government grant being considerably increased. Besides this generous grant the school has no fixed income, and is entirely dependent on voluntary contributions. Appealing as it does to the sympathies of every class and creed, the work has aroused widespread interest and encouraging support in its efforts to train these afflicted children to become useful, happy and, as far as possible, independent citizens.

VILLAGE WORK.

In 1892 Miss A. Scovell was sent out, specially supported for work in the villages around Kandy, which remained her centre until 1896 when the present Mission House at Gampola was first rented. The C.E.Z.M.S. was then assigned the women's work in the Gampola district, thirty-six miles long by thirty-four broad, and Miss Scovell and Miss E. S. Karney carried on a zealous evangelistic campaign in the numerous villages, besides running a very successful dispensary in Gampola itself. Through this elementary medical work touch was obtained with many of the surrounding villages, patients taking back the Gospel message to their homes. The C.E.Z.M.S. relieved the C.M.S. of the ten girls' schools in the district and opened five new ones. Miss K. Gedge worked in Gampola from 1898 to 1902, and then took charge of the C.M.S. and C.E.Z.M.S. Training School for vernacular teachers at Cotta from 1904 until her marriage in 1909. Miss Johnson arrived in 1904 expressly for village work. Another valued helper was Miss M. R. Gedge who, after a period of honorary service in East Africa, came to Ceylon in 1900 and rendered useful help in various mission stations, both C.M.S. and C.E.Z.M.S., especially devoting herself to the English-speaking people. A Young Women's Christian Association branch of seventy members was started in Gampola in 1898 and Bible-classes formed, and these two branches of work were carried on by Miss Gedge on her arrival with much success. Living at Gampola, she also visited in the railway settlements at Kadugannawa and Nawalapitiya. Later this work among the railway employees and their families was taken up by Miss M. Peto, another honorary missionary, who, after service in North India, made her home at Gampola in 1910 and has since worked among the English-speaking people. Miss Scovell retired in 1903 and Miss Karney in 1905. Miss M. E. Lambe arrived in 1906 and from that time she and Miss Johnson have carried on the work. The Society having acquired the bungalow and compound, a new dispensary and sick-room were added in 1912, a boarding school was started and a preaching band formed. In this year Miss Karney returned to the Mission and developed the work at Talawa, a village near Anuradhapura, in which village she lived until her departure from Ceylon in 1915.

Some of the girls' schools taken over from the C.M.S. were given back to that Society in 1918, thus setting free the missionaries to devote more time to evangelistic work.

CHAPTER XVII.

THE GREAT WAR AND RECENT PROGRESS.

THE great war of 1914-18 had a less direct effect on the Ceylon Mission than on those of India, Uganda, Egypt, China and Japan. Ceylon sent no Labour Corps officered to a certain extent by missionaries as did Uganda, India, China and Japan, but this was mainly due to the inability of the Ceylon Government to finance such an effort. Apart from the enlightened and active patriotism shown in some of the secondary schools, the attitude of the mass of Sinhalese and Tamil Christians was that of sympathetic spectators of the conflict.

The Ceylon Mission played its part in the war as far as its numbers and position would allow. The Revs. A. K. Finnimore and A. G. Fraser served as Army Chaplains on the Western Front, while another missionary was accepted as a chaplain, but withdrew on account of an urgent call to return to Ceylon. Trinity College, Kandy, gave of its best, including seven of its staff, of whom two were killed. Fifty-four of its pupils, of whom eleven laid down their lives, also took part. Its contribution to the war was graciously recognized by the King, who presented one of the captured German machine-guns to the College. Mounted on a granite stand, this was unveiled by the Governor of Ceylon, Sir William Manning, in the presence of a large assemblage, in 1921.

The Rev. A. M. Walmsley served for a short time in the I.A.R.O. in Mesopotamia and in 1917 when compulsory military training for all Europeans under fifty was introduced, several of the members of the Mission preferred to join the local Defence Corps rather than be exempted by reason of their calling. The son of a T.C.M. catechist joined up in 1916 and fought throughout the Palestine campaign. Several old boys of our elementary English schools also joined up and served in Palestine and Mesopotamia and on other battle fronts.

The smaller boarding schools, both boys' and girls', contributed to the best of their ability to the various war funds.

In consequence of the war and the subsequent problems arising from it, the desire for greater political freedom has become more intense and more widely spread. The Christian community share to a great extent in this legitimate aspiration, the only difference being that their non-Christian brethren make more use of the Press and of public meetings to forward the particular ends which they favour. With many, 'self-determination' is the political war-cry and the object of their agitation. It is not the purpose of this chapter to discuss this movement, but simply to note to some extent its effect as seen in the manner of the reception of the Christian message. Among the masses of the Sinhalese there is a decided tendency to regard Buddhism as the national religion, while many, both Tamils and Sinhalese, regard Christianity as a religion of the West. Hence has arisen the somewhat widely-spread idea that to become a Christian is to become denationalized and to be out of sympathy with national aspirations. For this reason, the missionary body as a whole would welcome a far greater measure of self-realization for the Ceylonese communities than has hitherto been reached.

The 'revival of Buddhism,' which became noticeable early in the century, has received a further impetus from this national movement. Of recent years this revival seems to have taken the form of an attempt to demonstrate that the Buddhist system of philosophy is capable of adaptation as a working force in the modern movements of the day, many of which are essentially Christian in origin. Thus we have, as pointed out in Ch. III, Buddhist Grant-in-aid Schools run by a central organization, just as we have Christian Grant-in-aid Schools run by different Christian bodies; Buddhist Sunday Schools; Young Men's Buddhist Associations in emulation of the Young Men's Christian Association; and a Buddhist Literature Society is contemplated. Buddhists co-operate with Christians in Social Service Leagues and in other societies for the amelioration of suffering.

As regards the Mohammedans the most that can be stated is that their attitude is more friendly than in pre-war days.

Dealing with the congregations of Sinhalese and Tamil Christians connected with and owing their origin to the C.M.S., it should be noted that the ten years prior to 1918 have seen a considerable development in organization, especially in connection with the Diocese. Missionaries and Ceylonese clergy of the C.M.S., holding the Bishop's license, are naturally part of the Diocese as much as are the clergy more directly associated with it, their relationship to the C.M.S. being something additional. C.M.S. missionaries took a prominent part in the formation of the Diocesan Synod in 1880, and have ever since taken their share in its work and in that of the Diocesan organizations generally.

In 1909 the present Bishop of Colombo, Dr. E. A. Copleston, accepted the invitation of the Parent Committee to become Chairman of the C.M.S. Conference, and the establishment of this closer connection between the Bishop and the Society has been attended by much profit to the work. Whilst thus intimately connected with the Diocese, it is however natural that as the Parent Committee makes large grants to the Ceylon Mission and sends out missionaries from England, it should claim a certain amount of control and this up to the present has been secured by the Conference and the Finance Committee which together form the Local Governing Body of the Mission, and by a Patronage Board which controls the appointment of Ceylonese clergy to the charge of pastorates connected with the Society. The Parent Committee's Memorandum of 1900 forms the basis of the policy which has been pursued. Four Ceylonese clergy, elected by their own fellow clergy, and two laymen nominated by the Conference have seats on the Conference, and two of these are generally elected each year to serve on the Standing Committee.

A stage has now been reached in which the leading pastorates, Sinhalese and Tamil, have attained to a status of self-support and independence, receiving practically no grant from the Parent Committee for pastoral work, but assisted by grants in aid of the evangelistic and school work which nearly all of them have undertaken.

Thus, for example, there is now no District Missionary in Jaffna. The whole of his work has been undertaken by the four pastors and their Church Committees, with Chundicully, Nellore, Copay and Pallai as their centres, leaving only the English educational work and the training of vernacular teachers in the hands of the missionaries. In the Cotta District a similar step has been taken with the Nugegoda and Talangama pastorates, and in Colombo as regards the Sinhalese and Tamil pastorates. In Kandy the Tamil pastorate has become independent, and the Sinhalese congregations there, namely at Trinity Church, Katukelle and Gatembe, have been in this position for nearly forty years.

A remarkable feature of recent years has been the progress and development of the Tamil Christian pastorates in the planting districts. Whereas in 1900 there was but one ordained Tamil clergyman working in the sphere of the Tamil Cooly Mission, the Rev. A. Gnanamuttu of Kandy, there are now nine. These men are in charge of vigorous pastorates in Kandy, Dikoya, Dimbula, Nuwara Eliya, the Kelani Valley, Sabaragamuwa, Matale, Badulla and Gampola.

CHAPTER XVIII.

RECENT EDUCATIONAL DEVELOPMENTS.

THE past twenty years have witnessed a great and ever-increasing demand for education, and a correspondingly higher standard in missionary schools has been necessitated. The days are past when any sort of a weather-proof building would do for a school and when a teacher need have only sufficient education to impart instruction. Buildings, to satisfy Government requirements, must be of a much higher type, and teachers must, with few exceptions, be more or less experts. Thus the burden and expense of missionary schools becomes increasingly heavier. Secondary schools must have their laboratories and science equipment and all schools must have a certain proportion of trained teachers on their staffs.

A feature of the present demand for education is the desire to learn English. Parents will pay anything in reason and often more than they can afford for English education for their children. Pupils will daily trudge miles to supplement a vernacular school course with some instruction in English.

The importance of higher educational work is accentuated in these days of national aspirations. Ceylonese are taking a more and more prominent part in public life and although the few proceed to an English University, the many receive their deepest educational impress in the high schools and colleges of the island. Moreover, in connection with the progress of Christianity and the development of the Church of the future, it is increasingly necessary to aim at the training of men who will be fitted to take a leading part. It is a significant fact that with some few notable exceptions, the Ceylonese of outstanding capacity in politics, Government service and business, are Christians or have received their education in a Christian institution.

A distinction more or less defined may be noticed in the outlook and ideals of the Christian and non-Christian leaders. Christianity gives a wider and more altruistic outlook and, in many of the present-day leaders, tends to moderate the ambitions of the extreme Nationalists without, however, evincing any lack of sympathy with any reasonable scheme for the greater self-realization of the Ceylonese races.

The teaching of science, both pure and applied, has made great strides of recent years. The School of Tropical Agriculture is doing a great work and receives the support of the land-owning classes. Agriculture as a profession is beginning to compete with the practice of law and medicine and with the attractive Government service.

The world-wide movement towards Social Service has not left Ceylon untouched. The first Social Service League in the island was initiated at Trinity College under the leadership of the late Capt. N. P. Campbell. The movement has spread, and in Colombo and in other places similar organizations are working for the uplift of the masses. Some of these are even non-Christian, but when one remembers the pessimism of the Buddhist philosophy, the negative idealism of Hinduism and the fatalistic creed of Mohammedanism, there can be no doubt as to the source of the inspiration.

Higher education for girls is still largely in the hands of the missionary bodies at work in the island. The Buddhists have two institutions in Colombo and others are projected, whilst the Hindus have one school in the North. The Mohammedans, the most backward race as regards education, are beginning to bestir themselves, but so far only as regards the education of their boys. Signs are not wanting that in India the more enlightened Mohammedan communities are realizing the necessity for educating their girls, and it is hoped and believed that this movement will before long spread to Ceylon. There are two factors which mark the urgency of the higher education of girls. One is that the educated young Easterner feels the need of and demands a correspondingly educated and enlightened partner. The second is the increased scope for the work of women in social service. The pace at which the movement for the emancipation of women in the East is progressing leaves the historian breathless. During the last year or two, the claim for the franchise for women has been urged in India with no uncertain voice. The fulfilment of this claim is probably far distant, but that it has been made at all, is a momentous advance.

From a missionary point of view, the Boarding Schools for Girls are the most satisfactory in results. These, however, share with all other grades of schools, in the necessity for complying with the demands of Government for better buildings, more competent staff, and more up-to-date equipment. To keep pace with these demands is an ever-increasing difficulty and many schools barely pay their way.

A few years ago compulsory education was introduced and is gradually being enforced. With it came also the Conscience Clause, a copy of which is displayed in every school. A new policy of education affecting our vernacular schools, recently foreshadowed by the Ceylon Government, constitutes a problem for our Missionary Societies. The near future will witness a considerable modification of evangelistic effort, the chief notes of which will be more concentration and greater efficiency.

Within the sphere of the Tamil Cooly Mission the most noticeable development of recent years has been the increase in the number of Estate Schools. This is due chiefly to a Government ordinance requiring estates to make provision for the education of the children of their labour force. Though the ordinance fails in that it contains no clause for enforcing attendance, a large number of estates have provided schools and many of these are under the management of the missionaries. A smaller number are both managed and financed by the missionaries. Educationally, they are of doubtful value owing to the irregularity of the attendance, though this, we hope, will be remedied to a great extent by the provisions of a new labour ordinance which will limit the employment of very young children in manual labour on the estates. From a missionary point of view, the chief points in favour of many of them are that they provide a *point d'appui* for beginning work among the coolies of an estate, and that the school building is useful as a meeting-place for the Christians.

CONCLUSION.

It is hoped that the foregoing pages have given a fair and a readable account of the work of the Church Missionary Society in Ceylon during the century which ended in the year 1918 and that the reader will rise from their perusal with some idea of what God has wrought by this imperfect and unworthy instrument. He has given to all concerned in the work much cause for praise and thanksgiving for the measure of prosperity and progress which He has permitted them to witness, for the many souls brought into His Kingdom and for the moral uplift of the peoples of Ceylon.

At the same time there is much cause for humiliation when it is borne in mind that throughout the century there have been multitudes, young and old, rich and poor, educated and illiterate, who, although they have had the Gospel of Christ put plainly before them, have either deliberately rejected it or turned away from it with indifference, as though it were something which did not concern them. The proportion of Christians to non-Christians in the whole island is still a fraction below ten per cent. This constitutes a loud call to the Ceylonese who have embraced the Christian religion to

'Take up the torch and wave it wide,'

for the work of evangelizing the country must now be left more and more in their hands, and dark places still abound which need to be illuminated with Gospel light.

> 'Say not, "The struggle nought availeth,
>   The labour and the wounds are vain,
> The enemy faints not nor faileth,
>   And as things have been they remain."
>
> For while the tired waves vainly breaking,
>   Seem here no painful inch to gain,
> Far back, through creeks and inlets making,
>   Comes silent, flooding in, the main.
>
> And not by eastern windows only
>   When daylight comes, comes in the light ;
> In front the sun climbs slow, how slowly
>   But westward, look, the land is bright.'

A HYMN FOR CEYLON.

Jehovah, Thou hast promised
   The isles shall wait for Thee;
The joyous isles of Ocean,
   The jewels of the sea;
Lo! we, this island's watchmen,
   Would give and take no rest,
(For thus hast Thou commanded,)
   Till our dear land be blessed.

Then bless her, mighty Father,
   With blessings needed most,
In every verdant village,
   By every palmy coast;
On every soaring mountain
   O'er every spreading plain,
May all her sons and daughters
   Thy righteousness attain.

Give peace within her borders,
   'Twixt man and man goodwill,
The love all unsuspicious,
   The love that works no ill;
In loyal, lowly service
   Let each from other learn,
The guardian and the guarded,
   Till Christ Himself return.

To Him our land shall listen,
   To Him our land shall kneel,
All rule be on His shoulder,
   All wrong beneath His heel;
Oh consummation glorious,
   Which now by faith we sing;
Come, cast we up the highway
   That brings us back the King.

                        W. S. SENIOR.

APPENDIX A.

LIST OF CEYLON C.M.S. MISSIONARIES (Men).

Abbreviations.—Oxf., Oxford; Camb., Cambridge; Dub. Dublin; Dur., Durham; Isl., Church Missionary College, Islington; d., deacon; p., priest; m., married; S.M., Sinhalese Mission; T.M., Tamil Mission; T.C.M., Tamil Cooly Mission; T.C.K., Trinity College, Kandy; Ret., Retired from Ceylon; C., Curate; V., Vicar; Rec., Rector; D., Died.

1818

1. Lambrick, Rev. Samuel (Matlock)—m. 1827 Mary Ann Stratford. d. 1860. S.M. Ret. 1835. Tutor at Eton, 1816. Chaplain to Marquis of Cholmondeley, 1837. Compiled a 'Sinhalese Grammar and Vocabulary.' D. 1854, aged 85.

2. Mayor, Rev. Robert, son of Rev. John Mayor, of Shawbury.—m. September 4, 1817, at St. George's, Everton, Charlotte Bickersteth, daughter of Rev. E. Bickersteth of Watton, and Secretary of the C.M.S. S.M. Ret. 1828. V. of Acton and Rec. of Coppenstall, 1838. D. July 14, 1846, aged 55. A son, Rev. John Eyton Bickersteth Mayor, born Baddegama, January 28, 1825, became Professor of Latin, St. John's College, Cambridge, in 1872, and wrote several classical, philological and antiquarian works. He died December 1, 1910, aged 85. Another son, Rev. Joseph Bickersteth Mayor, was Professor of Classics at King's College, London, 1870-79, and died in November, 1916, aged 88.

3. Ward, Rev. Benjamin (Wellington)—m. Mary Meires. d. 1864. S.M. Ret. 1828. Hon. Canon of Carlisle, 1857.

Rec. of Meesden, 1859. D. 1879, aged 87. A son, Rev. D. Ward, Vic. of Upton, Cheshire, died in 1912, aged 85.

4. Knight, Rev. Joseph, born at Stroud on October 17, 1787. T.M.—m. (1) Mrs. S. B. Richards, D. April 26, 1825. (2) Mrs. E.S. Nichols, D. February 4, 1837—both widows of American missionaries. They were buried in churchyard of American Mission, Tellippalai, Jaffna. Wrecked off the Cape in 1838, died shortly after his return to Ceylon on October 11, 1840, and was buried at Cotta.

The four above missionaries were ordained by Bishop Ryder, of Gloucester.

1821

5. Browning, Rev. Thomas (Stroud)—m. Mary Stephens, D. 1839. S.M. Died at sea in July, 1838.

6. Bailey, Rev. Joseph (Dewsbury) S. M.—m. (1) Sophia Parkin, D. 1825. (2) 1834, Octavia Bulmer, D. 1864. D. at Cotta on March 19, 1844, aged 47, and buried there. Compiled a 'Church Hymn Book.'

1824

7. Adley, Rev. William (Canterbury) T.M.—m. (1) Lucy Coles, D. 1839. (2) 1841, Catherine Theodora Gauntlett, D. 1880. Ret. 1846. Rec. Rudboxton. D. 1889, aged 97.

1826

8. Selkirk, Rev. James (Harwich), St. Bees Coll., S.M.— Mrs. Selkirk died in 1876. Two children, Emily Jane (1831) and John (1832) were buried in St. Paul's burial ground, Colombo. Chaplain of Hull Gaol. D. 1880, aged 81. Wrote in 1844 ' Recollections of Ceylon.' Ret. 1840.

9. Trimnell, Rev. George Conibere (High Wycombe), Isl. S.M.—Ret. 1847. Mrs. Trimnell died in 1861. D. 1880, aged 80.

1827

10. Faught, Rev. George Steers, Isl. S.M.—m. Anne Le Clerc. d. 1870. Ret. 1836. C. Bradfield. D. 1873, aged 72.

Three children, Susan Margaret (1830), Marcus Steers (1835) and Godfrey Steers (1835), died and were buried at Baddegama.

1830

11. Ridsdale, Mr. William (Hull), S.M.—m. on April 7, 1832, at St Peter's, Colombo, Susan Dorothea, eldest daughter of Captain F. W. von Drieberg. Ret. 1836. A daughter, Mary Anne (1834), buried in Galle Face burial ground.

1831

12. Marsh, Rev. Joseph (Bonsall), Isl. S.M.—Died at sea, 1831.

1835

13. Oakley, Rev. William (Hertford), Isl. S.M.—Born October 3, 1808. m. 1839, Frances Mary King, D. in Kandy July 14, 1866. A tablet to her memory in Trinity Church, Kandy. Wrote ' The Lord's Supper not a Sacrifice,' ' Conversation on the Christian Religion,' ' Simple Truths of Christianity ' and several other tracts. Did not visit England after his arrival in 1835, and died in Nuwara Eliya on July 18, 1886, in his 79th year.

Mr. Oakley's only son sailed for England in the *City of London* in 1850, the vessel foundered and all on board perished. His only daughter, Mary, married at Kandy on May 10, 1867, Priestly Jacob, Head Master of the High School, Poona, son of the Rev. G. A. Jacob, D.D., Christ's Hospital, London.

1838

14. Powell, Rev. Henry (Reading), Isl. S.M.—m. Mary Ann Heath. Ret. 1845. Vicar of Bolton and Hon. Canon of Manchester. D. 1898, aged 84.

1839

15. Haslam, Rev. John Fearby (Halifax), B.A., Camb. S.M.—m. (1) 1837, Elizabeth Denton, D. 1839. (2) 1842, Sophia Elizabeth, daughter of Rev. J. Bailey, D. 1873. Compiled ' Vocabulary,' and ' Arithmetic '. Translated into Sinhalese Dr. Mill's ' Life of Christ.' D. in Colombo March 19, 1850. Buried in Galle Face burial ground.

The Haslams arrived on January 7, 1839. The first Mrs. Haslam died at Cotta on March 24, aged 25, and their daughter, Elizabeth, died on November 8. Both buried in the Galle Face burial ground.

16. Taylor, Rev. Francis W. (Luton), Isl. T.M.—m. Caroline Bella Price. Ret. 1849. V. West Thorney. D. 1887, aged 76.

1840

17. Johnson, Rev. J. Talbot (London), Isl. T.M.—Ret. 1849. m. Amelia Winn. Rec. Beccles. D. 1871.

1841

18. Greenwood, Rev. Charles (Cambridge), Isl. S.M.—m. Harriet Winn, D. 1872. Drowned whilst bathing in the Gindara river at Baddegama on June 21, 1850, aged 37.

1845

19. Pargiter, Rev. Robert (Cornwall)—d. 1846· p. 1847. T.M. m. (1) 1844, Charlotte Elizabeth Jones, D. 1849. (2) 1851, Anna Matilda Palm, D. 1900. Ret. 1864. C.M.S. Association Secretary, 1865-1885. V. Towersey, 1885. D. Charmouth, April 1, 1915, aged 98. Mr. Pargiter went to Ceylon in 1844 under the Wesleyan Missionary Society and joined the C.M.S the following year.

A son, Robert S. Pargiter, C.C.S., died as Assistant Government Agent of Negombo in 1876. A daughter, Mrs. John

Pole, died in Ceylon, and another son, A. H. Pargiter, died in Colombo in 1898. Another son, Rev. G. E. A. Pargiter, was Principal of St. John's College, Agra, 1883-91.

1846

20. Gordon, Rev. Alexander Douglas, Isl. S. M.—Ret. 1854. D. 1865.

21. O'Neill, Rev. James (Kilcoleman), Isl., B.D., Lambeth.—d. 1845. p. 1846. m. 1846, Elizabeth Adams, D. December 16, 1848, aged. 27. T. M. Ret. 1854. V. Luton. D. December 28, 1896, aged 75.

There is a marble bust of Mr. O'Neill in Luton Parish Church where he was Vicar for thirty-four years. A son, James Arthur, a physician in Devonshire; another son, Henry Edward, H. M. Consul at Rouen.

22. Collins, Rev. Henry (Maidenhead), Isl. S.M.—Ret. 1849. D. 1860.

1847

23. Wood, Rev. Isaiah, Isl. S.M.—m. Sarah Ann Spencer, D. 1873. Ret. 1861. D. 1889.

1849

24. Bren, Rev. Robert (Reading), Isl. T.M.—m. Sarah Jordan Brown. Ret. 1858. D. 1885. Wrote 'Christianity and Hinduism Compared' (Tamil).

25. Parsons, Rev. George (Bath), Isl. S.M.—m. Diana Alway, D. 1896. D. Colombo, April 18, 1866, aged 42. Buried in Galle Face burial ground. Wrote 'Exposition of the Thirty-nine Articles' (Sinhalese). A tablet to his memory in Baddegama Church. Eldest son, Rev. G. H. Parsons, a C. M. S. missionary in Bengal, for many years. A grandson, Rev. B. G. Parsons, C.M.S., Fuhkien.

1850

26. Pettitt, Rev. George (Birmingham), Isl. S.M.—Tinnevelly, 1833-50. Ret. 1855. m. Louisa Hare, D. 1892. V. St. Jude's, Birmingham. D. 1873. Wrote 'Tinnevelly Mission' (1850), 'Life of Rev. J. T. Tucker,' 'The Mirror of Custom.' (1862).

1851

27. Fenn, Rev. Christopher Cyprian, son of Rev. Joseph Fenn, Travancore.—Born at Cottayam. M.A., Camb. d. 1848. p. 1849. S. M. m. (1) 1859, Emma Poynder, D. 1870. (2) 187?, Harriet Elizabeth Christiana Morris. Ret. 1863. C. Ockbrock 1848-50. C.M.S. Secretary, 1864-94. D. October 12, 1913, at Tunbridge Wells, aged 90. Wrote (1868) 'Answer to Durlabdy Winodaniya.'

28. Higgens, Rev. Edward Thomas (Snodland), Isl. S.M.—m. (1) Amelia Dyke, D. June 9, 1854. (2) 1858, Annie Catherine Schon, D. 1911. Ret. 1900. D. June 11, 1901, at Chatham, aged 78. Wrote 'No Salvation in Buddhism' (Sinhalese). The first Mrs. Higgens, and their son, Edward Albert, who died on October 6, 1854, buried in Holy Trinity Churchyard, Kandy.

1853

29. Barton, Mr. Henry James (Ipswich), St. Aidan's, S.M.—Ret. 1862. m. A. Allen. Afterwards ordained and Chaplain of Poplar Sick Asylum.

30. Sorrell, Mr. Joseph, Highbury Training College, T.M.—Ret. 1860. Afterwards ordained. d. 1863. p. 1864, C. St. John's, Limehouse, 1901. Rec. of St. Nicholas', Holton, Somerset. D. November 11, 1916, aged 88.

1854

31. Collins, Rev. Richard, M.A., Camb. T.C.K.—Ret. 1880. m. (1) Frances Wright, D. 1862. (2) 1863, Frances Anne Hawksworth. V. Kirkburton. D. 1900. Wrote ' Philosophy of Jesus Christ ' (1879), ' The After Life ' (1894) ' Missionary Enterprise in the Far East,' and ' Introduction to Leviticus in Pulpit Commentary.'

1855

32. Whitley, Rev. Henry, B.A., Camb. Incumbent of Christ Church, Galle Face.—m. 1855, Marcia Paterson. Accidentally killed by the falling of a wall of school room, Galle Face, November 10, 1860, aged 34.

A tablet to his memory in Christ Church.

33. Hobbs, Rev. Septimus (Portsea), Isl. T.C.M.—m. 1849, Sarah Westbrook, D. 1898. Ret. 1862. 1842-55 in Tinnevelly. Rec. Compton Vallence. D. 1898, aged 82.

1857

34. Jones, Rev. John Ireland, M.A., Dub. Isl. S.M.—m. (1) Kitty Crawford Colclough, D. 1877. (2) 1882, Frances Matilda Sinclair. D. Colombo, November 12, 1903. Wrote ' Jubilee Sketches ' (1868), ' The Wonderful Garden ' (Sinhalese), ' Handbook of Sinhalese,' ' Answer to Durlabdy Winodaniya.'

Eldest son, Rev. Philip I. Jones, C.M.S., North India; second son, Beauchamp, died in Kegalle, and daughter, Mrs. H. W. Unwin, died in England.

1858

35. MacArthur, Rev. Charles Chapman, (Iona), Isl. T.M.—m. Annette Cohen, D. 1898. Ret. 1867. Rec. Burlingham. D. 1892. Wrote ' First Principles ' (Tamil).

36. Foulkes, Rev. Thomas (Holywell), Isl. T.M.—m. (1) Miss Maiben, D. 1853. (2) Mary Anne Ashley, D. February 6, 1859, aged 22. A tablet to her memory in Nellore Church. Tinnevelly, 1849-58. Madras, 1859-60. Only one year in Jaffna.

1860

37. Coles, Rev. Stephen, Highbury Training College. S.M.—m. 1860, Elizabeth Nicklin, D. 1898. D. Colombo, 1901. Wrote ' Essay on the Atonement.' Comp. ' Scripture Text Book,' ' Hymns for Children.' Trans. ' My King ' (Sinhalese), ' Picture Tracts.'

38. Tonge, Rev. Robert Burchall (Manchester), B.A., Lond. Isl. S.M.—Ret. 1867. Mrs. Tonge died 1875. C. Gresley.

1861

39. Clowes, Rev. Josiah Herbert (Yarmouth), Isl. S.M.— m. Susan Emily Seppings. Ret. 1866. C. Woodbridge, 1867-68. C. Newton, 1868-70. Diocesan Inspector of Schools, 1880-96. Rec. Weston. D. Beccles, May 16, 1911, aged 74.

A son, Rev. E. G. Clowes, Rector of Weston ; a daughter married Rev. E. A. Fitch, C.M.S., E. Africa.

40. Rowlands, Rev. William Edward (Worcester), M.A., Oxf. Isl.—Born October 30, 1837. d. 1861. p. 1864. T. M. Ret. in 1884 and rejoined in 1907. m. (1) 1863, Mary Blackwell Evans. d. 1877. (2) 1888, Emily Charlotte Adams, D. 1889. C. Watermen's Church, Worcester, 1861. Rec. Bonchurch, 1895-1906. Assistant Chaplain at Les Avants. 1906-07. Ret. 1918.

A son, Rev. H. F. Rowlands, C.M.S., Punjab, killed in earthquake at Kangra in 1905 ; another son, Rev. F. W. Rowlands, Japan Mission.

1862

41. Buswell, Rev. Henry Dixon, Isl.—d. 1862. p. 1863. T. M. m. 1862, Mary Sophia Cullis, D. 1892. Ret. 1865. C.M.S., Mauritius, 1866. Archdeacon of Seychelles, 1894.

42. Pickford, Rev. John (Sheffield), St. Bees. T. C. M. Previously eleven years in Tinnevelly.—m. Mary Turner, D. 1866. Ret. 1868. D. 1882.

1865

43. Allcock, Rev. John (Marston), Isl. S. M.—m. 1867, Harriet Elizabeth Gladding, D. 1899. D. Kandy, 1887.
Eldest son, Rev. W. G. Allcock. C. St. John's, Ealing.

1866

44. Good, Rev. Thomas (Kilbourne), Isl. B.D., Lambeth.—d. 1866. p. 1867. T. M. m. 1867, Susan Brodie. Ret. 1874. C. Baggotrath, 1874-78. V. Sandford Ranelagh, 1878. Wrote on ' Temperance.'

45. Mill, Rev. Julius Cæsar (Lodi, Italy), T.M.—Ret. 1869. m. 1867 Catherine Mary Schaffter. 1869-75 Tinnevelly. D. 1888.

1867

46. Fenn, Rev. David, M.A., Camb. T.M.—Only four months in Ceylon. D. 1878.

47. Dowbiggin, Rev. Richard Thomas (Hawkshead).— Born April 27, 1838. Isl. S. M. m. 1869, Letitia Ann Layard. D. at sea near Suez on March 8, 1901.

48. Griffith, Rev. Edward Moule (Birmingham), Isl. B.A., Camb. T. M.—m. 1867, Mary E. Skinner Marshall. D. Jaffna, March 13, 1890, aged 47.

49. Wood, Rev. David (Stockton on Tees), Isl.—d. 1867, p. 1869. T.M. m. 1869, Margaret Webster. Ret. 1892.. Rec. Willand, 1898. Wrote ' Brief History of Prayer Book' (Tamil).

A son, Rev. A. R. Wood, V. Thorpe-le-Soken; a daughter, Mrs. T. Gaunt, C.M.S., China.

1868

50. Clark, Rev. William (Southwark), Isl. T.C.M.— m. 1851 Mary Anne Baker. Ret. 1878. Wrote ' Expositiou of Prophecy,' ' Christian Minister.' 1848–68 in Tinnevelly. 1880–84 in Travancore. D. at Highbury in 1913, aged 88.

1873

51. Unwin, Rev. Gerard Francis, Isl.—d. 1873. p. 1878. S. M. Ret. 1878. V. Frocester.

1874

52. Cavalier, Rev. Anthony Ramsden (Sheffield), Isl.— d. 1874. p. 1875. T.C.M. m. 1876 Mary Grey. Ret. 1880. 1883–85, Tinnevelly. Secretary, Z.B.M.S. V. Mancester, 1915.

53. Dunn, Rev. Thomas (Wallhouses), Isl. —d. and p. 1882. Ret. 1881. m. 1874, Jane A. Ford. 1882–84, British Columbia. 1886–90, Japan. 1904–10. Rec. Weare Gifford.

54. Simmons, Rev. Jonathan Deane (Shiplake), Isl.—d. 1860. p. 1862. T.M. m. (1) 1860, Caroline J. Bolton, D. 1861. (2) 1864, Ada Van Someren Chitty, D. 1900. Ret. 1903. In Tinnevelly, 1861-74. D. March 27, 1914, Wokingham, Berks, aged 79.

1875

55. Smith, Mr. William.—Ret. 1878. D. at sea.

1877

56. Newton, Rev. Henry, M.A., Dub.—d. 1870. p. 1871. Incumbent, Christ Church, Colombo. Ret. 1885. C. St. Matthew's, Dublin, 1870-72. C. Christ Church, Leeson Park, 1872-73. Inc. St. Paul's, Portarlington. 1873-76. Perp. C. St. Mark's, Brighton, 1885-95. V. Christ Church, Surbiton, 1901-15. V. Haydon, 1916.

57. Ferris, Mr. William Bridger, Isl. T.C.M.—Ret. 1878. Ordained d. 1878. p. 1879. V. Christ Church, Worthing, 1898. Hon. Canon of Chichester.

58. Taylor, Mr. Isaac John.—Born November 1, 1847. Isl. T.C.M. Ret. 1878. S. India, 1878-80. Ordained d. and p. 1880. N. W. Canada, 1884-1897. V. Linstead, 1907.

1878

59. Schaffter, Rev. William Pascal, Isl. T.C.M., son of Rev. P. P. Schaffter, C.M.S., Tinnevelly.—m. 1861, Theresa Stammer, D. November 29, 1916. Ret. 1879. Tinnevelly, 1861-78.

60. Blackmore, Rev. Edwin (Exmouth), Isl. T.M.— D. Jaffna, 1879. Tinnevelly, 1874-78.

61. Pickford, Rev. Joseph Ingham (Sheffield)—d. and p. 1878. Isl. T.M. m. 1880, Mary Young. Ret. 1907. C. Wingfield, 1888-9. C. St. Mary's, Islington, 1897-98. V. Walpole, 1909.

1880

62. Fleming, Rev. George Thomas (Pimlico), Isl. T.M.— m. 1892, Minnie Frances Fleming, daughter of Rev. T. S. Fleming, formerly of the Chekiang Mission, who died on November 11, 1916, aged 90. D. Colombo, 1896.

63. Garrett, Rev. John Galloway (Boyle), M.A., Dub. S.M.—m. 1878, Eliza Margaret Bradshaw. D. Dublin, 1911.

Father of Rev. Geo. Garrett, C.M.S., Uganda, also of Second Lieut. William Oakley Garrett, killed in action in Mesopotamia, 1915.

1881

64. Glanville, Rev. Frederic (Exeter).—Born November 19, 1856. Isl. d. and p. 1880. T.C.M. m. (1) 1882. Frances Ann White, D. 1883. (2) 1885, Eleanor Keen. Ret. 1883- C. St. John Evang. Penge, 1880-81. C.M.S. Organizing Sec., 1885-1901. V. St. Matthew's, Kingsdown, Bristol, 1901. D. Bristol, May 15, 1914.

65. Balding, Rev. John William.—Born at Horncastle, March 20, 1856. Isl. d. 1881. p. 1884. S.M. m. June 10, 1884, Matilda Hall. Wrote 'Story of Baddegama Mission,' 'Story of Cotta Mission,' 'Centenary Volume of the Ceylon Mission' Eldest son, Charles John Balding, A.M.I.C.E., drowned at Felixstowe in 1912, aged 27; youngest son, Second Lieut. Reginald Norman, fell in action in Mesopotamia in 1917, aged 22.

66. Horsley, Rev. Hugh (Courtallam), M.A., Camb.— d. 1873. p. 1877. T.M. m. 1877, M.E. Rendall. In Tinnevelly, 1873-79. Ret. 1894. V. Oulton. V. Eastwood.

1882

67. Field, Rev. John (Schull), Isl.—d. 1880. p. 1881. S.M. m. 1872, Emily Jane Mattock. Ret. 1885. In Yoruba, 1877- 79. C. Pitt Portion, Tiverton, 1880-82. British Columbia, 1886.

68. Liesching, Rev. George Louis Pett.—Born July 18, 1856. Isl. d. 1882. p. 1885. S.M. m. 1882, Maude Edridge. Ret. 1901. C. St. Paul's, Dorking, 1892-3. St. Stephen's, Walthamstow, 1902-03. Bushbury, 1903-04. Bovington, 1904- 07. V. Little Horwood, 1907.

A daughter, Grace Liesching. Assistant Secretary of the Z.B.M.S., London.

1884

69. Ilsley, Rev. Joseph (Liverpool).—Born September 19, 1855. Isl. d. 1879. p. 1885. T. M. Ret. 1914. m. (1) 1881, Jeannette Morgan, D. 1905. (2) 1909, Isabella Jane Boesinger. In Tinnevelly, 1880-84. C. St. Giles', Northampton.

1886

70. Thomas, Rev. John Davies, Isl., son of Rev. John Thomas, Megnanapuram.—In Tinnevelly, 1863-86. m. 1863 Mary Jane Green. T. M. D. Colombo, April 18, 1896, aged 56. Buried in Kanatte Cemetery. Translated 'Whately's Evidences' and 'Butler's Analogy, Part I' into Tamil.

Father of Dr. J. Llewellyn Thomas, many years in Colombo, of Mrs. T. S. Johnson, C.M.S. and Mrs. E. A. Douglas, C.M.S.

71. Hodges, Rt. Rev. Edward Noel, D.D., Oxf. T.C.K.—m. 1877 Alice Shirreff. Ret. 1889. Masulipatam, 1877-86. Bishop of Travancore and Cochin, 1890-1904. Rec. St. Cuthbert, Bedford, and Hon. Canon of Ely. A son killed in France in 1916.

1889

72. Fall, Rev. John William (Bedale), M.A., Camb.— d. 1887. p. 1888. T. M. m. 1893, Ethel Berridge. Ret. 1897. C. Walcot, 1887-89. Jesmond, 1898-1900. Asst. Secy., C.P.A.S., 1900-02. V. St. Andrew's, Whitehall Park, 1902. V. Christ Church, Ware, 1917.

73. Perry, Rev. Edward John (Stratford), M.A., Oxf. T.C.K.—Accidentally shot near Alutnuwara on April 2, 1890, aged 34 years. Was of Worcester College, Oxford, and Pusey and Ellerton Scholar and had been a master at Merchant Taylors School.

1890

74. Napier-Clavering, Rev. Henry Percy, M.A., Camb.—
d. 1885. p. 1886. T.C.K. Ret. 1908. m. 1909, C.K.E.
Gedge. C. Monkton Combe, 1885-89. Rec. Stella, 1900-07.
Chaplain, Pussellawa. Clerical Secy., C.E.Z.M.S., London,
1912-16. Chaplain, Beaufort War Hospital, Fishponds,
Bristol, 1917.

75. Dibben, Rev. Arthur Edwin, M.A., Camb.—d. 1886.
p. 1888. S. M. Secy. of Ceylon Mission. C. Fairfield, 1886-87. St. John's, Chelsea, 1887-89.

1891

76. Carter, Rev. James (Netherseale), M.A., Camb.—
d. 1889. p. 1890. m. (1) 1893, Mary Fernie, D. 1899. (2)
1903, Agnes Layard Dowbiggin. T.C.K. and St. John's,
Jaffna. Ret. 1904. Asst. Master, St. Oswald's Coll., Ellesmere,
1888-89. C. Christ Church, Stone, 1890-91. C. Branston,
1904-05. Rec. Kineton and Oxhill, 1905.

1892

77. Welchman, Rev. William (Bristol), M.A., Camb.—
d. 1890. p. 1891. m. Elizabeth Marshall Griffith, 1892. T. M.
Ret. 1899. V. Holy Cross, Bristol, and Hon. Canon, 1901.
Army Chaplain in France, 1915-16.

A son, Lieut. Eric Welchman, fell in action, 1914, in France.

78. Simmons, Rev. Sydney Mainwaring, son of the Rev.
J. D. Simmons. Isl.—d. 1897. p. 1898. m. (1) 1897.
Beatrice Reynolds, D. 1907. (2) 1909, Helena Elsie Marion
Walker. S.M. Ret. 1915. C. Christ Church, Great Worley,
1915. Rec. Little Laver, 1917.

79. Carus-Wilson, Mr. Ernest Jocelyn.—m. 1898, Katherine Mary Chapman. S.M. Ret. 1899.

1893

80. Heinekey, Rev. Henry Edward, Lond. Coll. Div.—
d. 1889. p. 1890. m. 1892, Ellen Flora Harris. S. M. Ret.
1905. Compiled 'Sinhalese Birthday Text Book.' Only
child died and buried at Baddegama. C. St. Paul's, Stratford,
1889-91. C. St. Cuthbert's, West Hampstead, 1891-93. V.
St. George's, Westcombe Park, 1906. C. St. Thomas', Hull,.
1916. V. St. Peter's, Drypool, Hull, 1917.

1894

81. Mathison, Major Gilbert Hamilton Fearon.—m. 1906,.
Edith Mary Tucker. Ret. 1909: S. M. Formerly Major in
Alexandra P.W.O., Yorkshire Regt.

1895

82. Ryde, Rev. Robert William (Brockley), M.A., Camb.
T.C.K. and St. John's, Jaffna—m. 1897, Emily Margaret
Loveridge. S. M. D. Colombo, 1909.

1896

83. Hamilton, Rev. James, B.A., Dub.—d. 1876. p. 1878..
T.M. m. 1880, Wilhelmina M.B. Moore. Ret. 1897. Incumbent of Thornhill, Ireland.

1897

84. Townsend, Rev. Horace Crawford (Clonakilty), B.A.,.
Dub.—d. 1893. p. 1894. m. 1899, Mary Edith Grace Young.
T.C.M. Ret. 1903. C. Ballymena, 1893-96. Incumbent,.
Craig. Army Chaplain, France, 1915-17. Awarded Military
Cross (Fourth Class), 1917.

1898

85. Hanan, Rev. William John (Cahir), M.A., Dub.—
d. 1895. p. 1897. m. 1899, Miriam Clarke. T. M. C. Cahir,.
1895-8.

APPENDIX A

86. Thompson, Rev. Jacob (Liverpool), M.A., Camb.—
d. 1888. p 1894. m. 1888, Amy Beatrice Brockbank. St. John's College, Jaffna. Travancore, 1888-94. C. Blundell Sands, 1895-96. C. Peel, 1896-7. Brother of Rt. Rev. J. D. Thompson, Bishop of Sodor and Man.

A son, Lieut. H. B. Thompson of the Berkshires, was awarded the Military Cross in December, 1916, was wounded and missing the same month. Another son, Second Lieut. R. Denton Thompson, joined a Motor Cycle Signalling Corps, and a third son, Second Lieut. J. Cyril Thompson of the East Lancs., was taken prisoner.

1900

87. Butterfield, Rev. Roland Potter (Aylsham), Isl. M.A., Dur.—d. 1900. p. 1901. m. 1904, Clara Herbert. T.C.M.

88. Pilson, Rev. Arthur Ashfield (Birts Morton), M.A., Oxf. T.C.K.—D. April 30, 1902, at Nuwara Eliya, aged 29.

89. Purser, Rev. George Arthur, Isl.—d. 1911. p. 1912. S.M. m. 1911, Elizabeth Beatrice Sparrow, S.M.

1901

90. Booth, Rev. Wilfrid, B.A., Oxf.—d. 1895. p. 1896. m. 1904, Constance Magdalene Clift. T.C.M. C. Great Yarmouth, 1895-1900. D. Teignmouth, March 23, 1918.

91. Shorten, Rev. William Good, Isl. B.A., Dur.—d. 1901. p. 1903. S.M. m. 1907, Amy Kathleen Deering, S.M.

1902

92. Johnson, Rev. Thomas Sparshott, Isl. B.A., Dur.—d. 1902. p. 1903. T.C.M. m. 1905, Annie Elizabeth Mary Thomas, T.M.

1903

93. MacLulich, Rev. Archibald MacLulich (Clonalin), M.A., Dub.—d. 1899. p. 1902. T.C.K. Ret. 1909. C. Tuam, 1899-1900. C. Carrickfergus, 1900-02. V. Holy Trinity, Colombo.

94. Ferrier, Rev. John William, Moore Coll., Sydney, d. and p. 1912. L.Th., Dur.—m. 1901, Evelyn May Garland. S.M. Accountant of Mission till 1910 ; rejoined 1915, having been ordained in Australia.

1904

95. Fraser, Rev. Alexander Garden, M.A., Oxf.—d. 1912. p. 1915. m. 1901, Annie Beatrice Glass. T.C.K. Uganda, 1900-04. Army Chaplain, France, 1917.

96. Phair, Rev. Robert Hugh Oliver, B.A., Manitoba, Isl.—d. 1904. p. 1906. Son of the Rev. Archdeacon Phair of Winnipeg. S.M.

97. Storrs, Rev. Arthur Noel Coopland, B.A. Camb.— d. 1887. p. 1888. m. 1893, Anna Maria Louisa Fitton. T.C.M. Tinnevelly, 1889-04. Son of Rev. W.T. Storrs, C.M.S., India. Ret. 1904.

1906

98. Walmsley, Rev. Alfred Moss (Stockport), M.A., Camb. —d. 1906. p. 1907. m. 1906, Alice J. Murgatroyd, B.Sc., London. Trinity College, 1906-1911. S.M., 1911. Served in Mesopotamia, 1918.

99. Weston, Rev. George Thomas (Langley), Isl.—d. 1906. p. 1907. T.M. Ret. 1911. Planters' Chaplain, Matale, 1912.

100. Senior, Rev. Walter Stanley, M.A., Oxf.—d. 1903. p. 1904. T.C.K., 1906-1915. Incumbent of Christ Church, Colombo, 1915. m. 1907, Ethel May Poole, T.M. Author of ' Pisgah or The Choice,' the triennial prize poem on a sacred subject in the University of Oxford, 1914.

1908

101. Gibson, Rev. John Paul Stewart Riddell, M.A., Camb. F.I.A.—d. 1906. p. 1907. m. 1904, Kathleen May Armitage. T.C.K., 1908-1914. Training Colony, Peradeniya, 1914.

102. Saunders, Mr. Kenneth James, B.A., Camb. T.C.K.—Ret. 1913. Y.M.C.A., Calcutta, Rangoon. Trans. 'Dhammapada' into English. Author of ' Maitri—The Coming One,' 'Buddhist Ideals,' ' Two Heroes of Social Service (St. Francis and St. Dominic),' ' The Candid Friend, or Buddhism from Within,' ' The Vital Forces of Southern Buddhism in relation to the Gospel,' 'Adventures of the Christian Soul,' and several other pamphlets and articles.

103. Campbell, Mr. Norman Phillips, M.A., Oxf. T.C.K.—m. 1913, Lettice Margaret Armitage (a sister of Mrs. P. Gibson). Joined H.M.'s Forces in 1914, obtained commission as Captain in Royal Engineers, fell in action on May 3, 1917.

1909

104. Finnimore, Rev. Arthur Kington, Isl. M.A., Dur.—d. 1885. p. 1888. Inc. Christ Church, Colombo. T.C.M. m. 1885, Mary Elizabeth Hughes. In South India, 1885-90. Mauritius, 1893-01. C.M.S. Organizing Secy., 1901-08. C. Eastbourne, 1908-09. Army Chaplain, France, 1915-16. A son, Lieut. David Keith Finnimore, died from wounds in a military hospital on May 10, 1917. Another son, Major A. C. Finnimore, in the Royal Engineers; a daughter, Miss D. E. Finnimore, a missionary at Palamcotta.

105. Mulgrue, Mr. George Robert. T.C.K.—Ret. 1915.

1910

106. Gaster, Rev. Lewis John, Isl.—d. 1910. p. 1912. T.C.K. m. November 18, 1911, Harriet Elizabeth Hobson, S.M.'

1914

107. Houlder, Mr. Alfred Claude (Croydon), B.A., Oxf. T.C.K.

1915

108. McPherson, Rev. Kenneth Cecil, B.A., Oxf. T.C.K.—d. 1915. p. 1917.

SINHALESE CLERGY.

1. Jayasinghe, Rev. Cornelius.—d. 1839. p. 1843. Educated at Cotta Institution. First Catechist and Interpreter. Stationed at Talangama and Slave Island. In 1867, Trinity Church, Kandy. Editor of the Sinhalese *C.M. Record*. D. Colombo on November 18, 1876. Mr. Jayasinghe's name stands fourth on the C.M.S. List of Native Clergy and Mr. A. Gunasekara's fifth.

2. Gunasekara, Rev. Abraham.—d. 1839. p. 1843 by Bishop Spencer. Educated at Cotta Institution. Worked in Baddegama and died there on June 27, 1862, aged 60. The son of Bastian Gunasekara, who was born in 1773 and died in 1853. The father of Rev. H. Gunasekara, who died in 1916, Paul Gunasekara, a catechist and schoolmaster for fifty years, who died on January 3, 1917, aged 74 years, and Mrs. B. Karunaratna, a Biblewoman for many years. A grand-daughter married Rev. T. G. Perera, and another married Rev. A. B. Karunaratne.

3. Senanayake, Rev. Cornelius.—d. 1846. p. 1851. Educated at Cotta Institution. Transferred to Colonial Establishment in 1852 and died in 1886. Wrote a Sinhalese Church Hymnal.

4. De Livera, Rev. James Andris.—d. 1861. p. 1867. Educated at Cotta Institution. Stationed at Kandy and Nugegoda. Died December 23, 1868. At his examination for Deacon's orders by Bishop Chapman, he was offered his choice between the Greek Testament and the Sinhalese Bible and he unhesitatingly chose the former.

5. Gunasekara, Rev. Henry.—d. 1867. p. 1871. Educated at Baddegama Seminary and Cotta Institution. (1) Pupil Teacher, (2) Catechist, (3) Pastor. Stationed at Nugegoda, Colombo, and Trinity Church, Kandy. Retired in 1909.

Died May 24, 1916, at Lunawa. Mr. Gunasekara was married in 1870, and his widow died on November 1, 1916. A son of Rev. A. Gunasekara.

6. de Silva, Rev. Hendrick.—d. 1868. p. 1885. Educated at Cotta Institution. (1) Schoolmaster, (2) Catechist, (3) Pastor at Cotta, Nugegoda and Talangama. Died at Negombo on March 12, 1891.

7. Jayasinha, Rev. Daniel.—d. 1868. Educated at Cotta Institution. (1) Schoolmaster, (2) Catechist, (3) Pastor at Katukelle, Nugegoda and Cotta. Died at Cotta on January 1, 1887.

8. Wirasinha, Rev. Bartholomew Peris.—d. 1869. Educated at Cotta English School. (1) Schoolmaster at Cotta, (2) Catechist for sixteen years, (3) Pastor at Kegalle. Retired in 1894 and died in 1900.

9. Kannanger, Rev. Hendrick.—d. 1869. (1) Schoolmaster, (2) Catechist, (3) Pastor at Talangama, Cotta, Bentota. Retired 1885, and died on July 13, 1894. Father of Mrs. Wirakoon, Head Mistress of Baddegama Girls' Boarding School.

10. Perera, Rev. Garagoda Arachchige Bastian.—d. 1881. p. 1886. Retired 1916. The son of Garagoda Arachchige Don Abraham Perera and Thudugalage Dona Christina. Born at Talangama on December 19, 1836. Stationed at Balapitiya, Baddegama, Cotta and Colombo. Celebrated golden wedding and fifty-fourth anniversary of service with C.M.S. in 1914. Mrs. Perera died the following year. A daughter married Mr. H. C. Jayasinghe of T.C.K.

11. Amarasekara, Rev. Abraham Suriarachchi.—d. 1881. p. 1884. Stationed at Kegalle, Dodanduwa and Kandy. Retired in 1885 and became (1) Curate of Holy Emmanuel, Moratuwa, (2) Incumbent of Matale. Founder of Matale Mission to the Duriyas.

12. Kalpage, Rev. Johannes Perera.—d. 1881. p. 1887.

Kurunegala, Kegalle, Baddegama, Dodanduwa, Bentota. Died 1903 from the effects of a crushed finger, and buried in Kanatte cemetery. Father of Rev. J. A. Kalpage of Tangalle.

13. Amarasekara, Rev. Gregory Suriarachchi.—d. 1887. p. 1889. Educated at Baddegama and T.C.K. (1) Schoolmaster, (2) Pastor, Cotta, Nugegoda and Trinity Church, Kandy. Celebrated twenty-fifth anniversary of ordination to Priesthood in 1914. A brother of Rev. A. S. Amarasekara.

14. Botejue, Rev. Welatantrige Lewis.—d. 1889. Educated at Cotta Institution. (1) Catechist, (2) Pastor at Mampe and died there on May 13, 1895. Father of Rev. W. E. Botejue.

15. Seneviratne, Rev. Henry William.—d. 1889. Gampola. Retired 1902. Died in 1917, aged 80.

16. Colombage, Rev. James.—d. 1894. p. 1898. Educated at T.C.K. Baddegama and Kegalle. Retired and joined the staff of St. Paul's, Kandy.

17. Daundesekara, Rev. Frederic William.—d. 1894. p. 1910. Educated at Kurunegala and T.C.K. Colombo and Kegalle. Retired.

18. Botejue, Rev. Welatantrige Edwin.—d. 1896. p. 1901. Educated at T.C.K. Mampe. Ret. 1902. Incumbent of Ratnapura.

19. Perera, Rev. Theodore G.—d. 1896. p. 1898. Educated at Cotta English School. Talangama. m. a granddaughter of Rev. A. Gunasekara. Ret. in 1902.

20. Perera, Rev. D. Joseph.—d. 1896. p 1904. Colombo. Died in 1912.

21. Gunatilaka, Rev. Robert Teuton Eugene Abeyawickrama.—d. 1903. p. 1905. Baddegama, Dodanduwa, Cotta, Mampe.

22. Welikala, Rev. Don Louis.—d. 1903. p. 1905. Talangama and Colombo. m. a sister of Rev. J. Colombage.

23. Wikramanayake, Rev. John Henry.—d. 1903. p. 1905. Mampe, Nugegoda.

24. Wijesinghe, Rev. Charles.—d. 1903. Gampola, Kurunegala, Liyanwela. Ret. 1916.

25. Seneviratne, Rev. James Gregory Newsome.—d. 1909. p. 1913. Gampola.

26. Wickramasinghe, Rev. Benjamin Perera.—d. 1909. p. 1914. Mampe. Cotta.

27. Ramanayake, Rev. John Perera.—d. 1913. p. 1917. (1) Schoolmaster, (2) Catechist, (3) Pastor, Homagama and Dodanduwa.

28. Jayasundra, Rev. D. S.—d. 1915. Talampitiya.

29. de Silva, Rev. W. Bernard.—d. 1915. Educated at T.C.K. (1) Catechist, (2) Pastor. Baddegama.

30. Weerasinghe, Rev. C. B. Educated T.C.K. Master at T.C.K.—d. 1918. Kurunegala.

TAMIL CLERGY.

1. Hensman, Rev. John.—d. 1863. p. 1865. Educated at Cotta Institution. Teacher, Nellore, 1837. Catechist, Chundicully, 1840. Copay, 1848. Pastor, Copay. Died September 5, 1884.

2. Champion, Rev. George.—Born October 1, 1824. d. 1865. p. 1870. Educated at Batticotta Seminary. (1) Catechist, (2) Pastor, Nellore, and Chundicully. Retired 1902. Died 1910. Celebrated Jubilee of his C.M.S. Service in 1894.

3. Hoole, Rev. Elijah.—d. 1865. p. 1870. Pundit, 1850. Catechist, Chundicully, 1852. Pastor.

Died at sea July, 1881, on his way home from Bishop's Assembly at Colombo.

4. Handy, Rev. Trueman Parker.—d. 1865. p. 1870. Educated at Batticotta Seminary. School Inspector, 1850. Pundit, 1851. Catechist, 1856. Pastor at Nellore. Died May 17, 1885.

5. Peter, Rev. Pakkyanathan.—d. 1872. p. 1874. Teacher, 1856. T. C. M. Catechist, 1862. Assistant Missionary, Pelmadulla, 1892. Died June 15, 1895.

6. Peter, Rev. John S.—d. 1872. p. 1874. Retired 1877. T.C.M. Pastor, Kandy. Died 1906.

7. Gabb, Rev. John.—d. 1876. p. 1883. Retired 1883. (1) 1876-81, Mauritius. (2) 1881-83, Ceylon. (3) 1883-94, Madras.

8 Gnanamuttu, Rev. Arulananthan.—d. 1881. p. 1885. Retired 1897. Died 1906. Schoolmaster, Catechist, Pastor T.C.M., Dickoya, Kandy.

9. Samuel, Rev. Samuel.—d. 1878. p. 1881. Educated at Palamcotta Training Institution. Son of Rev. A. Samuel of Tinnevelly. 1878-84, Tinnevelly. 1884-95, Colombo. Died May 6, 1895, in Colombo.

10. Niles, Rev. John.—d. 1885. p. 1889. Copay. Died March 23, 1892.

11. Backus, Rev. John.—d. 1885. p. 1889. (1) Schoolmaster, (2) Catechist, (3) Pastor, Pallai, Nellore. Celebrated his fiftieth year of C.M.S. service in 1913. Mrs. Backus died December 17, 1916.

12. Handy, Rev. Charles Chelliah.—d. 1891. p. 1896. B. A., Calcutta University. T.C.K. Head Master of St. John's College, Jaffna. Died 1908.

13. Virasinha, Rev. Arulumbalam Russell.—d. 1892. p. 1900. T.C.K. Stationed T.C.M. Died 1914.

14. Daniel, Rev. George.—d. 1893. Catechist, 1858. Copay. Seventy-five years of age on retirement in 1912.

15. Williams, Rev. Charles Tissaverasingam—d. 1893. p. 1896. T.C.K. Pastor, Kokuvil, Anuradhapura, Kandy, Kopay.

16. Morse, Rev. Samuel.—d. 1893. p. 1896. Nellore. Died 1909.

17. Matthias, Rev. Arulpragasam.—d. 1893. p. 1898. Vavuniya. Copay. Retired after forty years of service in 1915.

18. Sathianathen, Rev. Aseervathem.—d. 1899. p. 1902. T.C.M. Nanuoya, Dickoya. Retired 1914. Died 1916.

19. Daniel, Rev. John Vethamanikam—d. 1900. p. 1902. Head Master of Borella Boys' Boarding School, Incumbent of Tamil Congregation, Christ Church, Colombo.

20. Satthianadhan, Rev. Tillainather David.—d. 1903. p. 1906. T.C.M. Badulla.

21. Arulananthan, Rev. Gnanamuttu Manuel.—d. 1906. p. 1908. Incumbent, Emmanuel Church, Colombo.

22. Pakkianathan, Rev. Asirvatham.—d. 1906. p. 1908. T.C.M. Lindula.

23. Doss, Rev. James G.—d. 1907. p. 1910. T.C.M. Dickoya.

24. Somasundaram, Rev. Sangarappillai Samuel.—d. 1909. p. 1911. B.A., Calcutta. Master in St. John's College, Jaffna. Chundicully.

25. Nathaniel, Rev. Gunaratnam N.—d. 1909. p. 1913. Jaffna. 1917 Matale.

26. Welcome, Rev. Jesson Daniel.—d. 1910. p. 1914. Anuradhapura.

27. Daniel, Rev. Samuel Chelvanayakam.—d. 1910. p. 1914. Pallai.

28. Paukiam, Rev. Paul Abraham.—d. 1912. p. 1914. Rakwana T.C.M. Died 1918.

29. Yorke, Rev. John Vedamanickam.—d. 1914. p. 1917. Avisawela T.C.M.

30. Thomas, Rev. S. M.—d. 1915. p. 1917. Wellawatte T.C.M.

31. Ratnathicum, Rev. J. S.—d. 1915. Jaffna.

32. Refuge, Rev. M.—d. 1915. Matale. 1917 Vavuniya.

LIST OF CEYLON C.M.S. MISSIONARIES
(WOMEN)

1821

1. Knight, Miss Jane (Stroud), T.M.—m. Rev. D. Poor, 1823.

1823

2. Cortis, Miss Hannah. S.M.—m. Rev. J. A. Jetter, 1823.

1827

3. Stratford, Miss Mary Ann. S.M.—m. Rev. S. Lambrick, 1827.

1841

4. Bailey, Miss Sophia Elizabeth. S.M.—m. Rev. J. F. Haslam, 1842.

1879

5. Young, Miss Mary (Louth), sister of late Bishop R. Young of Athabasca. T.M.—m. Rev. J. I. Pickford, 1880.

1881

6. Hall, Miss Matilda, sister of Rev. J. W. Hall and Miss Margaret Hall, and cousin of Miss E. Hall, of the C.M.S., India. T.M.—m. Rev. J. W. Balding, 1884.

1884

7. Young, Miss Eva (Louth), sister of Nos. 5 and 12. T. M.—m. Rev. H. Robinson, N. W. Canada.

1886

8. Higgens, Miss Amelia, daughter of Rev. E. T. Higgens. 1877 in service of I.F.N.S., Punjab. S.M.

APPENDIX A

1891

9. Child, Miss Beatrice. T.M.—Ret. 1898.
10. Denyer, Miss Ann Murton. S M.—Ret. 1915.

1892

11. Phillips, Miss Helen Plummer. S.M. Previously Principal of Clergy Daughters' School, Sydney.—Ret. 1905.
12. Young, Miss Emily Sophia. T.M. Sister of Nos. 5 and 7.—Ret. 1910.

1893

13. Heaney, Miss Kate, Highbury Training Home. T.M.—Ret. 1898.
14. Saul, Miss Mary, Highbury Training Home. T.M.—Ret. 1899.
15. Paul, Miss Annie Elizabeth, Highbury Training Home. T.M.—Ret. 1897.
16. Josolyne, Miss Ellen Maria. The Willows. S.M.

1894

17. Forbes, Miss Constance Cicele. S.M.—Ret. 1896.
18. Case, Miss Lizzie Ann, Highbury Training Home. T.M.—Ret. 1912. m. Rev. G. Hibbert-Ware, S.P.G.

1895

19. Luxmoore, Miss Caroline Noble. The Willows. S.M.—m. 1896, Rev. J. H. Mackay, Murree.
20. Finney, Miss Harriet Ellen, daughter of Rev. W. H. Finney, Birkin. The Olives. T. M.—Ret. 1904.
21. Loveridge, Miss Emily Margaret, Highbury Training Home. S. M.—m. Rev. R. W. Ryde, 1897.
22. Gedge, Miss Mary Sophia (Redhill). The Willows. S.M.

1896

23. Spreat, Miss Helen Mary Warren. T. M.—Ret. 1897. Died in London, 1898.

24. Wood, Miss Minnie Alice, daughter of Rev. D. Wood. The Olives. T.M.—Ret. 1898.

25. Dowbiggin, Miss Agnes Layard, daughter of Rev. R. T. Dowbiggin. S. M.—m. Rev. J. Carter, 1904.

26. Thomas, Mrs. J. D. T.M.—Ret. 1914. Remained on staff after the Rev. J. D. Thomas' death.

1897

27. Townsend, Miss Susan Henrietta Murray. The Willows. S.M. Daughter of Rev. H. W. Townsend of Abbeystrewry and sister of Rev. H. C. Townsend.

28. Earp, Miss Annie Louisa (Capetown). The Olives. S.M. Ret. 1915.

1898

29. Goodchild, Miss Amy Chanter, St. Hugh's Hall, Oxf. The Willows.—Principal of Chundicully Girls' School.—m. Mr. C. V. Brayne. C.C.S. 1906.

30. Thomas, Miss Annie Elizabeth, daughter of Rev. J. D. Thomas. The Olives. 1887-93 in Tinnevelly under C.E.Z.M.S.—m. Rev. T. S. Johnson, 1905. T.M.

31. Young, Miss Maud Lucy. The Willows. S. M.—Ret. 1899.

32. Franklin, Miss Valentina Maria Louisa. The Willows. T.M.—Ret. 1912. m. Rev. Ashton.

1899

33. Payne, Miss Harriette Edith. The Willows. T.M. —Ret. 1911.

34. Leslie Melville, Miss Lucy Mabel, daughter of the late Rev. Canon Leslie Melville, Welbourn The Willows. S.M.

35. Nixon, Miss Lilian Evelyn, B.A., Royal Univ. of Ireland. The Olives and Willows. Principal of C.M.S. Ladies' College, Colombo.—Ret. 1914.

36. Whitney, Miss Elizabeth. St. John's, N.B. Canada. C.M.S. Ladies' College, Colombo.

37. Howes, Miss Eva Julia. The Willows. T.M.

1901

38. Tileston, Miss Mary Wilder, B.A. Harvard Univ. The Olives.—Ret. 1902. S.M.

39. Dowbiggin, Mrs. R.T. S.M.—Remained on staff after Mr. Dowbiggin's death.

40. Beeching, Miss Edith Grace, Highbury Training Home. Pacific Mission, 1894. T.M. m. Mr. J. B. Dutton, C.C.S., 1906.

41. Lloyd, Miss Sarah Cecilia. The Olives. S.M.—Ret. 1907. Rejoined 1914. Died 1918.

1902

42. Vines, Miss Ellen Campbell, daughter of Rev. C. E. Vines, C.M.S., Agra. 1889, South India. T.M. m. Rev. W. S. Hunt, C.M.S., 1907.

1903

43. Board, Miss Annie Theresa (Clifton). The Olives. S.M.—Ret. 1907.

1904

44. Ketchlee, Miss Sophy Laura. The Olives.—m. Rev. A. N. MacTier, C.M.S., Tinnevelly.

45. Poole, Miss Ethel May. The Olives. T.M. Daughter of Bishop Poole, first C. of E. Bishop in Japan.—m. Rev. W. S. Senior, 1907.

46. Page, Miss Sophia Lucinda (Bath). The Olives. Principal, Chundicully Girls' High School.

47. Bennitt, Miss Edith Gertrude (Harborne), L.L.A. St. Andrew's Univ. The Olives. S.M.—Ret. 1908.

1905

48. Browne, Miss Constance Emily, B.Sc., Univ. of Wales. C.M.S. Ladies' College and T.C.K.—Ret. 1914.

49. Deering, Miss Amy Kathleen. S.M.—m. Rev. W. G. Shorten, 1907.

1906

50. Sparrow, Miss Elizabeth Beatrice. S.M.—m. Rev. G. A. Purser, 1911.

51. Tisdall, Miss Adairine Mary. The Willows. T.M.

52. Henrys, Miss Florence Emily. T.M. South India, 1902. Returned to India, 1917.

1908

53. Walker, Miss Helena Elsie Marion. S.M.—m. Rev. S. M. Simmons, 1909.

54. Hargrove, Miss Eleanor Mabel. Daughter of the late Rev. Canon Hargrove. The Willows. S.M.

55. Hobson, Miss Harriet Elizabeth. Grand-daughter of Rev. J. Hobson, C.M.S., China. S.M. m. Rev. L. J. Gaster, 1911.

56. Horsley, Miss Anna Frances, Newnham. The Olives. Daughter of Rev. H. Horsley. C.M.S. Ladies' College.— Ret. 1914.

1910

57. Ledward, Miss Mary Amelia. T.M.

1913

58. Kent, Miss Alys Emily. C.M.S. Ladies' Coll., Colombo. —m. Mr. H. S. Stevens, 1915.

1915

59. Morgan, Miss E. C.M.S. Ladies' College.

60. Opie, Miss Gwen Lilias Fanny, M.A., B.Sc. C.M.S. Ladies' College.

61. Higgens, Miss E. C. (In Local Connexion).

1918

62. Taylor, Miss J. R., L.L.A. Chundicully Girls' High School.

APPENDIX B.

NEW CONSTITUTION FOR THE CEYLON MISSIONARY CONFERENCE

AS APPROVED BY THE PARENT COMMITTEE OF MARCH 8, 1921.

LOCAL GOVERNING BODY.

The Local Governing Body of the C.M.S. Ceylon Mission shall be the Conference of men and women hereinafter referred to as the Conference.

CONFERENCE MEMBERSHIP.

The Conference shall consist of :—

(*a*) The Bishop of Colombo, if a member of the Church Missionary Society—Chairman.

(*b*) All ordained Missionaries of the Society.

(*c*) All lay Missionaries in Home, Colonial, or Local Connexion with the Society, both men and women.

(*d*) Eight Ceylônese, of whom six shall be clergymen and two shall be from the laity, one man and one woman, annually elected by the Conference. Among the six clergymen, those priests in responsible charge of Districts formerly under the charge of European Missionaries shall first of all be included. The remainder shall be clergymen in Priests' Orders elected annually by the whole body of Ceylonese clergy in connection with the C.M.S., provided that the six clerical representatives shall include at least two Tamils and two Sinhalese.

(*e*) Seven lay members, primarily to advise on matters of finance, who shall be appointed by the Parent Committee, and shall hold office for three years, being eligible for reappointment at the end of that period.

(*f*) Any additional members who shall be appointed to membership by express resolution of the Parent Committee on the recommendation of Conference.

Executive Committee.

While nothing shall be considered as outside the purview of the Conference as a whole, it should direct its attention more particularly to the larger matters of Mission policy, to receiving and dealing with the reports of its Committees, and to the opportunity for united devotion and intercession, devolving the main responsibility for actual administration, including finance, on its Executive Committee.

This Executive Committee shall direct the work of the Mission between meetings of the Conference, and shall consist of—

(*a*) The Chairman of Conference.

(*b*) The Secretary of the Mission.

(*c*) The Chairman and Secretary of the Women's Committee.

(*d*) The seven laymen appointed by the Parent Committee.

(*e*) Two Ceylonese, and four men and two women from the Missionary members of the Conference, to be elected by the whole body of the voting members of the Conference.

Finance Sub-Committee.

There shall be a Finance Sub-Committee of the Executive Committee to consider and when required report to the Executive Committee on matters of finance. This Sub-Committee shall consist of the seven lay members appointed by the Parent Committee, and three members elected by the Executive Committee, together with the Secretary ex-officio.

Made in the USA
Columbia, SC
10 June 2025